THE UNAVOIDABLE

"Hell, I guess it doesn't matter."

"What doesn't?"

"You were gonna find out sooner or later. You might not want to be with me after I tell you this. But you need to know it, the truth about me."

Now I'm afraid. This is it: He's going to tell me he killed somebody. Please, don't let this be over. Don't let us be over. "Tell me."

"I'm afraid that someday, I'm gonna do something really bad."

"Like . . ."

"Like something you can't fix. I get so *mad* sometimes."

"Everybody gets mad."

"Not like this. Not like me." His eyes shimmer. They're brown, but for some reason they seem dark blue now. "You're the only one who can keep me from doing it."

"Doing what?"

"Losing it."

OTHER BOOKS YOU MAY ENJOY

STAY WITH ME

Paul Griffin

speak

An Imprint of Penguin Group (USA) Inc.

SPEAK

Published by the Penguin Group

Penguin Group (USA) Inc., 345 Hudson Street, New York, New York 10014, U.S.A.

Penguin Group (Canada), 90 Eglinton Avenue East, Suite 700, Toronto, Ontario, Canada M4P 2Y3

(a division of Pearson Penguin Canada Inc.)

Penguin Books Ltd, 80 Strand, London WC2R 0RL, England

Penguin Ireland, 25 St Stephen's Green, Dublin 2, Ireland (a division of Penguin Books Ltd)

Penguin Group (Australia), 250 Camberwell Road, Camberwell, Victoria 3124, Australia

(a division of Pearson Australia Group Pty Ltd)

Penguin Books India Pvt Ltd, 11 Community Centre, Panchsheel Park, New Delhi – 110 017, India

Penguin Group (NZ), 67 Apollo Drive, Rosedale, Auckland 0632, New Zealand

(a division of Pearson New Zealand Ltd.)

Penguin Books (South Africa) (Pty) Ltd, 24 Sturdee Avenue, Rosebank, Johannesburg 2196, South Africa

Penguin Books Ltd, Registered Offices: 80 Strand, London WC2R 0RL, England

First published in the United States of America by Dial Books,
an imprint of Penguin Group (USA) Inc., 2011
Published by Speak, an imprint of Penguin Group (USA) Inc., 2012

1 3 5 7 9 10 8 6 4 2

THE LIBRARY OF CONGRESS HAS CATALOGED THE DIAL EDITION AS FOLLOWS:

Griffin, Paul, date.

Stay with me / by Paul Griffin.

p. cm.

Summary: Fifteen-year-olds Mack, a high school drop-out but a genius with dogs, and Céce,
who hopes to use her intelligence to avoid a life like her mother's, meet and fall in love at the
restaurant where they both work, but when Mack lands in prison he pushes Céce away and only
a one-eared pit bull can keep them together.

ISBN 978-0-8037-3448-7 (hardcover)

[1. Love—Fiction. 2. Restaurants—Fiction. 3. Family life—Fiction. 4. Pit bull terriers—Fiction.
5. Dogs—Fiction. 6. Ability—Fiction.] I. Title.

PZ7.G8813594St 2011

[Fic]—dc22

2011001287

Speak ISBN: 978-0-14-242172-7

Book design by Jasmin Rubero
Text set in Adobe Garamond

Printed in the United States of America

For my editor and friend, Kate Harrison,
and for Juan G., who dreams of happy endings

STAY WITH ME

A HUNDRED AND TWO DAYS.

That's probably about average, but it didn't seem close to that long, especially in the beginning, that first month or so. It was just getting to that sweet spot, where everything is perfect for a while. A short while. Before it starts to fade—little by little, usually. Not for them, though. For them, it was ripped away in the middle of an ordinary summer afternoon, in a little less than a minute and a half.

It happened in a city you may or may not have heard of, but you probably know them—people like them. You have a friend like her, and maybe you've worked with somebody like him. At minimum, you've seen them around, in restaurants, on the street, walking a dog or two. People said, *Hey, what's the big deal? It happens all the time.* And it does. Until it happens to you. Then it's something different all right, especially when you're left to wander the wreckage.

It started in an unremarkable way, the same way it starts for lots of people: A hint was dropped, an introduction was made. When you're set up like that, you think it'll never work out. But it can, and sometimes it does.

It *does*.

And then somebody does something stupid. Not stupid. Somebody loses control. And then . . .

A hundred and two days. And then it was over.

STAY WITH ME

THE FIRST DAY . . .
(Friday, June 12, just before the dinner shift)

MACK:

"Bad news," Vic says.

"There's another kind?"

"I lost the restaurant."

"Another tough night at the online poker table?"

"Catastrophic." The old man saddles a flipped milk crate and clobbers garlic cloves with his hand. Says it makes him feel one with the earth, except there's not a lot of earth up here in the city. Baked concrete, now, that we got. Back in Texas, there you had land. "I'm bringing you and Tony over to my other place," Vic says. "Didn't I send you there once, to fill in for Freddy maybe, Valentine's Day?"

"No sir." I only started working here three months ago.

"It isn't far from here. You'll still be able to walk to work. You'll like it there. Nice family atmosphere. Tony's mom works there. His sister too."

"He told me." He also said his sister would like me, but I don't think so. I'm no good at looking folks in the eye. I guess I'm taller than average, but I grew up small, didn't hit my growth spurt till later. I don't know. I steer clear of people as much as I can. Vic and Tony. They're the only folks I feel a little comfortable with. I don't mind it so much, being alone. You can't do anything about it. You've got to keep going. What else are you going to do? "What're you gonna do about the name of the other restaurant, Mister Vic?" He has Vic's and Vic's Too—or he did until he lost Vic's.

"It'll still be Vic's Too," he says. "Brand recognition. Very important."

"I see." No, I don't. How do you have a Too when the first one is gone? "My spot at the new place, dishwashing?"

"Freddy keeps smoking pot on the job, you're in," Vic says. "Till then, you're on delivery. You look disappointed."

"I like to clean stuff."

"I know," Vic says. "You're very good at it. The grease on those plates. You're uncompromising."

"Thought you just said I was good."

"I suspect Freddy won't last," Vic says. "I gave him half a dozen chances to straighten up, and he left me chapfallen every time. Six or seven more times, I'll have to let him go."

"I hear you. Yeah. I'm betting *chapfallen* means nothing near what I think it means."

"Are you seeing a picture of a fancy British guy falling off a horse?"

"I am."

"Yeah," Vic says, "then you would be wrong. It means he douched me." Vic looks about as smart as a thrown stone, but he's the king of the crosswords. "Very potent word, *chapfallen*. Remember it." Vic says *potent* a lot too.

"Why would I use *chapfallen* when I can say *douched* instead?"

"Because you might not want to say *douched* in front of a woman."

"I do see your point."

"You up for some Wiffle ball?" the old man says.

"I got a bunch more prep work to do."

"Ey, look at me."

"Yessir?" I look him in the eye, but a second later I'm back to looking at my sneaker laces. One's busted, but I have string in my pocket.

"You're fifteen, not fifty," Vic says. "I don't tell somebody to do something unless I'm sure I'm right about it. I know what I know. Right here, right now, for you, this is the right thing, this Wiffle ball. You need to do this."

"I need to do Wiffle ball?"

He studies the ball in his hand. "Kid, no matter how much money you make, you'll spend more than you have. You miss a chance at fun, you never get it back. Now go on out and tell Tony I said knock it off with the clams. You work too hard, the two of you." Vic grabs the Wiffle bat from where we keep it with the long breads and chucks it to me. "I gotta call this guy, then I'll be out."

Out back, Tony's shucking cherrystones. It's hot for early June, and I'm sweating, but Tony doesn't sweat. He's the coolest dude, eighteen but with old-man wisdom. I can't look him in the eye either.

The restaurant backs up onto an old house on the one side. The neighbor's dog hops the fence to hang with us. Dog jumps all over Tony. Tony's laughing and telling the dog all nice to sit, but the dog has Tony on his pay no mind list.

I make my hand a claw and poke the dog's flank, like his

mom would do. Dog spins and looks at me. I have no problem looking him in the eye while real quiet I grunt "Wait." Dog rolls belly up for me to scratch him. His tail beats dust from the concrete.

"I'm telling you, Mack, you gotta do it." Tony is always after me to start my own dog training business. "You'd make serious coin."

"I don't have the money for the school."

"You don't need the school," Tony says.

"You need the license from the school, or people don't think you're any good."

Tony claps my back to make me look him in the eye. "How much is it?"

"The school? Got no idea." I got the exact idea.

"What, like four or five grand?"

"Four. How'd you know?"

"Four is nothing," he says. "We'll put it on my credit card."

"Nah, I don't like owing folks. What if I can't pay you back?"

"So?" he says.

That right there is Tony in a minute. He's the line cook, and he doesn't make a whole bunch more than me. I tell him he was right in the first place, the school's a waste of money, but now he won't let up on he wants me to go to the school.

My mother showed me the way of dogs. She was from hill country, a migrant picker's daughter. Knew all kinds of towns and the dogs who ran their streets. She could rehabilitate some tough dogs, tell you what. We were out shopping for milk and such once. Mom eyed a dog, said, "Mack, see that straggly mutt gnashing his teeth at me? I'm-a have him rolling over for a belly scratch before you can say boo." I said that was a good name for the dog, Boo. She laughed. She had that dog eating apple bits from her hand. That's pretty much my favorite thing I remember about my mom. The old man forever complained at her, like "Get that dog out the house," and "That is a *stupid* opinion," and "Why can't you ever be *satisfied*? You think you gonna get better than motel cleaning work? *You?*" Face like he sucked a bag of lemons.

I woke up a rainy morning some years back to find him reading the note. My mother was watching an old movie a few nights before and imagined herself in it. It came to her that God called her to be an actress, and she had to go north to New York. Me and my father followed her there, but we never did find her. We tried Philly too, then Los Angeles. To ditch the old man she changed her name to Miranda something, and I would have done the exact same thing.

My father couldn't find steady work, so we shuffled back to Texas a few times before we struck out north again. We been here in the city almost four years now, and I don't think we're going anywhere, now that the old man has a regular job.

I saw her once on a commercial, Mom. One of them pills that make you crap. Late night. She was in the background. The old man pointed her out before he smashed the TV with a jug wine bottle.

Vic limps out back with his hands up for me to throw him the ball. He pitches pretty good, but the Tone has a world-class arm on him. He could strike me out easy, but he lays it right in there so I can crack it. We put electric tape over the ball to make it go far. The other side of the restaurant butts up on a tenement alley. The echoes are cool when the bat gets a good hold of the ball.

Vic huffs and puffs from chasing down the ball, and him and Tony are laughing because the dog won't leave my side even when I'm batting.

The Tone wanted me to pair up with him for this big brother after-school thing, but in order to do an *after*-school, you have to go *to* school, and to hell with that. Everybody calling you faggot and snapping at your ears? And even after you get tall, they still push the books out from under your arm and put pennies in your milk when you aren't looking, to choke you. Smacking the back of your head because you missed a belt loop, or telling you your fly is down when it's fine? In the classes, I couldn't stay awake. Making me look at all those boring books. Reading is just lame, I don't care what folks say. I'm a working man, saving up to get a little land somewhere, set it up good for me and a pack of pit bulls and maybe a nice lady, if one gets retarded all of a sudden and starts to like me even though I could never look her in the eye. I don't mean to say anything about retards. I like retards a ton—I'm no racist.

It's not like I never been with a girl before, but she didn't like me. She was sixteen or something. A few months back, I had a job delivering store circulars to the tenements. I saw her twice or so in the halls, and she never spent a look on me. But this one day, she does a double take and says, "Hot cocoa?" And I said, "What?" And she rolled her eyes and said real slow, like I was a moron, "Do, you, want, some, hot *cocoa*?" The slush kept getting in through the rip in my sneaker, so I was like, "Yeah, cocoa'd be real nice, thank you." We went into her apartment and next thing you know she was pulling me into her room and pulling down my pants and we smacked it up real quick. She hurried me out right after, said her folks were coming home soon, and I didn't get any hot cocoa either. I brought her daisies the next day and she told me to git. I found out she was using me for practice, because she liked this older dude, and apparently he was real experienced, and he didn't want the responsibility of making a girl not a virgin anymore. So I don't know if there's a girl out there for me, but you got to have hope. Doesn't cost you anything, hope. At least nothing I can see.

Word gets out Vic lost the restaurant to this online poker queen who calls herself Hammerhead, and Vic's selling the food cheap to clean everything out before he has to turn over the keys to the shark. I like it busy. I'm scrubbing pots and driving plates through the washer, making sure they're perfect. The bustle keeps me from hearing the hissing. It's not really hissing, this noise inside my head, but that's what I call it. Like when you roll the radio to static and dial up the volume? Like that. It reminds me of stuff I can't let myself think about anymore. I have to move on. Anyways, staying busy blocks it out, most times. I don't know. Just have to stay busy, I guess.

Come end of shift, Vic pays me cash. I missed the last few check-ins with my parole officer, and they scan the tax databases for AWOL parolees. Vic knows I've got a record. Burglary when my old man was out of town for a few weeks, looking for work, and I was damn near starving. I had this house staked out, knew when the folks were at work. A neighbor caught me sneaking out with three frozen pizzas and a pocket's worth of jewelry, which ended up being fake. Then this other time these kids got at me, shoved me into a trash can and rolled me down the school steps, which is another reason you shouldn't go to school. The radio static got real loud on that one. To stop it I got back at one of them boys with my knife. What else can you do? And anyways, he wasn't hurt that bad. Crying over a few stitches in front of that judge. Ten stitches in your thigh? I got more sliding into a gravelly third base once. Man up. You don't want to get cut, don't say bad stuff about my mother when you're rolling me down the school steps.

Me and the Tone leave work together. Like every girl we pass on the main street knows him. Tony says to one of them, "How'd your father make out with the operation, Jessica babe?" And I swear he remembers all their sisters' and uncles' names and their families' doings and "How's Marisol's baby? She's got to be two by now, right?" And don't you know the baby just turned two? Tony introduces me, and I can't look at them. I kind of mumble hey and keep my head down. Tony says we have to go, and the girls are all like "Aw, Tony, hang out. *Please?*"

We get to Tony's street, and he says, "Hang a left, come on up my way."

"I better get on home," I say.

"I'm just down the block there. I want you to drop a hi on my sister."

I get all red and I'm like "Nah."

"You're gonna be working together anyway now at the Too. She's cool, I swear."

"Nah, man."

"C'mon in and say hi to my mother," Tony says. "She's always baking something and she'll let you sip a half a cup of beer."

"Baking in summer?"

"I know."

"I'm up early tomorrow." My other job is I walk dogs.

"Okay, look, I'll grab us a pair of Sprites, and we'll sip 'em by the curb. C'mon, it's a nice night. Mack, I'm not gonna bring out my sister, okay?"

I force myself to trust him and grab some curb where the street slopes down by the sewer. Crazy stars tonight. Tony's up and down the block in a minute with the coldest Sprites. We sip with no need for words passing between us, and I'm real glad I answered that sign in Vic's window saying he was looking for a dishwasher that rainy day last March. I'll miss Tony maybe more than anybody I ever met. "Yo, Tony, man, the army, you make up your mind?"

Tony smiles. He's checking the sky. "See that slow mover way up there, the brightest one? It's a satellite."

"Nah, serious?"

"That thing just might still be sailing long after we're all gone."

"Yo, I hope you don't do it, man."

"Mack, if I go, I need a favor."

"You got it, man. Anything." I almost look him in the eye.

"Céce."

"Huh?"

9

"My sister. I need you to look out for her."

"What, like, keep the dudes away?"

"No, she can handle herself," he says. "It's just that she's . . ."

"Yeah?"

"You'll see."

"Tony, man, stay, man. You don't have to go over there."

He takes in the sky and then the neighborhood, which is kind of run-down but quiet with these little old one-family houses. He gets a little sad-looking, but he real quick smiles that away and punches my arm soft and heads up the block.

THE SECOND DAY . . .

(Saturday, June 13, morning)

CÉCE:

My mother, Carmella Vaccuccia, is insane. Would you name your daughter Céce, especially when you know it means chickpea? You say it like chee-chee. Like Vaccuccia isn't bad enough. It means little cow.

Carmella just has to go to Costco, because everybody needs sixty-two thousand rolls of toilet paper and four assemble-it-yourself closets to store them, all to save a nickel and a half, even though the closets never come out right because they cheat you on the screws.

I tell her, "Carmella, I have a bad feeling about this one, I swear."

"Babe, we're *not* gonna crash, *I* swear."

We borrow Vic's car, more rust than ride. On the way back from Costco this ninety-six-degree morning, the Vic-mobile's air conditioner craps out. Ma swerves to avoid hitting a sign that says AVOID SWERVING. The tire blows, and she plows the wall.

I look at her with slitted eyes.

She winks at me. "You don't have it."

"I *do.*"

"It isn't even *real,* sister."

"It *is.*"

ESP. Grumpy had it—my grandfather. The gift skipped over Ma, so I bear the curse doubly, I'm sure of it. For example, my neighbor's cat Lola? Thing was looking at me weird one day, and I thought to myself, That cat is gonna die, and it *did,* squashed by a Prius in silent mode. Swear to God. It was like a year and a half later when chica became wheel grease, but still.

We pull out the toilet paper, Ma's smashed beer, everything covered in hand soap and Heinz, to get to the jack and the slippery spare. Ma's like me with the big rack, bent over the tire to show her cleavage to the world. This little chump in a Benz convertible yells out the window, "Yo baby, you got some junk in that trunk," which around here means you have a big ass. He could be talking to either of us. Trucks are about to cream us because there's no shoulder for a loser to swap her loser tire. Ma's laughing. "Babe?"

"Yes, crazy lady?"

"Life is gorgeous." That smile. Her pimp gold caps. She, like, *dated* this dentist once, I don't even want to know. The woman is a mental.

We bring the car back to Vic. "Cannot tell you how sorry I am about the baked ketchup stink," Ma says.

Vic shrugs. "Don't sweat it."

"It's a potent scent, Vic."

"Potent is good."

"I'm gonna get the crashed part fixed, babe."

"Nah, leave it," Vic says. "Adds character. Anybody up for some Wiffle ball?"

"Always," Anthony says. He's working with us now at the Too. He grabs the bat and heads for the alley.

Peeking out of his back pocket is a picture of the American flag and that damned army brochure he's been thumbing the past few weeks. The recruiter called the house the other day and left a message for him. I deleted it.

I can hear them out there, Ant and Vic, talking about it between pitches. "Should I do it?" Anthony says.

"Family is the most important thing," Vic says, never mind Vic has no family except us. He leaves out the *I know what I know* and *You need to do this.* Because Anthony doesn't need to do this, and everybody knows this except Anthony. Vic's a vet. He did two tours in Vietnam.

"So, you're saying I shouldn't do it, then?" Ant says.

"Whatever you do, it's the right decision," Vic says.

"That's not helping me much," Ant says.

"It isn't meant to." Vic throws a moon ball, and Anthony creams it.

He better not do it. Great harm will befall him. I will be the perpetrator. I swear.

Lunch shift is hell. The restaurant is seven thousand degrees because like Vic's so-called car, his dive joint isn't hospitable to working air-conditioning. Plus there's my lip. I burned it on a slice and it looks like the herp. Here I am walking up to the giant table with all the cutie-pies from the fast-pitch league. "For your dressing, you want French, Russian, or creamy ranch?"

The guys are wincing as they try not to look at my mouth.

I suck my lip to hide it and head back to the kitchen to hang my order ticket. I nod to this dude waiting for his take-out. "Howya doin', Derek?"

"Super, Céce," he says, but his eyes say, *Except I just completely lost my appetite at the sight of that pus-leaking* bubble *on your lip.*

Lunch shift ends, and I'm sitting with my butt in the ice machine as I turn my crummy SAT II bio workbook upside down to read the answer I got wrong.

Anthony hangs his apron as he swings out the back door.

"Where you going?" I say.

"Buy running shoes."

"*Running* shoes? What's that supposed to mean?"

"Shoes you run in."

An hour and a half later, we're gearing up for dinner shift. Ant runs into the kitchen, tying his apron. "I ship out in two weeks," he says. Like he won the mega on a quick pick.

"Thought you were going out to buy running shoes?" I say.

"I did," Ant says.

"As you swung by the recruiting station?"

"After."

"My one and only brother slips out between lunch and dinner shifts and signs an army contract? How is this possible?"

"Two weeks." Ma nods. She smiles and winks, which means inside she's weeping. "No college, huh, babe?"

"When I get back."

Except he's not coming back. I *feel* it. He's going to die over there.

He got into a good school too, was supposed to start this fall, nice financial aid package because 1.a., we're broke, and 2.b., Anthony was an all-state quarterback.

Ant nods to Vic. "What do you think, Vic?"

Vic pats Anthony's shoulder. "Proud of you," he sighs. He gets back to mumbling over one of his stupid crosswords. "Prescient."

My girl Marcy is ready to slide out of her crappy polyester waitress skirt as she drools over Anthony. "Army uniforms are hot," she says.

I go out of my way to get her a job here, knowing full well she's the suckiest waitress alive after getting fired from two other places, and she pays me back by macking on my brother, in front of me, no less? She was voted eleventh-prettiest in our grade in a Facebook poll, never lets anybody forget it, uses tanning spray daily because she has this idea that orange skin will maintain her ranking. The sucky waitress thing isn't her fault, though. Her left arm is messed up from this, like, freak childhood accident. She has enough nuts and bolts in her elbow to open up a Lowe's. You kind of need two arms to be a rock star waitress, so we all cut her a ton of slack. Poor Marcy. She always wears long sleeves. She's like my only friend who's my age. One's enough. I can barely stand myself at this age.

Ant nods to me. "Howya doin', kid?"

"I hate you."

My brother is leaving me alone with crazy Carmella to go get his ass shot off in the desert. I need dessert. Cheesecake.

Now. I sneak into the walk-in fridge and hunker behind the Parmesan wheel and scarf a slice.

The door opens, and this guy comes in, kind of tall, clean cut, definitely nice-looking, but there's something wrong with him. He strikes me as both wounded and perhaps a little dangerous. His eyes. He's got a dark sparkle working there. He sees me behind the Parmesan wheel, and he freezes. I freeze too, cheesecake two inches from my blistered mouth.

"Sorry," he says. He drops his eyes and backs up.

"Foh whah?" I say, a plug of cheesecake in my mouth.

"Just need some grated for the takeout." Eyes on the floor.

I scoop some Parmesan into a to-go cup and hand it to him. "New delivery guy?"

He nods, but he won't look at me. "Hoping to get promoted to dishwasher."

"But don't delivery guys make more money than dishwashers?"

"I believe so," he says.

Wha? "Céce," I say.

"I know," he says. "Tony told me."

"You got a name?"

"Yep." Like five seconds pass. "Sorry about that. Mack."

I nod. "Mack, I don't have herpes."

"How's that?" His eyes flick to my mouth and then away.

"It's a burn blister."

"I see," he says.

"Pizza."

He nods, head down, eyes to the side. "I'm real sorry for your pain." He looks into my eyes for a sliver of a second and then his eyes go back to the floor and he backs out like a vampire stalking in rewind.

Burn blister. Dude wasn't even looking anywhere near my lip. I'm an idiot.

We're in the bathroom. I'm all about the Blistex and Marcy is doing her bit to keep the eyeliner companies afloat. "See the new delivery guy?" I say.

"He's weird."

"He won't look at you."

"He won't *look* at me," Marcy says. "And what's up with the way he talks? You ask him a question, and there's this pause before he answers. I was like, ''Scuse me, but do you know what time it is?' And you know what my hero says? 'Yep.'"

"You ask him for the time when we have a clock on every wall?"

"I was trying to get him to sleep with me, Céce, duh. So I ask for clarification, speaking big and slow for the lip reader crowd: 'What, time, is, it?' And he pulls this cheap loser watch from his pocket—a *watch*, like who wears watches anymore?"

"He wasn't wearing it, you just said."

"And he's looking at the *watch,* and it's like 'Well,' *pause,* 'it's about twenty-seven minutes past four. Or, no, wait,' *pause,* 'it's twenty-two past five.'"

"He's shy."

"He's *slow*. Either that or he's huffing rubber cement."

"He totally looks like Matt Dillon from *The Outsiders*."

"I know," Marcy says. "It's criminal, his gorgeousness.

Thank God he's stupid. If he was hunky *and* smart? I'd never have a chance."

"Who says you have one now?"

"He's the type to screw anything, trust me. Total player."

"Here's what I know about him," Ma says from the stall. "He's a nice guy." She comes out smiling, but you can tell she's been bawling.

I. Am going. To *kill.* Anthony.

"How can you tell he's nice when he's only working here for like thirty seconds, Mama V.?" Marcy says. "For all we know, he could be dealing meth to kindergartners, and the delivery boy thing is his cover job."

Ma rests her arm over Marcy's shoulders and kisses the Marce-arella's fake tan forehead. "He's nice because Anthony says he's nice."

We wrap dinner shift, and we're cleaning up the kitchen. Ma wants to talk with Anthony at the bar. "Mack?" Ant says, spinning a pizza. "Do me a solid, walk my sis home?"

I roll my eyes. "I'm *fine.*"

Mack is all about polishing the sink nobody is ever going to see way behind the dishwasher there. Freddy, our stoner dishwasher, did what he always does: Freaked and disappeared just when the rush hit. Mack jumped in and doubled on delivery, and he rocked it. He takes off his apron and waits at the door, holding it open for me, looking down at his sneakers.

Marcy struts by, swinging her falsies. Mack doesn't look. Marcy makes her fingers into an L behind his back and mouths *Looooser.*

"You live around here?"

"Yep," he says.

"I see. Where?"

"Downhill."

"I see. How do you like Vic's Too, as opposed to the now defunct Vic's?"

"I like it," he says.

"Good. Good."

"*Defunk* prob'ly doesn't mean what I think it means, right? Deodorized?"

"Huh?"

"Nothin'. Sorry."

"For what?"

He shrugs.

"My mother thinks you're a really hard worker."

No reaction.

"She was singing your praises to Vic."

He gulps, eyeing the cracks in the sidewalk. "Nice laugh your mom has."

"She's a wack job. What school you go to?"

He frowns. "I dropped."

"Dropped out?"

He nods.

"Oh." I trip on a sidewalk crack.

He catches my arm and keeps me on my feet. Even now he won't look at me.

"Thanks," I say.

"Yep." He takes his hands away fast. His hands are strong.

The hot breeze blows back the trees, and overhead is this minor miracle. A bright light arcs across the sky, but really slowly. I point it out through the glare of the streetlights. "Slowest shooter ever."

"It's a satellite," the boy says. "Tony told me." He's tracking it. His eyes are big and dark brown in the streetlights.

"You believe my brother?" I say. "Signing up like that?"

"Your brother's a really good dude."

"I'm gonna murder him. You have kind of an accent."

"Texas."

"Just a little bit. It's nice, I mean. Sorry." I put my hand on his arm the way I always do to people when I want to fake sincerity, except with this Mack, I find I *am* sincere: I do like his accent, and I am sorry if I in any way hurt his feelings, as I suspect they've been hurt enough. Yes, he's wounded, definitely.

He flinches at my touch, not violently, but like when you collect sparks crossing the carpet to pick up the empty beer can your loser mother left in the middle of the floor. I take my hand away from Mack's arm. This guy thinks I'm a freak. I suck my lip to hide my pustule.

Dog. Pit bull. Running at us.

I freeze.

"He's all right," Mack says.

I make a noise somewhere between a screech and a moan and hide behind Mack.

Mack goes "Tst!" and the dog stops and cocks its head. "Wait," he says, makes his voice deeper to do it, says it quietly. "Sit."

The dog sits.

Mack flicks his hand, and the dog trots off, wagging its tail. I'm still shaking. "How'd you do that?"

"He didn't mean anything but to say hello."

"But how'd you make him stop?"

"His ears were back easy, and his eyes were soft."

"Huh?"

"Nothin'."

"Thanks."

He shrugs, studies his sneakers.

"Wow," I say.

"Nah," he says.

We walk, and after a bit, I don't feel the need to fill the quiet. I keep sneaking peeks at him. First peek: nice face to frame those intense eyes, nose on the big side. Second peek: nice hair, thick, keeps it short. Third peek: good shape, skinny. Long legs.

I can't help but wonder what it would feel like to hold this boy's hand.

No. Friend material. Not even. Why would he want anything to do with me? He's totally hot, could get somebody much better looking than me. Still, he can't even *look* at me? Gotta be the lip.

We approach the rotting, double-mortgaged vinyl-sider that is my abode. The Vic-mobile is parked by the dead hydrant in front of our house. I smell the hand soap and ketchup wafting out of the smashed trunk a half block away. Ma and Vic are out on the porch. Vic slurps coffee over a crossword and Ma sips her cheap beer. Carmella salutes us with her tallboy. "C'mon in, Mack. I won't mind if you sip half a cup of beer. Just don't tell your mother."

Mack waits at the curb. "Better get going," he says.

"I have cornbread in the kitchen," Ma says. "You'll *love* it."

"Totally burned," I whisper to him. "She has this idea that starting up a cornbread business is going to get her out of insane credit card debt. We're in the trial stages."

"Yeah, nah, I gotta go." He heads downhill.

Smack me, why don't you? I spin to Ma and Vic. "What's wrong with that kid?"

"He's perfect," Ma says.

"Ten letters, second is *e,* to make a net or network," Vic mumbles over his puzzle.

"Reticulate," I say.

"Atta girl." Vic licks his pencil and scribbles it in.

I downloaded this vocabulary-builder thing for the gifted and talented test. You take it over the summer. Two parts, multiple choice and essay. I'm no genius, but when I'm not working I'm home studying, and I have a ninety-three average, so I have a shot at the multiple choice. But the essay scares me. You have to tell them about your gifts and talents and goals. My only goal so far is not to end up like my mother: never married, twice knocked up and ditched, alcoholic with crippling bunions because at forty she's been waiting tables at Vic's Too since she was my age. The only gift I have is ESP, but I can't write about that because people put you in the psycho slot if you think that kind of thing is real. If you kill the G and T, you can transfer to a rock star high school. That would get me into a decent college and after that a half-decent suburb, which one I don't care, as long as it's far away from here, prefer-ably something with off-street parking and mature shrub-bery that screens out the stinking world. I grab a sleeve of

Oreos and go upstairs to study. I have to find a gift or talent between now and that stupid test.

That Mack dude is gifted. I feel it in my gut. My ESP drives me insane.

THE SECOND DAY, CONTINUED . . .
(Saturday, June 13, late night)

MACK:

I stole looks. First was her hair, long and loopy and pulled back. Second, she has the prettiest face, open-like and up-looking. Third time I looked she was studying that satellite and I saw her eyes, deep brown, almost black. She has these little scars on her chin. I like that. When a lady isn't perfect, she's a lot more perfect, I believe.

I bet when you hold hands with a girl that cool you wonder if it's possible you're going to levitate like one of them monks I saw on a TV commercial once, which don't you wish that was real?

I head downhill and cut along the highway, and of course they're at it again. The dog fighters. At the end of the alley. They got it going on in the back of a van with the seats ripped out. I see through the back doors left open. Men drinking forties and throwing cash and jawing into their phones. And the dogs.

It's not loud at all. Pits don't bark much. They duck and twist like Galveston lightning till they clamp on at each other's throat. They try to roll each other, but neither dog goes over. They sway. Imagine slow dancing with a bear trap locked on to you. The men kick the dogs and stick them to make them madder. The dogs stay frozen like that, bound by their teeth.

I'm running at that van, tell you what, let them pop me. I reach into my pocket like I'm heavy with a pistol. My other hand is up like it's badged. "Yo, *freeze*."

The van jerks out of its idle and squeals away. They kick the loser dog out the back doors as they go. She's gasping in a puddle of old rain and mosquitoes and grease runoff from a leak in the Dumpster.

I stroke the dog's muzzle. Her tongue hangs long in fast panting. Her head is heavy in my arms. Her front left leg is cut. Pouch under her jaw too. Her eyes are rolled back. If she dies, I'll bury her in the park where nobody can mess with her. Up in the hills, where if you slit your eyes it's like you aren't even in the city.

I don't understand violence. I don't understand why it's got to be. And why does it have to be in me? I get so mad sometimes I could cut the world at the neck. A baby in a tenement cries out and cries on.

I pinch a sheet hanging from a fire escape and make a sling of it and scoop the dog. She's forty pounds, just where they want them for fighting. The small ones are the fastest. I see a lot of old scars. Going to be hard to rehab her, get her so she doesn't try to fight other dogs.

Here I am huffing and puffing along the highway overlook with this dog in a bloody sheet sling. Yet another truck crashed on the blind bend of the on-ramp just ahead, honking, fumes, feels like August instead of June. Gluey. I don't do real good in the humidity. Nobody does, but me less than most. I get a little hair-trigger.

This dude guns up the exit ramp in a Mercedes convertible, new, black pearl. He swings hard into the gas station and near about clips my dog, not to mention me.

I don't say a thing, but I must be giving him the eyes, because after he sizes me up as trash, he flips me off, slow style, like what are you gonna do about it? He does a double take on the bloody sling and the dog, frowns, revs to the gas pump. MD plates.

I'm wrapped in blood, and he leaves me? This man should not be a doctor. This man should not be.

Everything gets real quiet, like you mute the TV, see? Then there's the hiss of radio static. It comes on so bright and loud, I'm deaf and fighting blindness.

I follow this doctor. Nice clothes. Phone to his ear. He's jawing all loud and proud like rich folks do. But I don't hear what he's saying. I don't hear a thing but the hissing now. I'm grinding my teeth to keep from roaring out. The street shakes.

The doc does a double take on me, and I see in his eyes that he knows I'm going to cut him. I look down. My knife is in my hand. Dog is dangling under my arm, whimpering. I run my lock-blade tip over the doc's sparkly black paint job. I start at the back quarter panel, head toward the driver's-side door, toward him.

The Mercedes guns away without gassing up.

The radio static takes a while to fade. I walk a little, but my legs are weak. Have to sit. Practically fall to the curb. I'm empty. I think about what I almost did, and I want to be anybody else so bad. Being anger's slave is nowhere to be. I don't know. That static. If it was a real thing, like a piece of cancer, I would cut it out myself.

The dog trembles on me. Have to get her inside. That's the thing about dogs: They take your mind off everything. My legs are still shaking. I can't carry this girl home. And no way a cabbie will let me put a bloody dog into his Chevy. I don't have a phone. Somebody ripped the receiver off the pay phone, and I have no quarters anyway, and nobody to call. Except maybe Tony. *You ever need me, I'm there for you, day or night,* he said to me once. But most folks just say that.

I don't know how long it is before this dude pulls over. "You all right?"

"Fuck away from me, man." Dudes that pull over try to mess with me sometimes.

"I bring peace, friend," he says. "God's blessings."

"You better drive on, *friend*." I side-eye him.

He's staring real hard into my eyes, and I guess I look as messed-up as I feel, because he says, "Get in the car, and I'll take you to the hospital."

"Leave. Me. *Be*. Last time."

"The dog. What happened? Did it get hit?" He's got the Jesus sticker on his bumper and the cross hanging from the mirror.

"Just let me use your phone, man." I close my eyes. "Please."

I can't even get myself up from sitting on the curb, and he has to get out of the car to hand it to me. I pull the piece of takeout bag Tony wrote his number on from my wallet. I keep it next to this old picture of my mom. Her face is kind of worn off, but you can see what she was like, that she was the goodness.

"Tone?"

"Mack?"

"Sorry to wake you, man."

"Nah, man, I'm—I was awake anyway. What's up, buddy?"

Tony comes with Vic's car. His hair is all flat on one side of his head and standing up off the other. He had to be out cold after working that double today, on his feet fourteen hours. He studies the dog, then me. "Mack, it's gonna be okay, buddy. I promise." Puts his hand on my shoulder. Then he makes to scoop the dog.

She gets growly, and that snaps me out of feeling sorry for myself. "I got her." I scoop her and sit in the front seat. Tony runs the belt out for me to take it. I strap me and my pittie girl in, and Tony drives us to where I live.

Our spot is in the basement. Old man is out at the bar. Left two radios going. One has the ballgame loud. The other is on soft with old-style music.

I turn them both off.

Near-empty quart of Boone's Farm side-lies on the couch. I make to hide it.

"Mack," Tony says, "forget the bottle. Let's take care of the dog."

I grab towels and peroxide, cool water jug from the fridge. Tony carries that stuff. My strength is back mostly, and I carry the dog. We head for the roof. I have the keys to the service elevator. The old man is the janitor of this big old tenement. Most of the tenants in here are veterans and folks in rehab and sad nice folks like that. The kind who don't mind if you bring in a sick dog, even if it's against the rules of having no pets.

Elevator clunks Tony and me and my pit bull girl up twelve flights. She's panting crazy. I check her paws—sweating. Means she's terrified.

We walk the fire stairs the last flight, to the roof. Tony takes a second to study the view. You can see the park from up here, in the slots between where the line-dried sheets jig. The pigeons scatter and resettle. "They let you pet their heads with your thumb sometimes," I say.

"No, they let *you* pet their heads."

"Yo, Tony, man. Thank you, man."

"Thank *you*, brother."

"For what?"

"For this night. It's a gift."

"How do you mean?"

He doesn't say. He helps me get the dog inside the hutch—or that's what I call it. It's the housing for the elevators, to protect the engines that drive the cables. It's cinderblock and of a fair size, maybe as big as a two-room apartment. The engines are in the back, and there's a small janitor's workshop in the front. I like to hunker here. Sleep here sometimes too, especially after the old man comes in from a mean drunk. I like the hum and whir of the elevator cables.

I built a pen of chicken wire scraps I found in a construction site. Okay, I pinched them. But I had to, because I didn't have money, and I needed the wire, so that made it all right. It says you can do that in the Bible. I fenced the whole roof five feet high with it. I recuperate my dogs here. "When this one is good again, I'll ask my dog-walking customers if they know anybody looking for a nice pit bull. If she lives," I tell Tony.

"She'll live, buddy. With you taking care of her, I'm sure of it."

"She'd be a good dog, you know? For your moms maybe, while you're away."

"My moms, huh?" His eyebrows go up and he smiles. "You like her, right?"

"She's real nice."

"No, I mean do you *like* her like her?"

"Your moms?"

"Céce, bud. Yeah, I can tell: You're crushin' on her."

"What? Nah. Not that I don't like her. I like her, but not like I *like* her like her."

"Why not?" Tone says.

"I could never disrespect you like that."

"You're funny, man. Anyway, Céce's terrified of dogs."

"I kind of saw that." I tell him about the dog who came up to us on the way home. "But I could fix her fear, you know? This dog here would be real good for her."

"Then I guess you'd better try to get her to take the dog, right?" Tony pulls his phone and holds it out to me. "Call her."

"It's two fifteen in the morning—wait, ten after three."

"I guarantee you she's awake, pretending she's studying while she's watching *Polar Express*." Tony starts to call, but I clap his phone shut.

"Look, man, she's got to look a *hell* of a lot prettier than she is now before I'm ready to make that call."

"My sister or the dog?"

"What? No no, your *sister,* man. I mean your *dog—my* dog. This here *dog's* got to look as pretty as your *sister* is what I'm saying."

"So you *do* think she's pretty."

"I'll shut up."

"Don't. It's fun watching you twist."

"I need to rehab her first, Tone, my Boo here."

"Boo?"

"What I name all my dogs, boy or girl. Tony man, sorry, man, I swear: When the dog's all mended and trained, *then* I'll reach out to Céce. You can't rush these things."

"Of course you can," he says. "That's the best way, bud. Crash hard and fast. Nothing like it." He sighs and helps me wash my Boo. We brush her down with a peroxide towel and lay her out on a clean blanket. I get into the pen with' her. Tony sits against the far wall. The moon is on him when the clouds aren't dunking it. "Man, she's tough-lookin' though, huh?" Tony says. "That big pit bull head? Massive."

"My favorite kind."

"Seriously?"

"I love pits the most. They're true. Don't listen to what everybody says, that they like to attack folks. You've got more of a chance of a golden retriever turning on you."

"*Right.*"

"Serious. Pits are bred not to bite their handlers, especially in the heat of battle. If you torture them and bring out the fight in them, they'll be dog-aggressive, sure, but even so, most always they stay human-kind. You've got to go a long way into evil to turn a pit against people. They forgive easy as rain falls."

"I heard they cry like people. Like they tear up."

"No dogs cry tears. A pit bull's jaw doesn't lock either. Tell you what, though?"

"Tell me what."

"I seen pitties so sad and soulful. You see this girl's eyes, big and wondering? She feels real deep. You know what this girl wants, the only thing? To give and get love. Right, girl? Right Boo?"

"She's cocking her head there, huh? She likes that name."

"Best thing about pits is they take in the fun. They're the clown of the dog world. They have a ton of energy, which is why you need to exercise them a bunch and train them strict, and I do too. I include training free when I walk them."

"How much you charge?"

"Buck an hour."

"We need to get you a business manager," he says.

"That's all folks around here can afford. You string six dogs at once, you do all right. Sometimes the walk lasts two hours too, because I'm having so much fun I lose track of time."

Tony nods. "I've never seen you like this."

"Like what?" I hate when I let my softness show. Soft gets you killed.

"I think you need to let me help you pay for this dog training class. Just let me finish. As an investment, I'm talking. You'll rock the class, start your own business, and have a house-no-mortgage by the time you're forty."

"And what would be your end in all that?"

"The fun of seeing the good guy win one."

"The good guy, huh?" I can't figure out what he sees in me. He knows I been locked up. Being around him, I almost feel like what he's saying is true. That maybe I could be somebody. "Tony, man, I'm sorry for taking up your night like this, jawing your ear off."

"Stop saying sorry. I'm gonna run down to the bodega and grab us some sodas."

"I have Sprites in that little cube fridge behind you there."

Tony cracks us a pair.

"Yo Tone, I'd appreciate you not telling anybody about, like, what happened tonight."

"What, that you almost got yourself killed running into a dogfight to save a chewed-up pit bull?"

"I just don't like people knowing stuff about me, you know?"

He stares at me, and after a bit he nods. "All right, kid. I won't say anything." He's looking out the window and laughing quiet.

"What's funny?"

He shrugs, and we're quiet for a while, and my mind drifts back to that doctor. The knife in my hand. Mercedes gunning out of there. So close, though. Rewind the night back a little more, to Céce. No. She's too good to be in my dreams. Her, her mother, Tony: all too good. I can't imagine Tony overseas. I won't. They put a knife in *his* hand? He's not made to use it. He's made to lay knives down.

My Boo girl rests her big boxy head in my lap. She's looking up at me, and I know what she's saying. The language of dogs is quiet. Tell you what, if there weren't any dogs on this planet, I would check out right now.

I follow Tony's eyes out the hutch window. The sky is a mist with the stars trying to poke through, like a razor rash on God's gray face.

THE THIRD DAY . . .

(Sunday, June 14, an hour before dawn)

CÉCE:

The nightmare wakes me up. Gunfight in the desert. Anthony gets hit. I was cruising YouTube with Ma for soldier's-eye clips before I went to bed.

Why is he doing this? I know, *somebody* has to do it, but let it be somebody else. If anybody should go over there it's me, except I would be the suckiest soldier ever. Violence flips me out. When I see it, I freeze.

I trip myself to the bathroom and splash water on my face. Down the block a dog yips. Two dogs, barking now. Fighting. My hands are shaking.

When I was nine, we were at this block party, crazy hot out, too many people, music way too loud. I had to get out of there. It was either walk all the way around the block on a hundred-plus-degree day or cut through the neighbor's alley. I side-saddled the fence, right over the No Trespassing sign, picture of a guard dog, teeth barred. The homeowner wasn't lying: He had this giant German shepherd mixed with a pit bull—I'm sure it was a pit bull—but it was a horrible guard dog. It had been around for as long as I could remember, and

I never heard it bark. Besides, it was always tied to the fence behind the garbage pails on a short chain. As I walked by, it whimpered. It was filthy, matted, a choke collar embedded in its neck. It was panting. Its water bowl was empty. I cranked the spigot and filled it up. The dog drank the bowl dry and looked up at me. I went to kiss the top of its head. It jumped up and bit my face and didn't let go.

I opened my mouth to scream, and the dog got in there. It knocked me to the cement and shook me. Its jaw locked—that's how I know it was part pit bull.

How I survived that . . . How I got away . . . I can't . . . I can't remember.

Twenty stitches. I still have the scars. Those pit bulls are the worst. Their eyes? Creepy. Like they want to eat you.

I go downstairs and make a sandwich in the dark. Not seeing it makes it easier to scarf down. I'm two bites in when I see a shadow bent over the kitchen table.

Carmella Vaccuccia slurps a beer. "Hey."

"Ma, it's four fifteen."

"Cocktail hour."

"In the morning."

"Whacha eatin' there, babe?"

"PBJ."

She's eating one too. "You are your mother's daughter."

"You're absolutely *sure*? I'm doomed." I grab her beer and dump it in the sink.

"Don't turn on the light, Céce." Her voice is soft, sweet. Headlights from a passing car briefly light up two shiny streaks of mascara slitting her cheeks. I practically have to carry her up to bed. I tuck her in. She winks at me and slurs, "Howya doin', sister?"

"Carmella, the sister act is getting old. Could you be the mother for five minutes?"

She smiles. Those gold teeth. Anybody else would look four hundred percent retarded, but she's beautiful. Sometimes I want to hug her till I break her. The woman is demented.

I wonder if that Mack boy is working today.

I pop my head into Anthony's room. He's out?

Middle of lunch shift, Marcy sticks her head into the walk-in. "Céce Vaccuccia, why you hanging out in the refrigerator?"

I hide my third slice of cheesecake. "Cooling off, *duh*."

"God swapped June for August on us. Probably be like this till winter, and then overnight it'll be five billion below zero, freeze nail polish right in the bottle. You can't win, Cheech. You *can't*. They got it stacked against us."

"Who's they?"

"*Them,* chica. The system."

I pat the cheese wheel for her to sit with me. "Hang out."

"Ohmigod."

"What?"

"Ew!"

"What!"

"You totally made out with that loser delivery guy dude last night."

"*What?* No."

"I can see it in your eyes, you lovesick bitch."

"You need to pop another Lexapro."

"Tell me later. You got a tray of manicotti up and your tables are howling for their checks. And Céce, the manicotti? Vic totally went heavy with the ricotta this morning. Gonna feel like you got a Honda Element on that tray. I can't believe you swapped spit with that dropout moron."

"I. Did not. Kiss. The de*liv*ery boy."

"Ick." She leaves.

I'm totally bloated. Skirt zipper is gonna rip any old shift now. It's like I ate a ten-pound box of chalk and then somebody pumped hot gasoline into my stomach. Make out with Mack? Is she out of her half a mind? Dude won't even look at me.

End of lunch shift I'm at the bar, refilling the salts and peppers, thrill-a-rill. The salt is all clumps in the heat. While I'm spilling the condiments I'm checking my G and T practice test grid against the answer key.

I aced it?

Maybe not so remarkable, because Vic keeps quizzing me words all the time. Like last night, I was picking up an order, and he handed me my linguine red sauce and said, "Frenetic." And I replied, "Crazed, as in 'Marcy is running around in a frenetic state, trying to catch up on her orders, because Vic's Too, currently the one and only Vic's eating establishment, is slamming.'"

Of course, this is only the multiple-choice part. I still don't have any idea what I'll write for the essay, but I have a few weeks to cook up a really good lie.

Marcy flies into the bar and drags me to the bathroom. "Your psycho boyfriend?" she says.

"He's *not* my—"

"*Yah.* He's a felon."

"*What?*"

"Your mother was asking Vic about him because she, like everybody else who isn't you, can tell you're crushing on him."

"I'm crushing on a felon?"

"Vic's like, 'Well, I suppose you should know he's had some problems in the past.' And then your mother's like, 'What kind of problems?' And then Vic goes, 'Well, he has a bit of a record.'"

"What'd he do?"

"I don't know. I snuck out from where I just happened to be behind the trash compactor to run here to tell you, but it was probably something *wretched.*"

Ma comes into the bathroom. "You know what they have to say about those who gossip?"

Marcy hides behind me. "What do they have to say, Mama Vaccuccia?"

"Not a lot. Go fill those pepper shakers, girls. And Marcy, you keep sneaking around like that, we're gonna have to make you wear a bell."

Wow. A felon. It had to be something not *too* bad. A boy that quiet would never do something violent.

I head upstairs to get the linens for dinner. Vic lives up here in a little bedroom stacked with vinyl records and books flagged with pink stickies that say POTENT and bright red ones that say VP! I can't help but peek into the room as I walk past, because Vic never remembers to close doors when he leaves. He leaves his car door open half the time. He has one picture on the wall over his desk, this crappy printout Ma gave him. He framed it. Me, Ma, Anthony, and Vic a few Christmases back. It's a blurry picture. Ma set the timer and put the camera on the stairs and ran to be in the shot without bothering to check the auto focus, which was on a sweaty beer can she left on top of the TV.

Down the hall is another bedroom, the supply room. Anthony is at the window with a stack of pizza boxes that need folding under his arm. He waves me over. "Quick, check this out," he whispers. The exhaust fan blocks the window, but I can see through the grate: Mack is down in the alley. He pulls his broken plastic watch from his pocket, checks the time, frowns.

"So?" I say.

"Hang out," Ant whispers. "They used to meet like this back at the other Vic's."

"Who?"

A few seconds later this guy comes into the alley, older, slash scars from the corners of his mouth up to his ears, shabby-looking army coat in all this heat.

Mack checks the alley, all clear. He gives the guy money, they palm grip, the other dude says, "Dog Man, whatever you need, you let me know," and goes.

This Mack kid is not only a dropout felon but also a junkie? I'm crushed, until I remember I don't even know him. "Awesome, a meth transaction behind Vic's Too. Great crowd draw. We gotta tell Vic."

"No meth involved," Ant says. "It's a one-way. Mack's just giving him money."

"Anthony, wake up. There's a mothball being transferred in the palm grip."

"Cheech, I *know* this kid. I'd bet my life on it: It's charity, pure. He makes fifty bucks a shift and gives away ten of it. I feel like I'm a firewalker when I see stuff like this. Puts me on a totally different plane, faith restored."

"You're retarded."

"I swear, I ever get rich? Just to see what he'd do with it, I'm giving Mack all my money."

"What about me?"

"You can give him all your money too." He sighs as he leaves the window. "Feel bad for the dude with the smiley. He would've had to been held down to be cut twice."

"Ant, you're trying to find magic in the bottom of a mud puddle again. Can you please stop feeling bad for every-body?"

"Actually, kid, I can't." He messes up my hair and goes.

I pull the linens from the rack and count the creaks in the steps. When I'm sure he's downstairs, I bury my face in the napkins so nobody hears me. I can't breathe. In two weeks my best friend is on a plane, headed for boot camp.

(The next afternoon, Monday, June 15, the fourth day . . .)

After last period I head for the library, basically where people go to take part in the unending spitball war that has been plaguing my class since the fifth grade. How many times have I scratched a monster zit on the back of my neck only

39

to discover it was a masticated quarter page of *Warriner's English Grammar and Composition*?

Mustering a rare burst of initiative, I'd booked the back room for a study session for kids who were thinking about taking the G and T. I advertised it on my Facebook page and hung a lame sign on the announcement board. As I'm walking into the study room, my ESP zings me: I'm going to be the only one who attends the session.

I am correct.

I dump my backpack. Yupper, I left it home, the book I need. I'm hungry and grumpy and so flipping hot and why can't I stop wondering why the junkie dishwasher avoids me at work? Or am I a paranoid loser? "Or am I both paranoid *and* shunned?"

"Who you talking to?" Nicole Reeni swings into the room. She's breathless, spitballs in her hair.

"Thanks for coming, Nicky," I say.

"What are you *talking* about? G and T study session? I'd rather pick the corn out of my crap."

"I want your life, Nic."

She drops six quarters into the soda machine, *clunk* goes the Fanta Zero, and the Reenster bounces.

One more week of school, and then I go from working weekends to slinging hash full-time at the just barely air-conditioned Too in a one hundred percent synthetic fiber uniform that went out of style in 1954. I so rule this Earth.

THE NINTH DAY . . .

(Saturday, June 20, morning)

MACK:

When she laughs, she snorts the tiniest bit. I like that. I couldn't stop thinking about it all week, her smile. Her. I double-checked the schedule. She's definitely on tonight.

"I shouldn't mess with this girl, Boo. Why start something that can't last?"

My girl Boo cocks her head. She's bouncing back good. Cuts look clean, closing up nice. She's eating. She's strong enough to take with me on my dog walking rounds.

"Boo."

She cocks her head twice. Brown eyes, big and pretty.

First dog I pick up is another pit, big red-nose goofball. What happens next all happens in about a second and a half.

Boo goes for Red's neck, just like I knew she would. I say "Ey" as I bump Boo's shank with the back of my sneaker. She spins to me. I snap the lead hard to pull her behind me and put myself between her and the other dog. Her eyes bug on me. Her ears go from high and forward to back and soft. I'm standing tall and strong, my head up high and proud as

41

I lock eyes with her and say real quiet, slow and deep, "I got it." Meaning that I got the situation under control. I won't let anybody hurt her, dog or human. Dogs don't know what you're saying, but they know what you mean. Now her tail goes soft too and into a nice easy slope. Her hackles flatten. Her eyes are soft on me and only me. Rest of the walk she's an angel.

I wouldn't trust her alone with another dog yet or maybe ever, but as long as she's with a human who will take the lead, she'll be peaceable. They only fight because they're scared the other dog is going to get them first, and wouldn't you be if your whole life was fighting?

Before you know it, six dogs are trotting along behind me, nice slack leashes, and it occurs to me I wish I could play guitar. Never let a dog walk in front of you, especially when you're going through a door. There's leaders and followers, and I wish I didn't have to be either one. For my probation once they made me run rec center track. Winning made me feel worse than losing. I felt good when I quit. But with dogs, you have to force yourself to be a winner. Losers make them nervous.

Thing about walking dogs is it goes pretty good with thinking, and I can't quit dreaming of Céce. We're holding each other, and I'm not afraid to look her in the eye.

Tony keeps pushing hints. Did I know that Céce loves movies, and wouldn't it be sweet for her to have somebody to go with after Tony heads south? I don't like movies too much because you can't talk to her and you don't know if you should hold her hand or when to kiss her and how far does she want you to go and stuff like that. I'd like to walk with her again instead. Her, me, and Boo.

Me and the dogs climb through the cheat weed hills to where the grass softens and gets long in the swaying tree shade, and we lose ourselves in the wildwood.

This is my secret place, the graveyard. The people who owned this land before they gave it to the city are buried here. Ten crypts, all worn by rain and mossed over. Nobody comes to visit them except me, and they let me sip the quiet. I lie back in the high grass and watch the hot wind punch it, and the dogs settle in around me.

I see signs taped to the light poles. Land, cheap. Six hundred bucks an acre. Have to clear the trees yourself. Get me fifty acres, build a cabin of the deadwood, have like twenty pits with me, nobody messes with us. I wonder if Céce likes the woods.

She's going to find out about me any day now. Everybody does sooner or later. That I got a record.

Me and Boo drop off the other dogs. Up on the main drag the vendors are out with their tables and signs that say EVERYTHING A DOLLAR. A buck picks up a wrong-made soccer ball for Boo. Pits like to chew soccer balls, so don't take them to a tight match. I see real nice fake leather wallets and stuff. I nod polite to the old lady behind the table, just like my mom taught me. "Ma'am, you got any ideas about what a girl would like in the way of a present?"

"What's she like?" lady says.

"Reckon she's fifteen, about so high."

"Fifteen and so high, you got to get her a phone case." She points to a bin of a thousand pink phone cases. They're a little moldy, but other than that they look pretty good. Thing is, I heard a rumor that girls don't like to wear phone cases. "What else you got?"

"How much money you got to spend, chico?"

I fish my pocket. "'Bout a sourbuck."

"Gets you a gorgeous little piece of magic." She dumps a bucket onto the counter, and all this real sparkly jewelry comes out, stickpins with diamonds on them shaped out into letters. "Will you just look at these?" she says. "Stunning, no?"

"*Whoa.*"

"What's her name?"

"Like Céce."

"*Chee*-chee? You kidding?"

"I don't believe I am at all."

"Lovely name." She hunts for a *C*, can't find one.

"Is that there a . . . wait. That one. That a *Q*?"

"*G,*" she says.

"I'll take it." I swap her the ten bucks for the *G*, pull my army knife and clip the little thing off the *G*. It passes pretty good for a *C* now. Old lady's nodding at me.

I walk away eleven bucks lighter for two items, which is about the way it always goes for me at the Everything A Dollar table. The lady chucks me a moldy phone case. "On the house."

I study the pin in a slash of sunlight twice bent off the tenement windows. The diamonds come alive. I look at Boo. She wags her tail. We head off. I'm pretty sure I'm levitating.

A hawk's wings are lifting me. I have a sparkly *G*-turned-*C* stickpin in my pocket.

I stop off in the basement to grab a water jug before I head up to the roof to bed my Boo for the night while I'm at work.

Pops is watching afternoon TV. "Get that goddamn dog out of here."

"I will."

"Y'all take that goddamn mountain of trash to the curb like I ast you last night?"

"I did."

"Make sure you double-check the door is shut on yer way out. Woke up this morning and the goddamn thing was left wide open, mister."

That's because you left it open when you stumbled in smashed this morning, I don't say. "I will," I say. I pull my pay from my back pocket and fork him my share of the rent.

Don't he just count it too, before he shoves it into his pocket. "Don't be late for work neither."

"I won't."

"I got *no* time for latecomers in my book. Be on time or be gone." He sips beer and burps and his phone rings, and he picks it up, and he's like "Oh, yeah, hey, how y'all doin', missy? Sure, we can forty-up right out back if you want," and I ain't even in his world no more.

Boo's going to sleep good tonight after all that walking we did today. She's curled up in her pen and snoring. I put a street-found air conditioner in the front window, but it's cool enough out. I raise the side windows and get the fans

I found at the construction site pulling in a good strong breeze. Found this CD player in the trash too. Had a disc of soft piano music in it. I keep it on loop for Boo. I don't use the radio part of it, because when the wind changes, you get static sometimes, and I don't need that at all.

I'm heading out of the hutch when this old stoop-back crank Larry comes up to the roof to hang his wet sheets. Larry is the brand of idiot who catcalls at the ladies when they're getting off the train. I see him out on the street, telling them what he would do to them if he got the chance. He nods at the elevator housing. "You better not have another dog in there. I'll call the cops. When is it going to sink into that bag of dirt renting space in your skull? No dogs allowed in this building."

"No cats either." Larry has cats, which I don't mind. Cats are sly, but they're all right sometimes, especially the ones who act like dogs.

"Filthy, dogs are. The stink gets into my sheets."

Why can't folks just leave folks alone? Serious, why do they always need to mess with you? I force myself to head for the stairs.

"Look at him running away now. Look at him go. Queer bait. If I kicked that dog in front of you, you wouldn't do anything but bawl like a baby hungry for the tit."

And that's when it comes, just a flicker of it, that low note of a hiss always hanging deep in my mind. A sound that can't decide if it wants to swell or fade. I tell myself to keep walking, but I'm not me anymore. I'm a rag puppet trying to get free of the strings. Getting jerked up high and fast into a sky hot enough to char the blue from itself. No air up here. Rib cage is caving in like these two fierce arms are clawing me from behind. The invisible hands turn me around real, real slow. I hear the hissing so loud that I can't quite hear myself, or whatever is making me say "I'm warning you, man, first and last." I sound like I'm underwater.

"Waste of life. You warn me? I was in the navy. The only reason you're standing here free on this roof to disrespect me is because I fought for your right to do it."

"Thank you for your service, but if you mess with my dog, I will hurt you, man. That's no promise either. That's a threat. I mean the other way around." I'm shaking bad.

Larry hangs his sheets, laughing at me. I can't hear him. Just the radio static now. He mouths *Punk* as he heads downstairs. I make my hands into fists to keep myself from reaching into my back pocket and pulling my lock-blade. I'm liable to break my fingers, I'm balling them so tight.

Takes a while for the heat to float off me, and then I drop hard back into my body, and I'm so heavy with the fear of what I almost did, I have to sit down. My mind is so crunched up there's room for only one thought: I have to give Céce the pin. What's the worst that could happen? I scare her off?

That would suck.

The minutes click by a little faster, and time becomes real time, and I'm back in the everydayness of things. I double-check the padlock on the elevator housing door. Only the old man and me have the key for it. Good solid door. Heavy metal to keep out the thieves, or at least Larry.

THE NINTH DAY, CONTINUED . . .

(Saturday, June 20, afternoon)

CÉCE:

We take the bus for the air-conditioning that isn't working anyway, and it T-bones a soda truck. A couple of people are faking whiplash for lawsuits, but everybody's okay.

"I had a vision I was in a bus accident," I say. "Couple of years ago. Swear to God. Let's just leave it at that."

"Let's," Anthony says as we hike toward the Too. "Look," he says, "you're perfect for each other."

"My brother wants to set me up with a dropout drug addict convict. I rock."

"Why do you have to think the worst?" he says.

"Because that's how it usually turns out."

"I know things about him. Things I can't tell you. Trust me. I'm not saying you have to go out with him, but let him be a friend to you. He'll help you."

"With what? And what things can't you tell me?"

"I can't tell you."

"Trying to make him mysterious to get me to go out with him isn't working."

"Yeah it is. Cheech, I'm out of here in a week. You need a friend. I trust him."

"We got all we can handle with Vic watching out for us."

"*You* need *Mack*."

"I don't *need* anybody. And by the way, I'm not going to the airport with you to say good-bye."

"Why?"

"Because I'm *pissed*, Anthony." I walk on ahead. Like he has to tell me to hang out with the dude. I find myself very attracted to sad people. I seriously hope this guy isn't going home and firing up a mothball after work.

Vic's at the bar with Ma. "Ameliorate," he says.

"Relieve," I say. "As in, 'Ma sank into our cheap, cruddy, scratchy brown couch and drank a six-pack of Bud Light last night to try to ameliorate the stress of my moron brother's looming departure.'"

"Potent sentence," Vic says. "Image-laden. Well done."

"Cheers," Ma says, sipping what I hope is a Virgin Mary.

Mack's behind the dishwashing machine. I play cool, or try to. "Lemme guess, Freddy's being an idiot again?"

"What?" he says.

I do the lamest Freddy impersonation, the way he calls in, "'Uh, yeah, Céce, wondering if you could talk to *Vic* for me. Uh, see, thing is, I find myself under the *weather* today. *Cough-cough!* Can't seem to get rid of this *cough-cough!* Tell him it's *potent*, this cough, Céce, you can't *envisage* a more dire respiratory condition.'"

Mack looks away, no smile for me, no eyes either, gets to work. Dude thinks I'm a total geek. Note to self: Don't ask him to play Wii tennis.

I check the wall clock. It's getting to be that time: his daily drug deal. I grab Marcy from the bathroom. "Can you stop looking at yourself for five minutes?"

"Depends on what you're offering for an alternative. And don't say wiping down the silverware."

"I need your opinion."

"Is it about the felon? You ever notice how he pinches the inside of his wrist when he's nervous? It's a shame, really. He's got the nicest ass."

"You ever see him with that dude out back? Do you think he's—"

"Yes."

An hour later we're slammed. Me and Ma are running food to our tables and Marcy's because my girl doesn't do too well when we get busy. Vic's whomping garlic and tossing it into Anthony's pans, ten going at once. Half hour later the customers are pouring in, and we're in the weeds. Me and Ma are starting to confuse the orders. Marcy is catatonic. Even Vic is a little edgy, mumbling his crossword vocabulary list, "overwhelmed, overcome, *in*undated." Mack washes and reracks and double-times it out to the floor to help us bus our tables without being asked, but even he's falling behind.

We're at the point where we'll lose it, and the customers will walk out.

Then there's Anthony. He turns up the radio, classic rock station, perfectly clear reception because Vic has the satellite subscription working. Ant makes the pepper grinder his microphone and sings with Bruce Springsteen, *"Tramps like us, baby we were born to run."* He's got this incredible voice. Ma flashes back to her slutty youth and joins in totally off-key. She's working the broom, air guitar, totally cheesy but at the same time endearingly cute in only the absolutely saddest Carmella-Vaccuccia-trying-to-be-cool sort of way. Vic whomps garlic to the drumbeat. Me and Marcy are singing backup with our atrocious voices. We go back out to the floor to serve, and we're beaming, and the customers love it. Who doesn't like a happy waitress?

I'll always remember this. My big brother making everybody feel good, his arms caked with sweaty flour, his apron filthy with deep-fry grease and tomato sauce. Doesn't sound like much of a moment, but I have a feeling this might be the last time we're all together like this.

Mack has the smallest smile working behind those dish racks. Wait, a second ago, was he looking at me?

We close out the register with lots of money in our pockets. Ma and Vic are playing slap cards at the bar. Anthony says he's got to say good-bye to some friends. "Mack buddy, you walk my sis home?"

"That all right with you?" Mack says.

"Sure, whatever." My heart makes a clicking sound. I wonder if he can hear it. I try to cover by nonchalantly swigging a soda, and I spill Pepsi on my boobs. Loo. Ser.

We're slow-walking the main drag. Kids on Harleys rip up and down the street. Mack clears his throat, says to his worn-out sneakers, "I been to jail. I expect you already know, but I thought I should tell you, just in case. I, some folks are scared to be with folks who been locked up."

"No. I mean, no, I'm not scared. This is nice, you walking me home. I appreciate it." I'm scared to ask, but I have to know. "What happened?"

He tells me what he did.

I nod for a long time, and now I clear my throat. "So you never killed anybody."

"No. No."

"I'm glad. I mean, for *you* I'm glad. I didn't mean—"

"No no, I know." He nods, still won't look at me. "I, you, like the other night. The dog. The one that jogged up on us. You was—you were scared."

"I was bitten once."

His eyes flick to my scars, then away. "Did you try to kiss the dog?"

"Well I, how did you know?"

He shrugs.

We're in front of CVS now. "Mack?"

He's startled, hearing me say his name. "Yep?"

"I gotta grab a couple of things, okay? Wait here. I'll be back in five." I head in. Ma told me to pick up a roll of toilet paper on the way home, because when we wrecked Vic's car, the four hundred rolls in the trunk got skunked with beer and ketchup. But I don't want Mack to see me buying a loser item like toilet paper. Figure I'll pick up the smallest roll Charmin offers, just to get us through Sunday, and hide it under a cool item, perhaps a giant bag of Skittles, for instance.

CVS is having a huge toilet paper sale. All they have left are sixteen-packs.

Problem: We're down to using travel-pack tissues at home. Now I have to walk around with sixteen rolls of Charmin.

When I come out of the store, two bikers are stopped at a red light. One has his radio blasting some faraway station, more static than music.

Mack looks weird all of a sudden. Mad. He's staring at the biker.

The biker's friend doesn't like that. "You got a problem, bitch?"

"Let's go," I say.

But Mack is someplace else, his eyes locked on the biker.

The light changes, and the biker's friend waves off Mack with "Pf, you ain't nothin'." The two Harleys jerk away, busting up the night with their sawed-off mufflers. Car alarms go *blant-blant-blant*.

He's back now, sort of. He's wobbly. He puts his hand on the mailbox to keep his feet. "You know like when you're crouching, and you stand up too fast?" he says.

"Except you weren't."

He's looking at my hand on his arm. He doesn't pull away this time. He catches his breath. "I can show you how to greet a dog, if you want."

"Greet a dog? I'm worried about you. Are you hypoglycemic?" That or he totally dropped a Seconal while I was in CVS. "Here, have some Skittles." Of course when I pop the bag I spray three trillion Skittles all over the street.

"My dog," he says, bending to clean up the Skittles. "I want you to meet her."

"Yeah, no, I don't think so."

"She's the sweetest little pit." This guy. His eyes. That dark sparkle.

"Anybody ever tell you that you look like Matt Dillon from *The Outsiders*?"

"That good or bad?"

"Hello, it's only one of the best movies ever in the YA genre."

"I don't know a whole lot about movies or . . . whatever that French-soundin' word you said was. Come drop a hi on my dog."

An hour ago, I thought my night would be inventing lies for that stupid Gifted and Talented essay, and now this boy with the dangerous eyes is asking me over to his place to meet his pit bull. I push my bottom lip over my top to shave my sweat 'stache. I swallow hard. I nod. "Okay. Do you need any toilet paper?"

We go straight up to the roof of his building: scary. He unlocks the door to the elevator engine housing: scarier. He calls it "the *hutch.*" I see a sleeping bag. I see myself in tomorrow's news, *Girl Who Should Have Known Better, 15, Murdered While Resisting Advances of Ex-Convict Meth Addict.*

"You live here?" I say.

"Sometimes."

"And what about the other times?"

"Cellar." He holds the door for me. "Go on now," he says.

The entire *Saw* franchise flashes before my eyes as I step into the dark of the elevator housing. He follows me in. One thing keeps me here: Anthony's word. If Ant says Mack is good, then Mack is good.

The hutch roof has one of those old glass box window vents, with the wire woven through the glass and the moonlight weaving through that. I wait by the door while he unlatches the hellhound's pen.

The dog: fawn with a vanilla bib, huge brown eyes, *huge* head, jaw that could crumble cinderblock. She yawns shark teeth and shakes herself awake, wagging her tail faster when Mack turns on the light. "Easy," Mack says to the dog, his voice deep, firm. He stands next to me. "Don't look at her."

"Don't worry," I say, my eyes clamped.

"Don't talk to her. Don't touch her. Not yet. For now, just ignore her. Let her smell you when I call her over."

"Can't we just go mess around on your computer?"

"I don't have a computer."

"*What?* How do you Hulu?"

"Boo, come."

I tremble as his wolf demon sniffs me. She nudges my hand with her snout.

"Don't pet her," Mack says. "Just keep looking at me."

Except that *he's* not looking at *me*. "I have DVR back at my house. Please. The season finale of *The Biggest Loser*—oh, my, *god.* What is she doing?"

"That's how they say hi."

"She's sniffing my butt."

"Exactly."

"I have two gift certificates to Cheesecake Factory, but they expire in nine minutes. If we leave right now—"

"Okay, now look at her. Open your eyes."

The dog is sitting at my feet, wagging her tail, her eyes on me.

"Okay, that's enough," he says. "Look at me again, like she's not even there. Now, real easy—don't bend over her. Keep standing tall. Good. Let the back of your hand rest soft at the side of her snout."

"No way."

"Don't come from up top. They have bad eyes and don't

like stuff coming at them from above. Come from the side, where she can see your hand, nice and slow, and then you let her sniff it, and then you brush down the side of her neck with the back of your fingers, real easy. Go ahead."

"Nuh-uh."

"Yep."

"Nep."

"I promise, she may drench you with licking, but she won't bite."

"And what about you?"

"Trust me," he says.

"Ha!"

"*Trust* me." He takes my hand and brings it to the side of the dog's face. His hand is rough with calluses. Together we stroke her neck and under her snout. The dog leans into my leg and licks my hand. But I'm not looking at her. I'm looking at Mack. He feels my eyes on him, and he stops moving my hand through the dog's fur.

"You did real good," he says, taking away his hand.

I won't let him go. I squeeze his hand. Why won't he look at me? I can see it in his neck, his pulse, as fast as mine. I want to bite the beautiful vampire's neck.

He slips his hand from mine. "We better get her down to the street," he says. "She's been holding it in all night."

They walk me home, Mack and Boo. When he hands me the leash, the dog pulls ahead of me. "Pull back hard on the lead," Mack says.

"She'll bite me."

He takes the leash and swings the dog behind me. She stays there all the way to my house.

"You want her?" he says.

"Uh, *no*."

"She likes you a ton. She'll cuddle you all night."

"I can't."

"Your moms?"

"My mother loves dogs."

"I figured."

"Why?"

"She's the type."

"And what type am I?"

He looks away. "I'll be holding her for you. Give her to you trained perfect too."

I scan Palazzo Vaccuccia. The windows are dark. I step so I'm facing him and a half step closer. "We could crank the air conditioner, and you, me, and Miss Boo can watch *Polar Express* with the director's commentary. My mother made peppermint cornbread. It tastes gross, but on the upside it's filling and not completely stale, baked fresh four days ago."

"In all that heat?"

"I know."

He scratches the back of his head as he checks the sky.

"Satellites?" I say.

"None up there tonight. None I can see."

"Come on in with me. Just for a little bit. For like a Pepsi or something."

"I'm a Sprite man." He strands me there, not even a walk the girl to her door.

It's definite now: I am the fattest, ugliest girl in the city.

He gets a few steps away when he stops. "I wanted to give you something." He digs his hand into his pocket, and for a second I'm seeing him pull that knife, the one he used to cut the kid who rolled him down the stairs. He takes his hand out of his pocket, and it's empty. "Wanted to, to give you a little bit of advice."

"Ad*vice*. Okay?"

"When you walk a dog, if you choke up on the leash a little, you have more control over her."

"I see."

"You did real great though, Céce. With Boo, I mean. You don't know it, but you're a dog person." He goes with his dog. She watches and studies and worships him.

Four o'clock in the morning. I'm doing a droolly face plant in my notebook when a crash downstairs wakes me up. My stupid practice essay is sticking to my face, some crap I wrote about wanting to be in politics, because I thought it would make me seem community-minded.

Anthony is down there before I am. Ma slumps against the wall at the bottom of the stairs. The leave-your-crap-here table is on its side. Grumpy's dusty glass figurines are all over the floor.

"Ma, did you fall coming up or going down?" Ant says.

"Uhhh. Pp." *Plas*tered. Her nose is bleeding, a splinter of glass in the bridge.

Ant pulls it out. "Cheech, you gotta watch her while I'm gone."

I want to rip off my skin and crawl through salt. I'm

screaming, "Why, Ant? Why're you going over there?" Then I start in on my mother when Ant calms me down with a gentle hand to my shoulder.

"Hey, kid?" he says, his voice soft, easy. "Breathe. It's gonna be okay. Cheech, look here. I swear. Let's get her upstairs."

We get her into bed. The overhead fluorescent is on its way out. "Are the lights flickering, or am I losing it?" she says.

"Both," I say.

"Where's Anthony?"

"Getting towels and ice."

"*Towels* and *ice*?"

"For your nose, Ma. You're bleeding all over yourself."

"I can't even feel it."

"Fantastic."

"Céce Vaccuccia?"

"What?"

"I love you like a crazy person."

"You *are* a crazy person, Carmella."

Anthony comes back with the ice. Ma won't let go of his hand. "Anthony, don't go, honey. Please, babe. Stay."

THE TENTH DAY . . .
(Sunday, June 21, morning)

MACK:

Sun comes up hazy between the condo towers they're building past the reservoir there. I guess I slept some last night.
I'm studying the *G*-turned-*C* stickpin. Boo whines to pee. I
take her down to the street, and we walk the reservoir and
then pick up the rest of the dogs. The whole morning I can't
think of anything except that I'm the biggest idiot in the city
for not holding on to that girl's hand.

When we get back, I set down a pot of cool water. While
Boo's drinking I go to the other side of the roof. "Boo, come."

She looks up, gets back to her water.

"Boo, come." This time I show her inside my hand, peanut butter wiped on it.

She bolts across the roof to lick my palm clean. I try it
again and again, then without peanut butter, and still she
comes to me every time, even if it's just for a scratch under
her jaw. Now is the hard one: "Wait."

Nope, dog won't stop following me, her peanut butter man.

"Wait." I say it strict and deep as I walk away from her, but
she keeps following me. She's too tired for training after all

our walking. I pen her and rest with her. By mid-afternoon I can't stand it anymore, dreaming of Céce but not seeing her.

I'm not on the schedule tonight, but I show up at Vic's Too just at the time Céce is getting off brunch shift. I wait out front, by the mailbox.

Her mom comes out first. Her hair is dyed bright pink. She has a Band-Aid on her nose, but she's smiling her pretty gold teeth. Her eyes are pink too, means she danced hard with the bottle last night. I want to help her, but my experience is adults get mad when kids try to help them. She musses my hair. "Couldn't stay away even a day."

I can't tell if she's talking about Vic's Too or Céce, and either way I'm too sick with the crush to pretend I'm not interested in her daughter. She knows. She winked at me when she caught me staring at Céce last night.

Céce comes out kind of mopey.

"I gotta go buy limes," her mom says.

"For your cornbread, ma'am?"

"For tonight's bar fruit. Lime cornbread, though. You're a genius." Mrs. V. pinches my cheek and heads off for the market.

"Hey," I say.

"You're not on the schedule tonight," Céce says.

"Happened to your mom's nose?"

"Ask me about her hair instead."

"Okay?"

"When she gets depressed, say like when her only son is leaving in a week to go get himself killed, she dyes it a bright color. Last time it was orange."

"What triggered that?"

"When my grandfather died. She went to the funeral with her hair blow-dried to look like a flame. She wanted me to do it too."

"You got the prettiest hair, though."

She rolls her eyes, hand on a cocked hip. "What do you want from me?"

"I just want to be with you. You want to go for a walk? Hit the park maybe. There's a couple of sweet hiking trails. I was gonna bring Boo, but it's too hot. You like the country?"

"Why are you doing this?"

"Doing what?"

"You have me up on that roof last night, and it's like, I don't know."

"I know."

"You know what I mean?" she says.

"I know. I don't know. I'm an idiot."

"I mean, it's like if you want to be friends, that's okay, but I just have to know which way you want to go."

"No, I definitely don't want to be friends. I mean I do too. Hell, look, I got something for you."

"More dog-training advice for the dog I don't have. Can't wait. Lay it on me."

I pull the stickpin from my pocket. It's kind of crusty with sweated-up dog biscuit crumbs. There's this dot of chipped glue where one of the diamonds fell off. Damn.

She takes it gentle from my hand and stares at it. Now that she's holding it, I see it's way not good enough for her. For the prettiest girl you ever seen, you need to do better than a junky piece of plastic that like a kid in fourth grade would give to a crush. And on top of that you can tell it isn't a real *C* to begin with. She shakes her head. *Knew* I should've gave her the phone case instead. "I'm sorry," I say. "I'm just the lamest."

"It's so, so beautiful." She pins it to her shirt, and she's misty in those dark brown eyes. She grips my hand. I let her keep it. We thread fingers tight all the way to the park. "I'm afraid to ask you," she says. "That guy in the alley."

"Which guy?"

"The one you're flipping tens to."

"He told you?"

"I saw you from the window."

"Spy, huh?"

"Mad?"

"Never be mad at you."

"Just so you know," she says. "I trend toward intensely emotional."

"I like that about you. That emotional stuff."

"I should be on meds," she says.

"You are a med."

"I'm a *med*?" she says.

"You're like a happy drug to me. You're kind of like perfect."

"What?"

"I went on a ride once at one of those fun parks. It's sort of a coaster. I forget the name of it, but it kind of makes you want to puke. It's real cool. The freefall thing. That's what it's like with you."

"The puke-inducing freefall?"

"I mean that from the bottom of my heart."

"Okay, so I'm looking at you right now, right?"

My eyes flick to hers, then away. "Looks that way."

"I feel myself leaning in," she says.

"You are. You have a cherry gum smell on you. That's like my second-favorite flavor."

"How I'm holding off from ramming my tongue down your throat, I have no idea," she says.

I have no answer to that. I'm pretty sure I'm about to drop backwards and smack my head on the trail rock, and then she's going to be ankle deep in dumb brains.

"But first I have to know about this guy you meet behind Vic's every day, in the alley. What's his name, your friend? You don't know, do you? Yet you give him money."

"He needs it."

"But you need it too."

"I got, I have enough to spare somebody a little."

"But why you?" she says.

"Somebody has to lend him a hand, I guess."

"You're not lying to me, right? I can't tell because you won't look me in the eye."

Still can't look her in the eye. Wouldn't be able to say the stuff I'm saying. "Never lie to you. Promise and swear."

"I'm praying you're for real." She says it more to herself than to me. She grips my jaw and turns my head so I have to look at her. "Mack Morse?"

"How'd you find out my last name? Tony told you, right?"

"I saw it on your time card," she says.

"You really are spying on me."

"You're a curiosity." She kisses me and leans back to look at me. I try to work up the courage to kiss her back, because who knows if this will happen again, her getting all mental like this. A breeze starts up the trail and dips and comes back stronger and stays. I'm trembly, and I look her in the eye as I lean in to kiss her, till my eyes cross. We smack mouths a little too hard. "Damn, sorry. Did I chip your tooth? No, you're good."

"You too." She sucks my bottom lip. I feel her breathing on me, from her nose, on my mouth. Sounds gross but it isn't. It's warm. She breathes fast and light like when a pigeon lands on the bench top real close to you and they look at you with a cocked head like you're a freak and you can see a purple rainbow on their wings.

We're standing there, hugging, our hearts punching each other. "You want to go sit under that tree, in the shade?" she says.

This is so perfect right now. Right here. I can't move. I can't open my eyes. Ninety-odd degrees and my teeth are chattering. "Let's just stay like this," I say, and she's my world, and I'm her satellite coasting through the stars.

THE SIXTEENTH DAY . . .

(Saturday, June 27, just before dinner shift)

CÉCE:

He comes into the walk-in for take-out Parmesan and finds me having one of my spontaneous meltdowns. I'm an ugly crier, face gets all scrunched up. Mortified he's seeing me like this. "I'm totally PMS-ing."

"I don't mind."

"I do."

He sits next to me on the cheese wheel and puts his arms around me. He's thin but really strong. I bury my head in the space between his neck and shoulder. "I think I'm getting snot on your shirt," I say.

"A little snot never killed anybody," he says. "Not right away anyway." And that's the exact moment I fall in love with Mack Morse. My mouth aches from all the kissing this past week, like I've been doing push-ups with my lips.

"I got six points lower on my SAT II bio than I thought I would."

"That's better than seven points lower. Better than nine lower too, for another example."

"Carmella was so drunk last night she fell asleep on the toilet."

"Better than wetting the bed."

I tell him about The Anthony Nightmare.

Mack Morse doesn't tell me to stop crying or try to hush me. He doesn't even say it'll be okay. He just lets me talk, and he listens to me. And he strokes my hair.

"Three days, he's on that plane, and I'll never see him again. I swear, I just *feel* it." I pull a slice of cheesecake, and we split it. "That commencement scene was insane. The whole place exploded when they called his name. They were cheering, *Coooooooch*, and To-*ny*, To-*ny*, like at the end of *Rocky*."

"I heard of that movie. I wish I could have seen it."

"We'll Netflix it."

"Tony's graduation, I meant."

Somebody had to stay back to line cook lunch. Vic trusted Mack enough to leave him in charge. Here I am bitching, and I didn't even think to ask him how he made out. Holding down the fort at the Too isn't easy when all you have for help is Marcy. "How was lunch?"

"Slow. I think we turned fourteen. One big take-out hit, though. Forty pies. Some slow pitch tournament going on up at the reservoir fields."

"Did Marcy at least spin a couple of the pies? No, because she was worried about her nails. The cuticles. Getting flour in them. I'm gonna kill her."

"She was a bit, well, blue today, I think."

"She wants to jump you, and she's pissed you won't look at her. *Blue*. You mean bitchy."

67

"I'd never say that about a girl. Come to think about it, I probably wouldn't say it about a dude either. Yeah, nah, I definitely wouldn't. For a *dude* who was acting nasty I would probably say he was being a—"

"Mack?"

"Yeah?"

I know him two weeks, and I feel compelled to tell him I love him. But that would be like giving a guy a blow job on the first date. Must keep impulsive psycho persona in check. Must. Not. Scare away this boy. "Kiss my neck."

He does.

"You know I'm bananas, right?"

"My favorite fruit," he says.

We talk between kisses. "Have no idea what I want to do with my life," I say.

"Because you can do anything you want."

"Yeah right."

"Yeah," he says. "Right. Look at all the stuff you do so great. Doing good in school. Looking after your mom. Being a good sister. A good friend to Marcy, the best girlfriend to me."

"You did not just call me your girlfriend."

"Pretty sure I did," he says. "You're gonna draw blood from my neck, you bite any harder. It's got to be tough choosing from a ton of opportunities. It'll come to you, what you're called to."

"How 'bout you?" I say. "Your dream life. What're you called to do?"

"Tell you what, right about now, I'm hoping it's being with you."

"Before I suck your tongue out of your head, two questions."

"Tell 'em."

"1.a., do you or do you not love cheesecake?"

"I love what you love."

"Totally correct answer. 2.b., do you or do you not believe in ESP?"

"If you do."

"Has to be yes or no."

"Let's say I have a picture in my half a mind. I see you and me at the fun park, on that freefall thing. If that comes true, then I guess I'm seeing the future."

"Can you read my mind?"

"Oh, yeah, of course," he says.

"Then what am I thinking?"

"Right now?" He puts his hand up my shirt.

"You *are* a mind reader." I pin him against the tiramisu tray. The stickpin he gave me digs into my boob. I know this is corny, but I'm never taking it off. I'm seeing stars, flashing lights. A phone camera flash. Marcy jumps back from the door.

"We just got Facebashed." I run to bitch her out, and I smack right into Carmella, arms crossed, tapping her foot.

Mack comes out with his hand in his pocket to hide his hard-on and ducks out the alley door to where he keeps the delivery bike. "Sorry ma'am," he says as he goes.

"Sorry Ma," I say as I try to squeeze past her.

"Just a minute, sister. C'mere."

"I gotta fold napkins, babe."

"Don't babe *me,* chica. Look here." She leans close and looks into my eyes. She nods. "Okay."

"Okay what?"

"Let's just keep it that way," she says.

"What are you not talking about?"

"You *know* what I'm not talking about." She grabs a rack of pizza dough and swings it into the front kitchen.

I follow her, head down.

"Slut," Marcy hisses.

"Not yet," I say.

"Prude."

Vic's reading the paper. He puts it to the side, dips his head, and looks over his glasses at me. "How's the studying coming?"

"Huh?"

"Hello, the G and T?"

"Yeah, no, good," I say. "Ready to rock."

"Define *circumspect*."

I shrug.

"Look it up." He winks as he heads out to the bar.

Now it's just me and Anthony. He's got his arms folded and he's nodding. "Better be good while I'm gone, kid."

"You practically smashed us together in the first place, so shut the flip up."

He headlocks me and knuckles the top of my head.

"I'm still not going with you to the airport."

"Yeah, you will. After an hour's worth of Ma's begging and your repeated, adamant refusal, you'll fly out of the house as Ma is pulling out of the driveway."

"Will you stop being such a dick? You're hurting me." I pinch his arm to free myself of his headlock.

70

Marcy was right: Mack pinches the inside of his wrist sometimes.

(Three days later, Tuesday, June 30,
morning of the nineteenth day . . .)

"Céce Vaccuccia, you need to stop hugging your pillow." Anthony is at my door with a basketful of folded laundry under his arm, rifling balled socks at me. "I'm being generous, using the word *hugging*. Let's go, breakfast is on the table."

"I'll die if I have to eat another slice of cornbread."

"Then you've been spared, because this morning she made corn *muffins*."

A last sock ball bounces off my head.

Total sex-dream hangover. My tongue hurts, means I was glomming in my sleep. Alarm clock says 7:30, and for a second I think it's a school day, but this is *the* day. He's leaving this afternoon.

He makes me go with him to say good-bye to his teachers. They're cleaning up, getting ready for summer school, which is always crowded around here.

"Oh man, *another* Vaccuccia?" Anthony's English teacher says. "Say it ain't so."

It ain't so. I'll never fill my brother's shoes.

Everybody tells him they're proud of him and praying for him. "Not that you *need* prayers," Mrs. Hardwick says. "You're going to be just *fine*, Anthony."

He's going to be in a war zone in six months. He has nine weeks of basic training, and then they send him to San Antonio for specialized training for sixteen weeks, unless for some reason he doesn't make it through boot camp, which is impossible. The guy runs a 4:30 mile and his GPA was 98.61.

He signed a 68-W contract: combat medic. My big brother. For all intents and purposes a father to me, even though he's only three years older, thanks to the fact that my crazy mother is a loser magnet. In the back of our fridge is this leftover takeout that's been there for three months, and that's longer than any of Ma's idiot boyfriends ever hung around.

Here's my problem with the 68-Whiskey assignment: Take out the line medic, and you cripple the platoon. 68-W's get shot at a lot.

The airport is mobbed. Mack and Ant do that man-hug thing: bang chests, pound backs way too hard—guys are idiots. Next up is Carmella. She's got her head buried in his chest, and she's bawling. He's laughing as he whispers something to her, and pretty soon she's laughing. Next up is me.

I am so out of here. I turn away, but he pulls me back and swings me off my feet. He throws me high, like when we were kids in the public pool, and he taught me how to swim. He lets me drop, breaking my fall at the last second. I'm trying not to be light-headed, but my stomach is still floating up there, and I can't help smiling. When he puts me down, I shove him away and run for the parking lot. I am not saying good-bye. If I don't say it, maybe he won't die.

I won't even be able to talk to him for the first couple of weeks, and then only for a couple of minutes on Sundays, if the drill sergeant feels like letting them use their phones. No e-mail either.

Ma hangs on to Mack's arm as we walk back to the Vicmobile. He gets the door for her. "Such a gent, Mack." She settles in behind the wheel. She's wearing giant sunglasses, her hangover hiders. You'd never know she's been crying if you didn't catch the tear splat on her boob. She's smiling, but her lips are trembling. "Your ESP giving you anything on this one, babe?"

I hold her hand. "It's telling me everything's gonna be fine." I don't tell her that last night I had a vision. Anthony is walking through a busy street and a car parked next to him explodes.

She nods. "We're all set, then."

"Absolutely." For the next six months anyway. Till he deploys.

Ma turns the key and the car won't start. Mack notices she left it in gear when she parked.

"Oh."

Out on the highway, we get stuck in standstill traffic, and the jets look like they're going to land on us. I climb out of the shotgun seat and swing into the back to be with my boyfriend. He squeezes my hand. Having him here, right now? I'm suddenly calm. I was spinning so fast when I ran out of the terminal. But he's given me something to focus on: him. He's clutching a bunched-up envelope. "Tony gave it to me," he says. "Feels like there's a quarter in it."

"Open it."

"Maybe I ought to read it later."

"I wanna see," I say.

He hesitates. He pinches his wrist.

"What's wrong?"

He tears the envelope and unfolds the paper, a blank page wrapping a thin chain and a medallion. He spills them into his hand. The medallion is worn down, but you can still make out the engraving, a peace sign.

"He had that around his neck for as long as I can remember," I say.

"Mack?" Carmella says. "Put it on, babe."

He does.

Ma nods. "It looks good on you."

THE TWENTY—THIRD DAY . . .

(Saturday, July 4, afternoon)

MACK:

The skies clear, the heat drops off, the air dries out, and Tony's peace medal doesn't stick to my chest. The restaurant is closed, but Vic and me are in the kitchen spinning pies for Mrs. V.'s barbeque. She comes in to check the eight trays of Fourth of July cornbread she had me baking all morning. "They're perfect," she says. "You are the *king*."

"All I did was put 'em in the oven, Mrs. V."

"How many times do I have to tell you: Call me Carmella."

I nod, but no way I'm calling her that.

She paints the cornbread with red, white, and blue cake decoration.

"Icing on cornbread, huh?" Vic says.

"Never been done before," Mrs. V. says.

"No, it hasn't," Vic says.

"Mack, is your father coming?"

"He has to work, ma'am." I hate liars, especially when they're me. I didn't even ask the old man. I need him getting smashed and talking trash and getting into a drag-out rumble in front of Céce?

"Mack, get that last round of pies into the oven, and then I need you to come out to the bar," Vic says.

"I do something wrong?"

He taps his temple. "I know what I know." He checks the pie dough to make sure I spun it okay. He nods, says "Good," and leaves.

Vic never finished high school either. He started with a takeout-only window, and he's in business thirty-five years. Tell you what, I like working for him better than anybody. He's got me doing a lot more cooking now.

I check my pies and swing out to the bar. Vic has the radio and TV and computer going with three different news shows, and he's got the paper out for the crossword. I don't mind the Too's radio, because with a satellite there's no chance of static. Either you get a perfect clear signal, or you get nothing, which is the way it should be.

Vic flips his laptop to me and explains how the bank and the bills work, and how you need to pay them on time but not too early either.

I'm nodding, but looking at the screen gives me a headache. All those words and numbers and click on this word and drag that one to there and type that number. I want to ask Vic to slow it down a little, give me a chance to catch up, but when I used to do that in school, they called me retard.

"You getting this?" Vic says.

"Absolutely," I say.

"You need to know this stuff."

"Why?"

"This dog training thing. Tony told me about it. You need to do it."

"I'm doing it," I say.

"Professionally. The school. The certificate. I looked into it. Ey, look at me. I wouldn't tell you to do it unless I was sure. I'm giving you the money. You pay me back when you can. I made calls to dog trainers on the east side. After you have the certificate, you can make between fifty and a hundred an hour."

"I heard that."

"You don't look too excited," he says. "You're making eight dollars an hour now. What am I missing?"

"I can't see anybody giving me fifty an hour for anything legal."

"When does the next training class start?"

"Fall."

"Perfect. Done."

"Look, Mister Vic, I don't mean to be a contraindication, but I'm too young to start a business like that, all professional. Hell, I'm but fifteen."

"You're fifty, not fifteen, and don't forget it. Fun is important, but so is work. Kid, no matter how much money you make, you can never have enough. You miss a chance to work, you never get it back. You're going to the school."

"I'm a little confused here. Are you, like, firing me?"

"The restaurant business, people come and go. I try to help them, but usually the person can't get it together, and they move on, and that's okay. Once in a while, you get somebody like Carmella, and you see she has to stay. You work for me, you need to have a dream. Carmella's is mak-

77

ing people smile. She can get that here. Tony too. He could be CEO of a multinational corporation, but that's not what he's meant to do. You watch, he comes back a hero, and then he runs this place."

"The hero part, yeah, but the restaurant business? I don't know. I pegged him for an athlete or president or maybe a teacher-type, the cool kind."

"Trust me," says the guy who lost an entire restaurant in one hand of cards with a woman named Hammerhead. "Tony's like his mother, has to see the joy face-to-face. He needs to be here." He taps the bar top hard and twice. "But for you, this job is to help you for the next one. It'll kill me to lose you, but by the time you turn eighteen, if you're still working here, yeah, I'll can you. Working here is too safe for you. You're like me, a gambler."

"If I'm like you, then I should stay working here."

"Dog training. That's what you're made for."

I don't get it, what these folks see in me. "What about Céce? What's her future?"

Vic's eyebrows go up with a smile. "Céce has maybe the most special thing of all coming her way."

"And what's that?"

Vic nods and smiles with his eyebrows up and says, "I know what I know," and I have no idea what the old man means half the time.

"The school," I say. "If I do it, I have my own money saved."

"Even better. Kid, just do exactly as I say, and you'll be fine. And do yourself a favor and look up the word *contra-indication*."

"Céce used it the other day."

"Not like that she didn't. C'mon, let's get the food into the car."

Vic drives slow and whistles "God Bless America" over and over. Mrs. V. is on the phone with Céce. "Relax, sister, we'll be there in five minutes." She clicks the phone and turns to Vic. "Cheech says the yard's packed already."

"You put out the word there's free pizza and beer, what do you expect?"

"And Independence Day cornbread," Mrs. V. says.

"And Independence Day cornbread," Vic says. "Mack, which building is yours?"

"I can jump out at the corner. You all go on ahead. I'll be over there in a few."

"Nah," Vic says. "We'll pick up the dog and drive over together."

"Nah, man, I don't want Boo stinking up your car."

"The car already stinks," Vic says.

"Better I walk her over for the exercise." The car stops at a light, and I hop out. "I'll see you all over there." I turn the corner, and my old man is out on the stoop with his lady friend, and they're good and twisted already, tipping rotgut forties and smoking a blunt in the broad daylight and arguing way too loud about God knows what.

Me and Boo are at the gate to the yard. If she passes this test, I'm going to start leaning hard on Céce and Mrs. V. to adopt her. When we're strolling the park, she's a typical pit bull, real good with folks, especially kids. Today is about seeing how she does in a packed crowd. And this is a block party all right, music blasting, folks spilling out into the street. I open the gate and go in first.

Boo's eyes are soft, ears back easy. Her tail wags nice and slow.

This lady says, "Get that dog away from me!"

"She's a peach," Céce cuts in. She sets a big bowl of chips onto the picnic table to stroke Boo's muzzle. "See?" she says to the lady.

"You're getting more relaxed around her every day," I say.

"Still a little freaked out when she tries to lick my face. My Boo-Boo," she says.

"No baby talking to her now."

She makes her voice really deep, "My Boo-Boo," and that's pretty funny to me. She takes my hand and introduces me to people. They're nice. Her mom is smiling at us.

The kids go crazy over Boo. She's gentle with them, even when this one girl pulls her tail. She's clowning too. She grabs a paper plate and taunts the kids to chase her to get it back. She's tearing circles around the yard.

"Wait," I command her, but I'm not in her world right now. She's all about having fun with the kids, and that's when I know it for sure: She'll be leaving me soon. I nudge Céce. "She's ready to go."

Céce nudges back twice as hard. "We'll see. You gonna be sad when she leaves?" Céce's smile is crooked and she has nine freckles on her nose. I want to kiss them, each one.

"Sad? Nah. I'll have another beat-up Boo within the month."

Boo jumps into Mrs. V.'s lap for a belly scratch. Mrs. V. mouths to Céce I WANT THIS *DOG*.

They have a tiny aboveground pool back here, perfect for Boo. Vic and the other old people are sitting around the edge, slow-kicking their feet in the water. They're sipping and arguing and laughing. The sun's high and clean, and the ripples in the water are gold bands almost too bright to look at.

I could live like this, I think. If Céce was with me. She's got the prettiest long brown hair. Her eyes are so dark and shiny you can see your reflection in them, and you look better than you do in real life. "Why you with me?" I say. We're filling the ice tubs with two-liter Sprites. "You're smart and crazy pretty and cool. Sometimes I wonder if you're with me just to see what it's like to go slumming."

"That's got to be it. Let's go inside. The basement. It's cool down there." She pulls me toward the back door to the kitchen.

"I better not."

"You're afraid to go inside my house," she says. "Why?"

Somebody taps a plastic fork on a plastic cup, and everybody does the same, and now it's quiet, except the music is still on loud with one of those old-school metal bands. "I'm on the highway to hell," the singer keeps screaming.

"Just wanna toast Tony today and everybody else looking out for us," this old man says.

Mrs. V. nods thank you. She's smiling, but she doesn't look the dude in the eye.

Céce tugs on my T-shirt. "Let's get Boo and go to your place."

"Let's hit the park, catch the fireworks," I say.

"Sunset's three hours away."

"If we get there early, we'll get a nice patch of grass."

"That dude you give money to," she says. "Where's he live?"

"Why?"

"Wanna meet him."

"I don't think he'd like that. Maybe in front of you he'll be embarrassed he's got to take money from me."

"You swear that's all you're doing, giving him money?"

"What else would I be giving him?"

She studies me. "Okay. Can we stop off at the church on the way to the park?"

"I only like church when it's empty."

"Saturday afternoon?" she says. "It'll be empty."

"We'll only start making out. I heard if you get a boner in church, they send you to hell."

"The dreaded church boner problem." She nods. "Well, then I guess we ought to go to Taco B instead. Frutista Freezes. Cherry Limeade Sparklers."

"I'll sip off yours," I say. "Thanks for saving me."

"Saving you?"

"From going to hell."

Kids at the park entrance have the M-98 crackers and bottle rockets going. I hate that sound, a sharp whistle bleeding into a hiss. Boo doesn't like it either. Her tail is curled under and flicking fast.

Céce strokes the back of my neck, and I can breathe again.

We take Boo into the hills, past the spot where we kissed that first time. "Want to take you to my most secret place," I say. "Only thing is, it's a little scary."

"Obviously I like scary."

"I warned you then."

"As long as it's someplace where we can lose our shirts, I'm down." She takes my hand. "Show me."

We're lying in the graveyard, her, me, and Boo. The grass is tall and clean and hides us. The trees give a nice swaying cover. It's nice: At last, I finally have a human being to share my secret place with. I kiss her breasts, but she starts breathing a little too fast, so I come right back up to kissing her mouth. I don't want her to think I'm into her only for her prettiness. But I also don't want her thinking I'm not into getting down with her, in case she wants to get down, and I kind of think she does because she grinds on me sometimes. Hard. That and she moans sometimes a good bit too. Or maybe that's me, except I hope not. Only girls are supposed to moan.

I suppose I could ask her about it, what she wants me to do. Nah.

I'm kind of afraid if we do it, she won't like me after. But I don't know how much longer I can drag it out. I swear, like half my blood supply is in my dick. My hands and feet are cold this crazy hot Independence Day, and I'm light-headed. You can't survive long like this. She puts her hand on it, and now she's got my fly down, and she's trying to get at it, but I'm wearing those fake fly underwear, and why in God's name do they do that? Damn dollar table gets me every time.

"Does it hurt?" she says. "Being hard for so long?"

"Psh, nah."

"Tell the truth."

"It kills."

She's mad nervous. Her hands are shaking on me. "I'm gonna take care of you," she says.

I check to make sure Boo's asleep. "Well, I, that'd be fine."

"Should I . . . I mean, do you want me to, like . . . Or will that make you think I'm a slut?"

I gulp, twice. I think she's talking about a blow job, but what if she's only talking hand job? "I, it's like, no, I could never think you're a slut."

"Except I'm not sure I believe you."

"Why?"

"Poor eye contact."

I force myself to look into her eyes, but by now she's looking down at my boner. "Wow," she says.

I can't tell if that means *wow, that's huge* or *wow, that's it?*

She's moving her hand now. "Cool," she says.

"Definitely."

You can tell she doesn't quite know how to do it, but no way I'm embarrassing myself to show her, and anyway it doesn't take long, and aren't I just embarrassed as hell anyway now with no tissues for the cleanup. She pulls a fold of Taco Bell napkins from her pocket.

I check to see if Boo is still asleep. No, she's looking at me. She looks totally bored.

Getting jacked off in front of a dog. I am lame.

Takes me a bit to catch my breath. I keep saying, "Wow. That was like . . . wow." Natural born idiot twice struck by lightning.

Cece's turned away, but she says, "Why do you pinch the inside of your wrist like that?"

I never realized I did. I stop doing it. "I don't know how to ask this any better, so I'll just say it. Like, can I do something for you now?"

"Like what?"

"Whatever you want."

And then she starts crying real hard. I knew I would ruin it. "I'm sorry."

"No no, it's fine. I'm fine." And even though she's crying she's sort of laughing too, and she's hugging me hard and stroking my face and kissing my neck, and we just stay like that for a time, and I get to wondering if maybe God loves me a little. I roll her onto her back and talk between kisses. "Been thinking."

"Uh-oh."

"Yeah. I don't want you to be embarrassed of me."

"What are you talking about?"

I comb her hair with my fingers and study its shininess. "Serious: Why do you like me?"

She thinks about it. "You're like the only guy I know our age who isn't retarded."

"I don't know what to say. Thank you."

She bites my lip. It hurts good.

"Maybe I'll head on back to school," I say.

She stops kissing me. She pulls back a little to look at me. She nods. "I think that would be really good."

"I don't mean like *school* school. Dog training school. Tony sicced Vic on me about it. They both said I'd do real good there. Actually, they said I'd do well. I almost have to believe that, because the Tone would never lie."

"No, he would never lie."

"Vic would lie, though."

"I know, but only to do a good thing, like make an anonymous donation to pay for some kid's school, and then the kid says, 'Vic was that you?' and Vic says, 'What are you talking about?'"

"You been talking to him about it."

"He's been talking to me," she says.

"Bit of a meddler, Vic is, huh?"

"He knows what he knows."

"Just do what he says, and you'll be fine."

She's got a good grip on my hand. "Then we should just do what he says."

"I keep this Bible box hidden under my bed. It's pretty full of money, enough for the school. I need to spend it anyway, before my old man finds it. I just want you to be proud of me."

"I'm proud of you."

"I want to get rich for you, you know?"

"You don't have to get rich for me."

"I'm gonna do it anyway."

"Just keep kissing me."

"I tell you, Céce."

"Tell me."

I want to tell her I've got a picture of us. Her and me together forever. But it's too soon. "I'll tell you sometime."

"Tell me now."

"Sometime." I smile and look away and she tries to get me to look at her, and we're practically wrestling till we end up in a cuddle. We're on our backs and holding hands, and she's looking at me and I'm looking up at a sky that's got just one pretty little cloud in it shaped like a bent top hat. Boo tries to wiggle between us, and the fireworks start. They're far away. The crackles are soft, and the hiss can't reach me. The lights are bright and pretty and red, white and pale blue, and it occurs to me: I'm happy.

THE THIRTY-EIGHTH DAY . . .

(Sunday, July 19, late morning)

CÉCE:

Marcy shows up at my house with a bag of wet laundry. "My mother's drying a *blanket*. I'll be forty-six by the time the thing's not damp anymore." She pulls out my clothes to dry hers, and then she yanks open our fridge. She taps a head of lettuce and says, "I'll have that," and sits and waits for me to serve her. Our ratty old Maytag drones *eeeooooeek*-clu-*clump*, *eeeooooeek*-clu-*clump* as it spins Marcy's Skechers.

I rip the lettuce twice, dump it onto a plate that might or might not be clean, squirt it with expired diet dressing, this raspberry vinaigrette thing that tastes like mouthwash, not to mention it's been left out of the fridge since yesterday. "Here you go, Queen." I slap down the plate.

"You can't spare half a carrot?" she says.

Here I am with my PBJ, licking Skippy off the knife. Totally nick my tongue. "Canned beets?"

"Bleh. Like an ant farm in here."

"Cornbread crumbs."

"Idea: vacuum. You guys fuck yet?"

"What? *No.*"

"Serious?"

"How many weeks should I wait before I give him a blow job?"

Marcy sneezes Orange Crush. "*Weeks?* Are you flippin' retarded? The only rule with bj's is never on the first date, except if the date lasts longer than six hours. What are you waiting for? Céce, face it, he's a summer distraction, jump and dump."

"He's the one."

"Oh. My. *God*. This is sad. Look, here's the math: Céce Brainwave Vaccuccia plus Mack Moron equals zero. He should be with somebody like *me*."

"He's not a moron, okay? He has . . . Look, you don't know him."

"And you do? What, you been together a month yet?"

"Since Anthony dropped the hint, it'll be forty days this coming Tuesday."

"What are you guys doing for your anniversary? You are *so* gay. Cheech, this boy has one purpose in your life: to break you in." She pulls my hair to bring our faces close so I have no choice but to look into her totally overdone eyes. Quarter-inch-thick makeup coats her cheeks. The girl came over here to do laundry. "By summer's end you'll have screwed each other a hundred and fifty times—hopefully. At that point, you'll be thoroughly sick of each other. Perfect. He'll move on to some other crappy dishwasher job in some new crappy restaurant where he'll bone some other cutie-pie waitress, and you'll move on to some new crappy school after you rock the G and T, and you'll bone some new cutie-pie guy, except this one will have an actual working brain. New is good, chica. Ripping out your heart for a guy who didn't finish junior high? Not so much."

"You. Don't. *Know* him. You don't know us. We see each other every day."

"So do me and you."

"Yeah, but me and Mack don't get sick of each other. We *do* stuff together."

"Hunting for satellites up at the reservoir with his *nasty-looking* pit bull? I'd rather tweeze my mother's shoulder hair."

"We tell each other things."

"What things?"

"We treasure each other's *secrets*, Marce. This is forever, him and me. I *feel* it."

"*Yeah*, and I'm so sure he feels it too. Wake up, Céce: He's after you for your rack. I gotta get outta here before I blow a half a head of rotten iceberg all over your kitchen. Call me when my sneakers are dry."

I'm trying to lead the ants outside with a rotten banana when my phone rings. Note to self: Either get a new phone or figure out how to change Hannah Montana ring tone.

"*Yo!*" Anthony says via live video stream courtesy of a handheld phone.

"Yo," I say.

"*Where's Ma?*"

"Put her in the shower on a plastic lawn chair with a sippy cup full of high-test coffee."

"*Nice!*"

"Oh my god, why are they not feeding you down there? What happened to your hair?"

"Forget about me. What's up with you? Quick, I have like two minutes before my sergeant gets back. Why so mopey, sis?"

"Marcy's a bitch."

"C'mon, what's wrong?"

"Nothing. The G and T. I'm just nervous about it."

"Liar. How's Mack?"

I fail miserably at trying not to grin. "He doesn't own a computer, and he hates TV. He doesn't own a *phone*."

"And this means?"

"Opposites attract."

"Knew *you guys would work out. The peace medal. It's doing its thing.*"

"It's *so* doing its thing. My ESP is in overdrive: We're meant to be together. It's real, Ant, the way I feel. I swear."

"A hopeful Céce Vaccuccia. Stunning. Yo, I gotta go. Tell Ma I love her like a crazy person."

Sunday nights we close at nine. Dinner shift is almost over. Mack's helping me restock. We're upstairs grabbing linens and each other. I push him against the wall and suck his lips. "If I told you I had a really important request, and that I needed you to say yes, would you ever say no to me?"

"If it's that important, then no."

"I want to go to your place."

"I don't think—"

"Don't think. Just say yes."

He nods, but he's miserable. "Hopefully he won't be home," he says.

✕ ✕ ✕ ✕ ✕ ✕

We walk down this dark dirty alley lined with old mattresses, to the basement. The lights are on. We hear staticky music. "He's home," Mack says. "Let's go to the roof."

"I want to see your room."

"My *room?*"

"What you hang on your walls, baseball crap or movie posters. Whether you're PS3 or Wii, the color of your bedspread."

"Céce, I sleep on a foldout cot in the kitchen. There's nothing of me in that place, except that Bible box full of money, and even that'll be gone soon."

"At some point, don't I have to meet the people in your life?"

"The only person in my life is you. Please. The roof."

Up here, above the streetlight glare, no moon, I see lots of satellites. The wind comes cool, and the sheets float. Pigeons leave the hutch roof, circle and resettle.

I'm sitting cross-legged, scratching under Boo's jaw. Boo's sitting between my legs, facing me. Her head rests on my shoulder to look at Mack, who's sitting behind me, against the half wall that fences off the roof. He's giving me the most righteous neck rub. "It occurs to me," I say.

"Uh-huh?"

"I have a pit bull in my lap. This pit bull has a massive head. This head is largely jaw. This jaw is less than six inches from my face, and I, a face bite victim, am petting this pit bull, and my hands aren't shaking."

"I'm telling you," he says.

"You've cured me."

"You cured you."

"In a month. Gently. Little by little. Unbelievable. I'll take her."

He kisses me, but I push him away.

"Under one condition," I say.

"Anything," he says.

"The first night she sleeps over, you sleep over too."

He's quiet.

"Tuesday night. My mother's going down to the shore to get trashed with her friend, this other Bud Light bride from high school. Julie has this popup camper for the overnight. Carmella won't be home till late Wednesday afternoon."

"Céce, sneaking behind your mom's back like that—"

"Mack? I'm sick of dry humping in the graveyard, you know? Of bringing ants home. I want to be *indoors* with you. To *be* with you, indoors."

He stops rubbing my neck. He gets up. He crosses toward the far side of the roof, and Boo follows. "Wait," Mack says as he keeps walking away.

But she won't. She only stops when he stops, and she leans against his leg. He can't get her to quit following him.

"You're up in the country and she's off leash," he says. "She sees a jackrabbit on the other side of the road with a truck hauling down it. You've got to be able to stop her in her tracks before you can call her back to you." He studies Boo. "It's the last thing she needs to learn, and then she's perfect."

"Instead of *wait*, try *stay*."

"You can use whatever word you want, so long as you use the same word every time."

"*Stay* is better."

"Try it." He heads across the roof. Boo follows.

"Boo, stay," I say.

The dog stops and sits and looks back at me.

"Boo, come," I say.

She comes to me for a belly scratch.

Mack jogs across the roof and chucks his arm over my shoulder and kisses my forehead.

"Before she found you, she must have been trained with that word," I say.

"Nope. You're magic."

Boo wiggles between us and slashes our legs with her tail and play-barks at us to stop glomming.

Pounding beneath our feet gets me jumping. "What is that?"

Mack frowns. "Larry. He's banging on his ceiling with a ball bat."

Some dude shrieks up the breezeway, "Make that dog stop barking, dirtbag. Hey, you hear me up there?"

Mack yells down the breezeway, "It was just for a second, all right? It's over now." He's so calm and strong with the dog, but now he's off-kilter. He's pinching the inside of his wrist again. "You won't ever hear her again, all right?"

"Motherless liar," Larry yells up.

"What'd you say about my moms, old man?"

"Mack," I say, but he doesn't hear me.

"I hear that dog bark again, it's dead," Larry says.

"What'd you say about my *moms*?"

"I'll tell her you said hello," Larry yells up. He's snickering.

Mack's eyes are spacey, the way they were that night with those two dudes on the motorcycles. He's pinching his wrist so hard. I stop him. I hold his hand.

"Just keep holding my hand," he says. "Don't let go."

"I won't."

He's trembling. I lead him into the hutch. He slumps against the wall. I crack him a Sprite and sit next to him, and he rests his head in my lap. I trace arcs across his forehead with my fingertips, until the fret lines soften.

"You're the only one," he says.

"The only one?"

Boo's upset because he's upset. She wiggles next to him and nudges his hand with her snout, but he won't pet her. I reach out to Boo.

"Don't," Mack says. "Wait till she's not scared. If you pet her when she's scared, you're rewarding her fear. My mom taught me that. Sorry. I keep telling you the same stories. About my mother, I mean. Hell, I guess it doesn't matter."

"What doesn't?"

"You were gonna find out sooner or later. You might not want to be with me after I tell you this. But you need to know it, the truth about me."

Now I'm afraid. This is it: He's going to tell me he killed somebody. Please, don't let this be over. Don't let us be over. "Tell me."

"I'm afraid that someday, I'm gonna do something really bad."

"Like . . ."

"Like something you can't fix. I get so *mad* sometimes."

"Everybody gets mad."

"Not like this. Not like me." His eyes shimmer. They're brown, but for some reason they seem dark blue now. "You're the only one who can keep me from doing it."

"Doing what?"

"Losing it." He looks away. "I had this counselor once who tried to teach me a trick. She said when I got mad, I should put myself in a favorite dream and live there until the anger left me. But it never worked. Because my dreams all seemed so far away. But now with you, when I'm near you, holding your hand . . . If I fly off and wreck somebody, they won't let us be together anymore. As long as you're with me, it'll be okay." He strokes Boo's neck. Her tail slaps the floor at his touch. She rolls onto her stomach for a belly rub. He gives her a quick scratch and squeezes my hand. "Tuesday night. I'll stay over your house, Céce." He checks the moon. "It's getting late. I better get you home."

He gets up and tries to help me to my feet, but I say, "Wait. I need a minute to think about this before I do it."

"Before you do what?"

"Shh, just gimme a sec." What does that mean, *something you can't fix?* I have no doubt he can cause some serious damage—he's all muscle. He's all heart, though. All mine. He needs me.

He's right: As long as I'm with him, it'll be okay. "Okay," I say.

"Okay what?"

I pen the dog and grab the sleeping bag and go to the back of the hutch and spread it out under the open ceiling hatchway.

He looks at the sleeping bag. He looks at me. "This can't be a one-shot deal," he says. "One of those, you know, you try this out to see what it's like, and then you move on."

96

"Never leave you. I promise."

His fingertips trace the lines of my ribs. I can feel his heart beating through me. The tip of his thumb rides a soft slow circle around my belly, winding into the button. I feel myself breathing faster as his thumb arcs down, and his fingertips are at the band of my underwear. Under the band now . . .

It happens fast: We're naked. He's kissing me everywhere. "You got any—"

"Yes," I say. The ones they give you in school. To carry with you, just in case.

His hands are shaking as he gets ready and my hands are shaking as I help him and then it happens and I take in the biggest breath and then another one and I can't let the air out of my lungs. Hot tears coast over my cheeks into my ears. I'm holding his face and touching his open lips, and still I can't breathe, and he's looking at me. Looking into my eyes. And he isn't turning away. And finally I let the air out, but right away my lungs pull in another huge breath, and I can't breathe, don't want to breathe, just want to stay like this.

"You done this before?" he says.

I shake no, and somehow I whisper, "You?"

"Not like this." And he's shivering and I'm shivering and I swear the sky is shivering. Through the hatchway the stars are falling and drifting down on us like that first soft snow, the kind that comes at the end of the fall.

THE THIRTY-EIGHTH DAY, CONTINUED . . .
(Sunday, July 19, late night)

MACK:

I can't stop looking at her. She's all goose bumps. She's curled into me and shivering, but the room smells like heat. I got my arms around her. She's looking up through the roof hatch. Boo snores on the other side of the wall. "I'll introduce you to my old man," I say. "You're going to be coming over here all the time, and you'll run into him sooner or later."

We just stare into each other and smile for a bit, me and this beautiful girl, her long bangs half covering her face. I brush back her hair to see her eyes better. "Céce, I'm not like him, okay? I have my mother in me, not him."

A squirrel peeks in through the hatch.

She yelps and digs her nails into me. "They're everywhere. You can't even hang your laundry anymore without one crawling into your bra and making a hammock of it."

"I'm not real familiar with that situation."

She wrinkles her nose and nose-to-noses me. "Hey?"

"Hey back."

"I'm gonna be coming over here all the time?"

I kiss her full and hold her and tell her, "I wanna do it again so bad. To be with you. Can we?"

"Make the squirrel stop watching us."

"Tsst!" I say, and the squirrel jumps away.

"This is Céce."

"*Chee*-chee?" the old man says all slurry. He's flopped

back in front of the TV with a box of doughnuts, crumbs all through the hair of his chest, too bombed to stand up.

"Hello," Céce says. She shakes his hand, and the old man won't let go. She doesn't like the way he's looking at her.

I don't either. I didn't think he was going to be this bad. He's eyeing her head to toe, and slow. "Reckon we better be going," I say.

"Nice to meet you, Mister Morse," she says.

"Nigha meea."

I have to get in there to pull his hand from hers.

He winks at me, gives me a thumbs-up. "Attaboy, Cario. Thaw you wuzza." He burps. "Faggot." A loud commercial comes on and his eyes drift to the TV.

We're outside. "He called you Cario," she says.

"My name. Macario."

"What's it mean?"

"Blessed."

We're quiet on the walk home. My arm's over her shoulders. Her arm's slung low on my back, her thumb hooked into my belt loop. She's walking Boo. Boo listens to Céce perfect. My legs are weak. I love her so bad. I want to say it to her. I better wait.

"He's not like that when he's sober, though, right?" she says.

"He's like that, just sober."

"Yesterday I woke up with Carmella in my bed. She was holding my hand. The lightning, she said."

"Lightning?"

"The thunderstorm. The woman sleeps with a Snoopy night-light."

"I like your mom a ton."

"If Anthony dies, she'll go from beer to liquor. After that, it won't be long. I'll wake up one morning, and she'll be dead on the couch with some DVD menu music on perma-loop. *Pretty Woman*. You ever see that one?"

"Hey?" I pull her close. "Tony's not gonna die."

She studies my eyes. "I believe you."

"I been wanting to send him a letter. To thank him for the medal. Can you help me write it?"

She hugs me. "We'll do it right now. C'mon." We're just a couple houses down from her house.

"I need a little time to figure out what I want to say."

"My mother made Christmas cornbread."

"In July?"

"I know," she says. "Red and green icing." She pulls me toward the house.

I hold up. "I'll come in Tuesday night."

"Promise me."

"We'll make dinner and sit at the table and make out, but not when we have food in our mouth, of course."

"Of course," she says.

"After that, we'll write the letter to Tony."

"And after that?"

"Man, you're cute when you're pouty, and I think you know it too." I walk her to her door and kiss her good night. She watches me back down the porch steps with Boo. "Don't know how I'm gonna look your mom in the eye at work tomorrow."

"Anthony was dating this girl for two years, and he was a junior in high school when Ma finally sat him down to talk birds and bees. Ant told me he chewed a hole in his cheek to keep from laughing. Slutty as she was in her youth, Carmella apparently assumes everybody's a virgin now. The last twenty-five years of soaking her brain in Bud Light must've eaten away the part of her brain cerebrum that's supposed to initiate reasonable suspicion."

"Say that last part in English. Sure, the cerebrum."

"Or is it the cerebellum?"

"Your pick."

"*Hate* bio. Don't worry about my mother, baby. The woman is out to lunch when it comes to this stuff."

"Yeah huh? Good luck."

"Good luck?"

"The kitchen light just went on. I better git."

THE THIRTY-EIGHTH DAY, CONTINUED . . .
(Sunday, July 19, late night)

CÉCE:

Ma's sipping in the kitchen. I walk by fast for the stairway. "Night."

"Cheech babe, can you c'mere for a second?"

"Yeah, babe?"

"Sit. Spend a few on the old lady, catch me up on you."

"Would so love to, but I gotta study. G and T's just around the corn—"

"Just for a sec. Grab yourself a hunk of Carmella's Christmas Confection there. I'll take one too. Yeah, no, the one with the headless snowman painted onto it. The top part was burned. I had to chop it off. I'm saving the good pieces for Anthony's platoon."

I sit, smile, force myself to look her in the eye. "Howya doin', Carmella?"

"Hangin' in, you know. *You?*"

"Oh you know. Everything's good."

"Excellent." She's nodding. She's squinting. She's drinking *coffee*. I am so fucked. "So looks like my Tuesday trip to the shore is getting canceled."

"Julie crash the camper again?" Shit.

"Weather's supposed to suck out loud." She drowns her creepy headless snowman in her coffee. "But Mack can still stay over."

"What are you *talking* about?"

"I'm going away, and you're not gonna try to swing the overnight? Hello, we share DNA. If you're gonna do it, and you are, then you're gonna do it someplace safe. You keep sneaking around, and that's how accidents happen. If you trust me about nothing else, trust me on that one. The apartment downstairs, the storm door. You have your own entrance. I don't have to know when you're down there, and I don't want to. Be respectful. Be discreet. Tell me you're using birth control."

"I totally cannot be talking about this with my mother— ew."

"I'm serious, Céce."

"With your pink hair and your gold teeth and your busted nose."

"Right now, I'm your best chance at not ending up like me."

"You think we're stupid?"

"I think you're fifteen. And thanks."

"Ma, look, I didn't mean it like that."

"Yeah you did. Condoms?"

I roll my eyes and nod.

She nods. "I'll take you to the doctor for a prescription."

"I told you, we got it covered."

"Doesn't hurt to have a backup." She holds my hand. "Just. Be. Careful."

I roll my eyes the other way. Why am I so bitchy to her when she's being so cool? "We *will*, okay?"

"I'm talking about being in love with each other so soon."

I'm about to tell her I'm not in *love* with him, but that would be a lie. "I do. I really do love him. And he loves me, I think. He's the one, Ma. He is. I *feel* it." Tears from nowhere. I am such a tool. She pulls me into a hug. I'm sitting in her lap. She's rubbing my back and hushing me. I bury my face in her pink hair. It smells like burned pumpkin. "Ma? He makes me feel like I can be somebody."

"You *are* somebody, honey. You are so awesome."

"No, Ma. You don't get it. He makes me feel like I can be somebody else."

THE THIRTY-NINTH DAY . . .
(Monday, July 20, morning)

MACK:

My life started last night. Here on in, everything I see, I *see*. Like the way Tony was always looking up at the sky. I don't think I need to look down to my sneakers so much anymore. To hide. I don't think I slept last night, thinking about her, about us, but I am *awake*.

The Too is closed to customers today, but we're in for annual cleaning. It's hard to hear her with all the fans sucking the stink of fresh paint out of the place. Mrs. V. and me are at the bar. She has her arm over my shoulders. "We understand each other?" she says. She puts her hand to my chin and tilts my head up so I have to look her in the eye.

"Yes, ma'am."

"Am I that old?"

"Sorry, ma'am?"

"Why won't you call me Carmella?"

"I will." I almost said *I will, ma'am.*

"Mack, Céce gets excited about things. She dives in fast and deep, you know? Sometimes before there's enough water in the pool. I know, this is a hard thing to hear, but you

104

understand what I'm saying, right? Look at me for a second. You love her, right?"

Sweat pushes through me. "Yes."

"And you're absolutely sure, of course."

"Yes."

"But here's my thing: You know you need each other, but you don't know each other."

But we do, I want to say. We know each other's secrets.

"Mack?"

"Yes ma'am?"

"Take the time, okay? To find out who she is, to let her know who you are."

"We will, ma'am."

She shakes her head. "The two of you, I don't know. I guess you'll be all right."

"Thank you, ma'am."

The news comes on the bar TV. They give the war report. Triple suicide attack. Car bombs.

Mrs. V. switches the channel to a game show.

I head off to clean the ice machine. Marcy's there in the back, with Céce. "How you doin', Marcy?"

"Suicidal, *Macky*. You?"

"Good."

"*So* happy for you." She turns to Céce. "Cheech, how's that herpes thing workin' out? You still contagious?"

We're at the Dumpster, emptying the trash buckets. Céce's looking over her shoulder to make sure nobody's spying. "How weird was that with my mother, right?"

"She was real cool."

"What'd she say?"

"That she loves you a ton."

She stops with the trash emptying. Then she gets back to it.

"Any word from Tony?" I say.

"Text that said he can't talk this week. Apparently if somebody in the platoon screws up, everybody loses privileges."

"I think I heard that."

She puts her hand on her hip, gives me mean eyes. "Where?"

"Recruiter came to the rec center a year or so back, was talking to the older boys about careers in the military."

"Mack, I swear, you will break my heart if you ever sign up."

"I don't think you need to worry about that."

"That's what all you boys say, and then you go off and enlist on impulse."

"No, I mean I don't think they'd have me, the army. I think once you do a bid, they unqualify you from military service."

"A bid?"

"Jail time."

"Oh." She looks at me different for a second, and it all comes back to me, that doubt I can't shake: This won't last. She deserves better than me. Why is she with me?

And then whatever she was thinking leaves her. She checks to be sure Marcy isn't snooping. She takes my hand and pulls me to the shade side of the Dumpster and kisses my eyes. "You ask your father if you can sleep over tomorrow night?"

"Not yet."

"My mother said that if you don't get permission—"

"I know. I'll ask him."

"You look like you think he'll say no."

"He won't give a damn about any of it."

"Then what's wrong?" she says.

I don't really know. I shrug off the feeling that something bad is going to come of this sleepover. I kiss her neck. I love her neck. If I rest my lips on her just right, to the side of her windpipe, I can feel her pulse in my mouth. Each time her heart beats through me, I love her more terrible. I don't know what I would ever do without this girl. I can't believe she's letting me hang with her. Over Céce's shoulder, I see Marcy in the window. She's got her phone up, waving to us.

"A picture's not enough?" Céce says. "You need video?"

"I need video."

Céce marches in to bawl out Marcy.

I turn over the trash barrel. It's hot out and Tony's peace medal sticks to my chest. I'm never taking it off, because as long as I'm wearing it, everything will be right.

THE THIRTY-NINTH DAY, CONTINUED . . .
(Monday, July 20, afternoon)

CÉCE:

We're just about done with cleaning day. I'm vacuuming a year's worth of stale crumbs from the bread warmer when

Ma comes in with burritos for everybody. "Vic," she says. "All the years we've known each other, have I ever steered you wrong?"

"Many times."

"Besides those times?"

"Never," he says.

"I have this fantastically awesome moneymaker idea for you."

Vic looks up from his laptop, squints through his old-man glasses at Ma. "Lay it on me, sweetheart."

"What would you think about adding home-baked corn-bread to the menu?"

"You mean like in a Mexican restaurant?" Vic says.

"Except it's Italian," Ma says. "Now how hot is that?"

Vic shrugs. "Let's give it a shot." He nods to his laptop, the news. "This guy got smashed in a rooftop bar, fell forty feet and lived. How's it go, God takes care of kids and drunks?"

"That's why I drink," Ma says.

And act childish, I almost say. Her hair is double bunned on top of her head. Pink cat's ears.

"Help me with the puzzle," Vic says. "Twelve letters, second's an *n*. Antiquated."

"Anachronistic?" I say.

"That's thirteen letters."

"Antediluvian?"

"Loser?" Marcy says. She pulls me into the bathroom. "Come to Cindi Nappi's party with me." She has about ten pounds of bronzer on, topped off with a pound of eye glitter, which only accentuates the fact that her poor eyes are a little too close together.

"Cindi Nappi? No thanks."

"Because she's like totally skinny, right?"

"All she does is brag about her new clothes and complain about boys."

"And? I swear, Céce Vaccuccia, you're like a six-hundred-year-old lady in a cutie-pie suit. There's this really hot guy who's gonna be there."

"I already have a really hot guy, thank you."

"A hot guy for *me*. It isn't always about you, okay? That dude Brendan from the east side. You know the one I'm talking about? His brother's in the Abercrombie catalog? I heard he might like me." She grabs my hands. Her right grip is stronger than her left. She's wearing tight sleeves today, and you can really see the difference: Her left arm is a lot thinner than her right. That childhood accident—

"You gotta come with me," she says. "Please? I need to make it look like I have friends."

"Only if I can bring Mack."

"What's it like, having sex with a criminal?"

"How do you know we—"

"Oh, Céce, *please*."

This is the ritzy side of town. People up here have actual backyards, the kind you see in the movies. Me and Mack are slow dancing by this beautiful pool. The yard is packed with prep school kids. Cindi Nappi's mom is always running for some office or other, and she sends Cindi to public school to show that she's *One* with the *People*, like her posters say. Doesn't matter that Cindi gets dropped off and picked up in a limo.

Then again, I don't take the bus either. I tell myself I walk for the exercise, but maybe I'm a snob too, just without the money. A few of them are here, at the party, the kids from my school. We don't cluster. We're all split off around the yard, like we're embarrassed of each other.

If I ever figure out a gift or talent to write about for the G and T essay, and I rock the test, I'll probably get offered a scholarship to go to a private school, the kind Anthony turned down, but I can't see myself at a private either. I can't see myself anywhere, except with Mack. It's starting to drizzle. "You wanna hit it?"

"Definitely," Mack says.

"Let's grab a drink on the way out."

As we head to the bar the other dudes are staring at him. They're in designer jeans and fluorescent tees covered with writing and rhinestones, two-hundred-dollar sneakers. Mack is regular old Levi's, white tee, bin kicks. All the girls are looking at him like they want to eat him slowly. He doesn't notice. The girls are giving me *you bitch* looks. I notice.

Mack pulls a Sprite from the ice.

"Have a beer, bud," this big dude says, holding out a forty to Mack.

"Thanks but I'm a'right," Mack says.

"Have one. It's cool."

"Nah, I'm a'right."

"You said that already."

I frown. I thread fingers with Mack and nudge him, like *let's go*.

Mack breaks eyes with the linebacker and turns to me.

We turn to go, but there's another linebacker waiting for us. "Where you from, cowboy?" he says, exaggerating Mack's slight twang.

I pull Mack toward the backyard gate.

The first kid slaps a heavy hand onto Mack's shoulder. "When'd you get out, *Hoss*?"

"How's that?" Mack says.

I'm gonna kill Marcy. Why does she have to broadcast everybody else's business? She even blogged about it on her slutty MySpace page, *My Best Friend Is Sleeping With a Convict*.

"You miss it, right, buddy? Getting plowed?"

He's moving too fast for me to see how he does it, but in less than a second Mack kicks the first idiot into the pool and flips the second one, a kid twice Mack's weight, onto the pool deck. He drives down at the kid's throat with his fist.

"Mack!"

He stops, his knuckles hovering above the kid's Adam's apple.

"No, baby. Please."

His hand softens. I grab it and hurry him out. We're at the street, half the football team catcalling "Oh *Macky*," and "*No*, baby, *please*," and "Rump *ranger*."

He's wincing, rubbing the back of his head, behind his ears.

"Is it the static?" I say. He told me about it last night.

He pulls me into an alley and holds me by the shoulders and presses into me. He has me up against the wall. He's kissing me, my neck. He's shivering, whispering into my ear, "Céce, I'm serious crazy in love with you. I know it's soo toon—too soon to be saying it, but you don't have to know somebody forever to know it's forever. I just need to let you know it, because we already done it, and putting a word to it can only help make it last. You're my warrant to be here, and I don't need anybody or anything else. If I ever lost you I'd just fade."

The rain's coming down, and I'm unbuckling his belt, and we're doing it standing up, in the shadows, in the downpour. He keeps telling me he loves me, and even after we're done he's still saying it, so I know it's true.

I want to say it back. I want to say it so bad, but I'm scared. Not here, in the alley. We need to be somewhere safe. Someplace where we can keep our secrets. My house. Tomorrow night. He's sleeping over. Mack, me, and Boo.

We hurry to the train. He rubs the shivers from my shoulders and kisses the trembling from my lips. We miss our stop. The bus says *Out of Service.*

The gutters are overflowing and the streets are shuttling heavy water, and we take off our sneakers. He doesn't want me to hurt my feet. He carries me on his back, and we're laughing all the way uphill. He's so tall and strong. He glides. He carries me to my door and waits until I'm safe inside. He tells me through the screen door one last time that he loves me, and then he turns and disappears in the rain.

THE FORTIETH DAY . . .
(Tuesday, July 21, morning)

MACK:

Tonight. Her house. In a real bed.

I can't think of anything else all morning, and my dogs know it. They're goofing off and nipping at each other and crossing leashes. Boo's out with me for my morning rounds. After three hours in the heat, she's done. I bring her up to the roof and water her and pen her, and she's asleep by the time I turn to lock the hutch door to head out for my afternoon rounds.

I'm off tonight, but Céce's working. Me and Boo are going to pick her up at the Too at nine. Tuesday nights are usually pretty slow, so Céce should be done with her tables by then. If she's not, Mrs. V. will cover the last table or two, and then she's heading down to the shore after all. I can't figure out if I'm more excited or nervous. I have this weird feeling. I don't know.

Sky's crazy, blue then brown, breezy then still, threatening conflagration, like that preacher used to say back when I was a child and my mother took me to church with her all the time to pray for money. Or maybe I heard Vic mumble it over a crossword. Or maybe I overheard Céce saying it, studying for the test between shifts. But somehow I know that word. I wish I didn't.

I drop off my dogs and collect my pay. I stop at the bodega and grab a six of Sprite for Céce and me, for tonight.

"You want a double bag?" the bodega lady says.

"Triple, if you can spare it," I say.

"*Triple?*"

"For my dogs. You know."

"Of course," she says, but she doesn't know what I'm talking about, and why should she?

"To pick up after them," I say.

"Doesn't matter," she says. "I'll give you four bags if you want."

"That'd be fine."

"Here, take five."

"I'll rip 'em in half and make 'em ten."

"Knock yourself out."

Man, she's cool. *Everybody's* cool. This is going to be the greatest day of my life, even better than last night. Tonight I will be in a real nice house with my girl. A home. I grab some flowers, daisies. Tell you what, I'm so excited about being alive, I can't stop smiling, and doesn't the bodega lady just smile too? She's whistling, and I carry her tune with me, out the door, the cowbell jangling like a laugh. I'm lit up just like the sky. Lightning falls all across it like God brushed a wirehaired jackal and pulled the dross from the comb and just tossed it down on us. The elevator's out again, and I haul the fire stairs for the roof to chill with

Boo for a couple of hours before we go pick up Céce. I can't barely wait till eleven o'clock or so, when I'll be kissing her long and slow, and we won't have to worry about anybody happening upon us, like that one time in the park when I was on top of her, and we heard owls hoot, except it was these kids watching from the thickets. But now we'll have a place to be alone together, for one night anyway. Her lips will be so warm and salty and sweet all at once, and her long hair will be black and shiny against the cool white sheets. It'll be so quiet, except for the whoosh of cars down on the highway, but even that'll sound nice because they're so far away.

My roof's quiet. Too. With the lightning, you'd think Boo would whimper at least. I unlock the door to the elevator housing. "Heya, girl, wake up."

The dog is on the floor, on her side.

"Boo, come."

Man, she's really out after that all walking.

"Boo?"

Wait, is she . . . She isn't breathing. I roll her head to me. Her tongue hangs slack and gray. Her eyes are sunk in. Oh, God. Oh, no.

What did I do? Was it too hot in here today? No, the air conditioner is on full blast. Too cold? She's no pup, but she's too young to have a heart attack. *Was* too young. Did I walk her too hard this morning? She walked farther and faster and on hotter days. I can't figure it out, how I killed her.

I ruined it. This is going to mess her up so bad, Céce.

I draw my Boo close to me and cradle her, and aren't I just lame, whispering to this dead body, petting it. Her limp like this in my arms, I feel it, that she's not here anymore, and I can't imagine where she's gone. It's all through her, the coming stiffness. The cold.

Then I look over at her water pot, full of bright green liquid. I sniff it. Antifreeze. Dogs go crazy for it. Like a milkshake to them because of the sweet smell. A tablespoon will kill a dog. Boo lapped up a lot more than that. It's all over the floor. In the window screen is a fresh rip. The glass is chipped out at a low corner. The holes are big enough to funnel through a length of garden hose.

I know what happened. I do. But I just don't want to let it be real, that a person could do such evil. If that's part of being human, I don't want to be a man. Right about now, I'd rather not be.

I can't help but see it, him, Larry: He waits till I'm gone. He takes out his knife and cuts the screen. He cracks the window with a punch of his blade and bends out the broken bit of pane. He funnels it through, the hose. As he snakes it into Boo's water pot, he's gleeful. Maybe he even calls her over with a gentle "Heya, pretty girl" as he lets the antifreeze run. Boo trots over, tail whirling, grateful for the sweet words and the sweeter drink.

He used kindness to cut her down.

I don't understand killing. How can it be, that killing is natural? That it has to happen? And it does have to happen. It really does now.

This time the static doesn't pounce. But that doesn't mean it isn't strong. It's the strongest yet, just taking its time to build itself pure. It creeps in, a growing itch to the back of my eyes, until the fingernails dig in hard, and I'm sure my eyes will leak their jelly. I don't know how long this goes on, me holding Boo, the inside of my head lighting up, the fever taking me from mourning to mad. No, this isn't mad, what I'm feeling now. This is moving into madness, sure enough. I can't hear anymore. Just the static, a tornado with ambitions, the kind that's bitter it wasn't born a hurricane. Outside the hutch window, the sheets are blowing horizontal. A dark gray one takes leave of the dry line and flies off like the Reaper starved for a fresh soul.

Boo's body slides out of my lap. After a second, she stills, her legs all wrong, her head like she'd never let it be in life, twisted so strange, like she's looking back over her shoulder too far, too hard. Her eyes. I think I know the last thing that came to them, the one thing that's stronger than love, apparently.

The rage swells like a heat blister in my throat, heart, balls. Behind my eyes, just clawed clean now.

I don't know if I'm being pushed out of the hutch or dragged, but I'm staggering across the roof, down the fire stairs to Larry's door. I see my fist pounding on it. Like I'm possessed, and I don't have the will to stop the demon. This isn't me now.

Larry's cursing at me from the other side of the door. He's fading in and out of the hissing noise, but I can just make out that he's saying, "I warned you I would get that filthy dog. Stinking up my sheets. Jumping around and barking up there. I *warned* you, dirtbag." He says it over and over, and he's laughing.

The worst of it is, she was so forgiving, my Boo. Men had wrung her out again and again, forced her to live a life of battle and fear so constant she couldn't have thought anything but that terror was the natural way of things. And she still had so much goodness spilling from her that she trusted her heart to a man again. To me. She believed in me. And I let it snatch her, the evil. She was sweetness and light, and this Larry is that darkness they say is between the galaxies, nothing out there. He was just made wrong. He can't be a man. We can't be the same. But we are. Oh, how we are.

I hammer Larry's dead bolt lock with a high kick, once, twice, I'm in.

Larry reaches for his baseball bat, mouth wide as his eyes.

The Sprite cans. I spin the bags tight to keep the cans in there real good. And then I walk fast at Larry and swing the six-pack at his face.

He bleeds bad. Spits broken teeth. He's still holding his bat, but limp, at his side. I slap it from his hand and hit him again with the cans. Bust his nose open.

On his knees, Larry. Looking up at me. I can't hear anything except the hissing now, but I read his lips: "Please. I'm sorry."

He sure is, boy, tell you what.

I peel off into my mind's darker streets and lose myself. I keep hitting him, and hitting him, and hitting him, until the cans explode.

Pink froth everywhere. Then it's a fast fade to shadows.

I'm sitting on the floor, must be a while later. My teeth click in the prickly hundred-degree heat. I scratch at a bedbug bite on my neck. One of Larry's cats stares at me from the kitchen counter. She flicks her tail. Another cat licks at the dishes piling the sink. Out the window the clouds are burnt rags.

The sound comes back with the cop's voice. "Son?"

I hear the echo of little kids laughing, playing chase down in the courtyard.

Blood slicks on the floor. A slug trail from when Larry tried to drag himself to the door. He made it halfway before I finished him.

"Yessir?" I say.

"Put down the bat, son."

Condo I-beam rising in the distance, ka-*kong*, ka-*kong*.

I see the bat in my hand. Slick. I start to remember it. Chopping at Larry after he was dead.

"Son, do you hear me?"

Church bells.

"Yessir," I say to that nice cop who three times called me son.

Céce would have stopped me. Just her touch would have been enough.

I'll never get to be with her again? That can't be right. She believed in me. She had faith that I was good. How could I let it come between us, the need for the stink of blood in my shirt? How could I let something so cheap one-up my love for her? It's awful and true: No demon made me do this. *I* did it. *Wanted* to do it. And I still think I was right to do it. That it had to be. I'm the demon?

I was a man, hers, and now I'm nothing.

My hand goes weak, and the bat bangs the sunburnt linoleum and rolls hollow and crooked across the sloped floor. With blood on my hand I touch my forehead, then my heart, left shoulder, right, in the sign of the cross. Then I fold my hands and I pray that Céce will forgive me.

Except maybe it's better she doesn't.

I look out the kitchen window, up to the sky. Across the street, a pair of sneakers strung over a power line turns in a hot wind that smells of ozone. The rain comes.

THE FORTIETH DAY, CONTINUED . . .
(Tuesday, July 21, night)

CÉCE:

He's late.

I'm waiting out in front of the restaurant. I keep replaying it: tomorrow, sunrise. Waking up with him in that double bed down in the basement. The light is good down there then. Clean. Boo will worm her way into our cuddling. She'll wake up with me every morning from now on, and I'll walk her around the reservoir. I'll lose weight and be able to eat more cheesecake.

He's never late. ESP. Push comes to shove, it isn't real, right? C'mon. Probably had to do something for his father. Haul trash, mop the halls, sweep the stairs.

Half an hour late. Why didn't he let me get him a phone? I was going to add another line to mine for ten bucks a month, and the phone comes free, but he said no. I head into the kitchen to tell Ma I'm going over to Mack's. Everybody's bunched around Vic's laptop. Vic downloads tomorrow's crossword every day at about this time.

They're not looking at the crossword. They're looking at me. They're pale.

I step closer, and I see they're on the breaking news link, local edition.

"Oh Céce," Ma says.

Vic almost catches me as I pass out.

(The next morning, Wednesday, July 22, the forty-first day . . .)

He was inside me. Moved in me. I felt him so clearly. His pulse. The sting of his desperate heart. Marcy told me it would hurt, but it didn't. It was perfect from the first stroke. It was blindingly clear to me: We were born for no other reason than to be together. He made me shake. I was a mess, but he didn't mind. He was shaking too. He draped me, his torso overtaking mine, gently, softly, our lower bellies brushing where the hair lightens. The throbbing was so sweet I saw colors I didn't know existed, and they shimmered to our rhythm, all kinds of gold, like sunlight through leaves. After: He held me, and I could cry in front of him and feel stronger for it. I was a seagull driving for the full moon. But now wires lasso my joints and pull me to the floor. A puppet flattened, chained to the dustiest ground.

They're calling him the Soda Can Killer. In the print edition, he comes up just before page six, where the gossip columns start. His mug shot looks nothing like him. He's not so much looking into the camera as looking through it, at something far, far away. He doesn't seem at all surprised. He looks tired and, oddly, relieved.

Oh my god. It's really hitting me now.

Mack Morse killed a man.

He hasn't called me. He's just gone. I'm dragging the pictures across my phone screen. Scrolling through smiles and touching and hugging Boo.

My Boo.

That man. Larry. How could he? How dare he? If he wasn't already dead, I'd claw him blind.

I need Mack with me so bad now. To keep me from wanting to break everything I see, windows, the TV, the bones in my hands, creaking.

I have to salvage what's left of us. I have to hold her one last time. Hugging the pillow doesn't work. Hugging myself hurts worse. I need her. I need Boo.

Vic drives me over there, to the roof. Yellow tape everywhere. A cop sits on a folding chair out front. "You can't go up there," he says.

"I have to," I say.

"Why?"

"Boo."

"*Boo?*" he says.

"My dog. Her body. I have to bury her. In the park."

"*Bury* her?" the cop says. "You can't bury a dog in a park."

"The graveyard."

"Miss—"

"You don't understand, Officer. That's *my dog* up there. I have to take her to her final resting site. My boyfriend's secret place."

"Your boyfriend?"

122

Vic hushes me and steps in. "Listen," he says to the cop. "You know Detective Escobar, right? He's one of my long-time customers—"

"Look," the cops says. "I can't let you through the tape. And anyway, the dog's not up there."

"Then where is she?" I say.

"They took the bodies. That's all I know."

I'm ripping the tape, heading up there. I have to see. To be sure they didn't just leave her there. I have to take her to his hideaway, our hideaway, where he buried the others, the ones he tried to save, the ones that didn't make it. That time he showed me. Beneath the pines. He marked their graves with smooth stones. I know it was wrong, but I couldn't keep my hands off him. I pushed my mouth down on him right there, I wanted to taste him so bad. He kept saying "Not here," but we did. Right there.

The cop is yelling, but I don't hear him. When he grabs my arm, I spin into him and shove him off and scream, "Don't touch me. Don't. You. Fucking. *Touch* me."

He and Vic drag me out and put me into the Vic-mobile. They hold my arms down, because if they don't I'll start smashing them on the dashboard again. The cop calls an ambulance, but by the time they get there, I'm spent, too tired to cry. They ask my name, where I am, and the day of the week, and I give them the right answers. The one guy says, "She's okay." I laugh myself into a coughing fit, because that's the funniest thing I've heard in the longest time.

A few hours later, we're in an old courtroom with a high ceiling. Marble floors, dark oak, ornate moldings everywhere.

But the windows are dirty. The lights are dark with bug cake. A thick filthy cobweb rope swings from the ceiling. The fans don't do any cooling, but they make a lot of noise.

Vic's detective friend knows a guy at the Department of Juvenile Justice. Mack is supposed to plead today sometime, could be anytime, depending on how full the blotter is.

It's full.

The place is packed. Me, Ma, and Vic are shoved into standing room only, way in the back. We bob and weave and go tiptoe to look over the crowd, but I can't see any sign of Mack. Every three minutes or so, the judge says, "How do you plead?" And some lawyer says for his client, "Not guilty, Your Honor."

Everybody's so mad in here. The heat. I have to step out for air. Ma comes with me, out to the courthouse steps. I try calling down to Anthony again, to tell him about Mack, but he's still in a communications blackout.

I still haven't heard from him. Mack, I mean.

"When's he gonna call me, Ma?"

"He'll call you, sweetie. Just give him a chance. He's probably . . . We better get back inside."

"But what if he doesn't, Ma? What if he doesn't call?"

And what if he does? What can he tell me, and what can I say? I keep seeing them, the words in the newspaper. What he did. The same person who clubbed somebody to death told me he loved me?

An hour later, the judge says, "Macario Morse, how do you plead?"

"Not guilty, Your Honor," Mack's lawyer says. He's the

same court-appointed attorney a lot of the others have. I can barely see Mack from back here. They gave him a clean T-shirt, but his jeans are spattered with dried blood.

He said I muted the hissing, but I'm really starting to wonder now: If I was with him, could I have saved him from himself? How do you do that, take a baseball bat to somebody's skull? His hands, once so gentle on my body, are fists now.

The judge is saying, "Bail recommendation?" when Mack cuts her off.

"Your Honor?" he says. Mack's lawyer tries to hush him, but Mack says, "I did it. I killed him."

The judge takes off her glasses. She nods to Mack's lawyer. "Is your client on medication, legal or otherwise?"

"I don't do drugs, ma'am. I don't drink either. I know what I'm saying, and I'm saying what I mean. I'm guilty. I don't want a plea deal either. I want to pay in full. He murdered my dog, I murdered him, eye for an eye, like that. He paid his due. What's mine?"

The judge gets mad and calls the district attorney and Mack's lawyer to the bench and gives them an earful.

Mack calls to the judge, "I want fast-track sentencing. That's in my rights. Give me fast-track."

I turn to Vic. "Why is he doing this?"

"Shh now," Vic says. "Easy, Céce. Deep breath."

"Why isn't he fighting this? Larry murdered Boo. All the newspapers said it: mitigating circumstances. I don't, he's, it's like he *wants* to go to prison."

A security guard tells me to quiet down, but mine is just one of many pleading voices.

I turn to my mother. "We could get him a lawyer and help put together an explanation for why he lost it. I know everything about him. I could help him with his case. He *needs* me, Ma. I can't desert him. I swore—"

"I demand fast-track," Mack yells.

The judge writes something in her file and waves her other hand without looking at Mack, and the bailiffs sweep Mack away.

*(Five days later, Monday, July 27,
late morning of the forty-sixth day . . .)*

He still hasn't called me.

We're downtown again, this time for Mack's hearing. This place is a lot different from last week's mahogany-paneled chamber. It's this small shabby room with plastic chairs. No dais this time. Just a wobbly, chipped Formica folding table. This dude slouches behind the table. Cruddy shoes, no jacket or tie. Ring around the collar. No way he shaved today. He's been texting for fifteen minutes solid. His fingers are flying, but otherwise he's emotionless.

Mack's father is here. He's nodding but not really listening as Mack's court-appointed lawyer whispers to him. Mr. Morse keeps checking his watch and hissing, "*Shit.* Be *late* again." I tried to say hello before, but he doesn't remember me now that he's sober, or hungover.

This isn't the trial. There won't even be a trial, because Mack pled guilty. His sentence won't come down for months, but today Mack gets to talk about what happened and more importantly, to offer his genuine remorse. That is, if he talks.

The guy behind the table isn't a judge. He's a court-appointed interviewer. Based on what Mack does or doesn't say, the interviewer will make a recommendation to a judge who will decide the final sentence. The interviewer also has discretion to offer an appeal to the district attorney's office, if he thinks the DA's penalty recommendation is too severe.

It's all too confusing. Why won't they just let me tell everybody about the real Mack? The one who gives away his money to strangers and risks his life to save abused dogs. The one who saves *people*. The one who loves me.

The one who killed a man?

I try not to imagine it. What his face looked like as he swung the bat at Larry's head. Would I have recognized him? How could that be Mack Morse?

They bring him in. He won't look at me or Ma or Vic. He's in a faded brown jumper, hands cuffed behind his back. He knows I'm here. When he came in, he did a double take on me before he dropped his head.

"Mack," I say, but the guard or whoever tells me, nicely, that I can't do that.

The interviewer dude keeps right on texting without any acknowledgment that Mack is sitting in front of him. He finishes his text and eyes Mack without a word for a long time. He flips open Mack's file and takes another long time to study it. Then he closes the folder quickly, takes off his glasses and rubs his eyes. "So you pled guilty straightaway, without even waiting for a deal offer. What's up with that?"

"I did what they said, the exact way they said it," Mack says. "Why waste everybody's time on jury duty? Lying about big stuff, like murder or love? It makes me sick. You do what you do, and as you reap you must pay for it in full. The Bible says that."

But what about us? What about what *we* did? What we had. What we made together. Doesn't he owe it to us to fight for it? To fight for me? Or was our love a lie, then?

"The Bible also talks about forgiveness," the interviewer says.

"I must've skipped over that part."

The guy nods and nods, and then he sighs. "Are you sorry for what you did?"

"Honest, mister? I'm not all that sorry. You didn't know Larry. He was evil. Everybody's playing it up like he was some sort of war hero, but my lawyer told me he had a dishonorable discharge—"

"We're not talking about the victim here. We're talking about *you*."

"Okay, do I wish I didn't do it? Yeah, I wish, but wishing don't mean I'm sorry. Wishing don't mean anything. It's done, and there's no going back." He sounds so different. Rougher. Harder accent. "What? You want me to lie, tell you I'm sorry?"

"I want you to *be* sorry." The dude pulls his pen and writes in his file. "I have to tell you, at first I thought that the ADA's petition that you be treated as an adult was extreme, but now, seeing you, I think you're well aware of what you did, and I think you think you were justified in doing it. You are aware you're being treated as an adult?"

"I been treated like a goddamned adult since I'm seven years old," Mack mutters.

"You have something to say?" the interviewer says. "Speak up."

"God-forsaken," Mack says even more quietly and to himself.

"Tell me what you just said."

"Fuck you, man. Just make your report and let me be on my way."

"You're leaving me no wiggle room here, son. I have no choice but to concur with the ADA's recommendation. Unless the judge sees something in you that I don't, I think you're looking at a long haul. I mean, given the heinous nature of this crime, your prior record, the fact you skipped out on probation? I bet the judge gives you fifteen to twenty-five, to life."

"What does that even mean?" I whisper to Vic.

"Shh," Vic says. He pats my hand gently, but his eyes are hard on Mack.

The interviewer explains to Mack that he'll be at a juvenile detention center until he turns eighteen, then he'll be remanded to an adult facility for a long time after that. Mack seems to know all that already. He shrugs. "We done?"

Two guards lead him out. His shackles clink.

"Mack? *Mack*. Mack, *please*." I'm screaming, "Look at me. *Look* at me," but he won't. He won't look at me.

THE FORTY-SIXTH DAY, CONTINUED . . .
(Monday, July 27, afternoon)

MACK:

Can't look into her eyes. Not hers, her mom's, Vic's. Won't.
I'm dead now. The dead shouldn't look on the living.

Maybe just a peek. One last stolen look. She came dressed
so nice. She probably thought they would give her a chance
to speak for me.

She's wearing that junky stickpin.

I make myself look away. If I lock eyes with her, she'll
have hope. She can't have hope here. Only one way this one's
going.

"We done?" I say to my interviewer.

"You're done, yeah."

"Thank you for your time," I say, and the interviewer
looks at me like I got three eyes.

They march me out.

Last night I had this weird thing, kind of a prayer I
couldn't stop thinking. I prayed my mom would be here.
If she knew about it, the hearing, I believe she would have
come. I do. I don't know what she would have done if she
was here. But it would've been nice to see her.

The old man is here, though. My lawyer got hold of
him. Figured maybe the interviewer would show some
mercy, me being Pop's only child and such. But with the
old man all in his dirty jeans and he didn't bother to wear
shirtsleeves, all them tats on his arms, I don't know what
my lawyer was thinking, bringing him into the building.

The guards escort us out together into a side hall and ask us if we want to say good-bye. We both shrug. They take us to a holding cell.

"Landlord tossed me from the building," the old man says. "I had to find me a new job too. Thanks a whole bunch, Cario. Best I could get is casual-status humpin' at them damn Roadway docks."

"Sorry to hear that." I am too. That was a sweet little janitor gig he had there. Near-free rent in that basement apartment, decent pay, nobody over his shoulder.

"Pulling the overnight in them trailers? Like a hundrit twenty, hundrit thirty degrees in there. Gonna be at least three, four years before I got enough seniority to get me a spot on a forklift. I'm fifty-one years old."

"I know."

"The hell was you thinking?"

"I wasn't."

"Damn right you wasn't. Damn right." He'd spit if wasn't nobody watching, but the guards are just a little ways off. "Thing is, boy? I think that dude back there is right. You ain't look too sorry to me."

I don't say anything. I'm sorry now all right. Being stuck in this here cage with this idiot, can't see a world outside of himself. *His* problems, huh? I'd damn near kill again to get me a spot working a truck or any other damned thing, just to get outside. I got nothing in my life but cages and idiots since last week, and how many more cages and idiots to come. Never mind what I told the interviewer, now I'm starting to feel sorry all right. Sorry about every damned thing.

Can't believe I'll never see her again. How can that be? How could I do that to her? To *them*.

Boo.

I'll never again have a dog at my side. I'll never again know the give and take of the purest friendship.

"Y'all are on your own now," the old man says. "Don't expect me to come visiting you. I got to work. Damn, dude. Hell is wrong with you?"

Where do you start with that one? You don't. You eat it. "My box," I say.

"Fuck you mumblin' about now?"

"The Bible box. The one Moms left me. I want you to have it."

"Now what all would I want with a fake wood *box*?"

"I owe you, man. You took me around with you, you know?"

"And right about now I'm damn sorry I did too."

"The box. It's under my cot. Check it out."

"Damn, I'm mad," he says.

"I know," I say. "You ought to be."

"You don't be telling me what I ought and ought not be doing, hear? *You*? Telling *me*? I wouldn't let you do my goddamn laundry for fear you'd—"

"For fear I'd fuck it up, I know, you done told me how many goddamn times?"

He grabs my shirt. I put up my hands to block him, but he gets a backhand in there before the guards pull him off. He says, "I'm all right. I'm all right." Straightens his greasy shirt. Stares me down long and hard, his eyes wet and angry. "You gonna have a hard time in there."

"I expect so."

"Damn. *Damn.* Shit." I never noticed it before: He's pinching the inside of his wrist. "I tried, boy. I *tried.*"

"I know you did."

"I just couldn't get it together, you know? I tried so *hard.*"

"It's all right, man."

"I don't get it, boy. Why didn't you hold out for a plea?"

I shrug.

"Maybe I'll come by on y'all's birthday," he says.

"You don't got to."

"You don't want me to?"

"I hate birthdays," I say.

He nods at me for a time, and then that turns to head shaking, and then he goes.

In the city pound, the mutts like me? The wild ones that bite? They put them down. I used to think that was flat wrong. That you could save any dog with training, with love. But now I know it: Once in a great while you come across a dog that is a killer down into his blood, the one who needs to be put away to keep the innocent safe, the one that's past redemption.

Every other row of seats is ripped out of the bus. They space the seats double to keep the riders from biting, kicking, strangling each other. None of that matters now. I'm the only rider this trip. The cuffs choke my wrists. The cuff chain loops through the seat-back rail four feet in front of me. The chain is short. I have to lean forward, doubled over like I been gut-shot.

The guard waves the driver through. The driver gears the

engine. The bus is green and hacks green smoke. The bus shimmies on its way over the one-lane bridge.

I made this trip once before, the time I cut that kid. Short bid, wasn't but three weeks. It looks different now, the island. I notice stuff more this time. Little things. Maybe because I know I'm not leaving. Not free anyway. The bridge has green railings. The paint's worn out like paint wears from hands on it, but I don't see any people walking this bridge. Not the time I was here before and not this time either. The island isn't green but for a few weed tree thickets and dying ball field grass. The island is rock, cinderblock and dirt surrounded by rolls of razor wire coming up out of the water. There's more than one jail on the island. One for the ladies, a few more for the men. And then there's the juvie unit. They thought of it last, for sure. It's a hard-shell dome tent. They put it right in the airport takeoff path, which is just a couple hundred yards across the water. Every thirty seconds the ground shakes. The planes look like they're going to drill the dome.

There's no cells in there. Just bunches of cots lumped in raggedy rows. Scratchy blankets. The floors smell like they swabbed them with outhouse buckets. I know, we don't deserve better, but I'm just saying, summer nights, like a hundred and some degrees in there under that tent, the jet thunder coming so patterned? You got a lot of angry boys in there. Going into the tent alone? Not having somebody inside? I feel like a bait dog about to get chucked into the pit.

I go to my chest to touch my peace medal, but it's not there anymore. They took it from me on account it's a weapon. I guess I won't get to write that letter to Tony after all. He's got to hate me bad by now. Good. That's how it's got to be.

If I cry, the driver will tell I cried, and then I'm marked for having the weak on me. I keep my eyes wide to let the water dry in the wells.

The way she didn't pluck her eyebrows. Didn't care what she wore and was the cuter for it. The taste of her mouth. How that girl held me. If only she was there that day, to quiet the hissing.

This evangel preacher lady, she's still doing her thing. I seen her when I was in here last time. We circle up in ratty plastic chairs, careful to avoid the ones with urine puddles.

Most of the fellas don't listen to the preacher lady. They just like the safety of being near religion. They bring their softback notebooks and sketch pictures and write songs and such. You have to sign the pencils in and out, and they're wrapped with tape like a football so you can't stab anybody with it. Some of the boys like to rhyme, and they make beats together, sort of soft, and all this is going on while the preacher lady gives her sermon, but she doesn't mind. "Maybe it doesn't seem like it," she says, "but God loves everybody just as much as everybody else."

And ain't that just scary for the truth in it.

"Listen here, boys," she says. "There was an old man, and he had two sons. One did everything right, and the other everything wrong. The bad one ran out with all his father's money and blew it on a big fat crack-smoking party while the good one stayed home and worked for his father night and day and took care of the old man. The bad one came back broke, hat in hand, and the good one was like, 'Pops is gonna stomp you, lazy, selfish fool.' And don't you know," the minister lady says, "the father has a big block party for the boy who came back, and he takes him into his arms. The other son, the one who honored his father and stayed by his father's side, he's mad. 'Why you giving him a block party after all the bad things he did?' And the father says, 'Because my son was lost, and now he found himself.'" The preacher smiles at us, suspicious. "Now, what do you all think about *that*? That seem fair?"

Nobody says anything, because they weren't listening, busy doing their drawing and rhyming and stuff. But I don't think that's fair, that the slacker got a better deal than the good brother. I don't say anything, though. I don't like to talk out loud in front of preachers unless I absolutely have to.

The preacher lady sips water. The tent flaps are open to let in the air, what there is of it in the heat. Just past the flaps are concrete courts, rusted hoops, no nets. Weeds fork through cracks in the blacktop patches. The stalks twitch in a hot breeze that comes, goes, and never comes back.

One of the fellas a couple seats down from me, he's nodding off in his chair. He's drooling, spun out. Must have fake-swallowed in front of the nurse and stockpiled his T-bars and double dosed. Thorazine is no joke. He pitches forward.

I catch him before he smacks his head on the concrete. I hold him with my arm over him to keep him from sliding out of the chair.

This kid under my arm here, he's what you call a ragdoll. Throw him this way or that, and he doesn't care anymore. He falls asleep on my shoulder.

Everybody's catcalling faggots and dick smokers and what

all. Teakettle whistling. But I stay with this ragdoll kid, because you can't let somebody fall and hit his head on the concrete. I scan the hecklers and zoom in on the loudest, a big old country boy with eyes so light blue the color bleeds out into the white part. He's got his sleeves rolled up to his shoulders to show off the desecrations to his flesh, a pair of gothic crosses and white pride lightning. He can't be older than seventeen, otherwise he wouldn't be here, but he looks twenty-five easy, lots of confidence in those nasty eyes, that smirk. This Blue Eyes is a wannabe boss all right. He'll be expecting me to crew up with him and his boys, for sure, starting out at the bottom. I smile at him. "What you in here for, son?" I say.

"You just called *me* son?" Blue Eyes laughs, says all proud, "This time? Grand theft auto, bitch. What you in for, stealing a apple pie?"

"Just a little old murder is all. I'm two-five to life, baby."

One of Blue's punks cackles out, "I seen him on the TV. He's the Soda Can Killer."

That just gets a big old laugh.

They think that's weak, huh? Swinging a Sprite instead of a nineratchet? They keep it up, they'll know true violence.

The kid with his head on my shoulder is awake now. He's looking at me, too out of it to wipe his own nose. I put my arm around his shoulder tighter, to better hold him upright, to hell with what everybody thinks.

From the corner this guard watches me. He has a mustache trimmed real neat. He's kind of short. His eyes are fierce on me, but when I look at him, he looks away. He's been watching me since I came in.

The preacher lady comes around offering Bibles.

"You gave me one already, ma'am, last time I was in here."

"I think I might remember you, child. How are you, baby?"

"Good, ma'am."

"Did you bring it with you, your Bible?"

"No ma'am, but I don't deserve the Bible no more."

"Of course you do." She tries to put it into my hand, this little hardback pocket Bible, but this other guard, a huge one, comes up and snatches the Bible from her. He waves that tiny Bible in the preacher lady's face.

"Now ma'am, I warned you about this last time you came in. I was nice to you, told you all printed matter has to be softback cover."

Preacher says, "And I told *you*, the company that donates them only had hardback books this time."

"That's not my problem," the guard says.

"Then what *is* your problem?"

"'Scuse me?"

Preacher says, "Even when I brought in the softback that time, you wouldn't let me give them out."

"That's because those had staples. Has to be softback with a glue binding."

Preacher yells, "You are going to deprive these young men of the saving grace of the Holy Word?"

Guard says, "Now, you know it's not about that."

"It is about that," preacher says. "It is *exactly* about that."

"I'm a religious man myself," the guard says as he walks off with the Bibles. "But next time you try to give one of these boys a hardback book, I will have you arrested."

The preacher huffs back to the middle of the circle. "Let's sing," she says.

The boys stand and hold hands, except for me and the ragdoll kid. I don't like singing much. Maybe if I was good at it, but I'm the worst. I hate the sound of my voice.

I help the kid back to his bunk. While he sleeps I sit at the foot of his cot and look at the TV, but I can't tell you what's on it. All I see is Céce and me being together, and damn it but I can't even beat off with all these kids and guards around and the moth-trap lights up there that never turn off.

That other guard, not the one who took away the Bibles but the one with the mustache, the dude who's following me from a distance all the time? Well, he's staring at me again. And when I look at him, he again looks away.

I'm trying so hard not to think about her, what she's going through. She's got to move on. I don't exist anymore.

THE FORTY-SEVENTH DAY . . .
(Tuesday, July 28, morning)

CÉCE:

I'm down in the basement, looking at the bed. I spark a ciga-
rette I bought loose off some dude in the street. First puff, I
throw up. I can't even smoke right.

Anthony called while we were at work last night. He
sounds happy on the machine, sort of. When I replay the
message, I hear he's faking.

I don't want him to know about Mack.

(The next morning, Wednesday, July 29,
the forty-eighth day . . .)

I make myself as pretty as I can be: not very. How somebody
as beautiful as him ever went out with me . . . I burn my
fingers on the curling iron. The last time I used it was right
after I saw *The Outsiders* for the first time, and I tried to
make myself look exactly like Cherry Valance, two and a half
hours frying my hair.

I raid Carmella's messy makeup cabinet. All this guck on

my face, and still you can see the bags under my eyes. Next I borrow a pair of Ma's heels. They're too big, so I put bunched toilet paper in the toes.

"Are you sure you want to do this?" Ma says. Pink eyes, totally hungover, forty looking sixty.

"Yep."

"Then will you at least let me come with you?"

"Nope."

"At least let Vic drive you. You said you would."

"I said I'd think about it." I leave.

Two trains and a city bus later, I'm at the gate with a bunch of women. They all smoke. None smile. We avoid each other's eyes. We're waiting for the shuttle to take us over the long skinny bridge to the island. Half an hour later, it comes.

The bus chugs over to Visitor Intake. "You'll have to leave that stickpin in the locker."

"Really?"

"Absolutely."

Four hours after I left the house, I'm in the waiting area. After another hour an older corrections officer says, "Macario Morse can't see you today."

"He can't see me, or he *says* he can't see me?"

"Yes."

"Which?"

"Miss—"

"I'll tell you what, sir. You go tell that sonuvabitch I'm not leaving until he gets his ass down to see me."

Folks stare.

This guard has seen it all and often. He pats my hand.

"Please," I say. "I have to see him."

The guard speaks softly into the phone. "Thanks." He hangs up. "They're gonna track him down for you."

"They don't know where he is?"

"They'll find him," the guard says. "Where can he go, right?"

"Oh. Right."

The guard pours me a cup of his thermos coffee. I hate coffee because it gives me a headache. I drink it anyway. All the other women are there with their men. They're henpecking them. They're loud. I swear I'm never going to lose it like this with Mack. The last thing he needs is for me to flip out on him. A baby cries.

This isn't like the movies, with the glass partitions and the old phone handsets. This is an open room. Everybody sits around wobbly tables spaced far apart, under lights that are too bright. Lots of guards in here. They see everything, but they allow a good amount of contact between visitors and prisoners. They patted us down and scanned us with metal detector wands before they let us in. I remember . . .

Mack and me at the shore with Boo, sunset. We're watching this old couple hunt the sand for gold, waving their metal detector wands back and forth, back and forth . . .

I'm the only one without somebody to visit. The guard lets me wait in his office.

"Need a medic," a young guard calls to the guard in the office. The young guard has a woman in cuffs. Her mouth is bleeding.

One woman says to another, "I saw it. She kissed a razor blade into his mouth."

The girl kicks as they drag her out. She's pregnant. Her

sweat suit is dirty. I'm self-conscious about what I'm wearing now. Bright pink blouse and pressed jeans I paid too much for. Ma's shoes, fake leather but looking fancy.

Dusty paper Christmas decorations from last year or maybe years before spin over the loud but feeble air conditioner. The heat makes me drowsy. I close my eyes to escape back to our day at the amusement park. We're . . .

. . . *on line for the Freefall, in the next-up box. Cloudless sky, furious wind. The rain stopped fifteen minutes ago, and the park is still pretty empty. We're going to get our own car, just him and me.*

"You, me, a bunch of dogs," he says. "In the country. A little house. Nothing fancy but real clean. Quiet. No computer or phones. Just us."

"Perfect," I say, "except we need a TV."

"The test. The one for the gifts and talents. You're gonna hit it out of the park."

"We'll see."

"Now Céce, c'mon. What happens after that? You have to move away?"

"No. I'd go to a different school, but here, in the city. I'm not going anywhere."

"But after that, you're going to college."

"Maybe."

"You better."

"If I do, I'll stay close to home and day-hop."

He looks away. "I just don't want to embarrass you, you know?"

"Stop saying that."

"I don't want to hold you back," he says. "You can have anybody you want."

"And I have you."

The car comes. The padded safety bars creak as we pull them down. We're sitting there in the dock, waiting. The ride attendant is on the phone. Something's wrong. I'm starting to squirm. Mack squeezes my hand, and I feel better.

"They made me take this test," he says. "A reading thing on the computer. When one word was on the screen, I could figure it out. But when you put two words next to each other, they would shimmer."

"Shimmer? Like—"

"They melt into each other. If I blink, they come together again for a second, but then they start to shimmer all over again, and I get a headache."

"Okay, so you're dyslexic. A lot of—"

"It's not dyc-dyslexia. Doctor called it an unquafilied. Wait. Can barely say it. Un, qualified. Neuro, logical. Processing disorder. If somebody reads to me, I get the gist okay. And if I dictate, I can make my way to communicate writing-wise, but who's ever gonna take the time to write down what I say?"

"I will."

He shakes no. "My handwriting is scratch. I type a word a minute, it comes out wrong. Vic gives me a takeout, I say, 'I don't need a ticket, just shout out the address,' right? Every time I apply for a job, I have to take the application home and get my old man to fill it in. Yeah, I get by, but getting by don't make me—doesn't make me a solid prospect for somebody like you. They made me take the IQ again too, back when I was locked up. They had to read it to me, modified this version they use for the blind, and I had to talk it back. I came out room temperature on an August afternoon."

"I have no idea what that means."

"That's how my counselor explained it. One hundred IQ. Flat average, fifty percent on the nose."

"You're so not *average*. You're gifted."

"Look, Céce, it's like the dude who gave me the test said: I have got to figure out how to build the little house that is Mack Morse with the toolbox God gave me. I'd do better if I kept things simple. Be a small farmer, grow one *thing*, tomatoes, sell 'em at street markets. That's why I get along better with dogs than people. Smartest dog is as smart as a three-year-old kid. After three, kids start getting mean anyway."

The car jerks upward. The chain pulling us up cli-cli-clicks. I'm getting dizzy.

"They made me take Ritalin," he yells over the clicking noise, "but it freaked me out. I wasn't me anymore, and I wasn't someone better, so I quit it. I'm never gonna get better, okay? This is the way I'll be for good."

"Okay," I yell back, over the clicking.

"Okay what?"

"I'm totally okay with this, with us, the way we'll be. The way we are together."

He shakes his head, looks over the rail. We're really high now, halfway up the tower. "I'm having a hard time figuring out where I fit in is all," he says.

"You fit in with me."

He double-squeezes my hand—I love when he does that. "I'm just saying, comes the time when you find somebody else, I don't want you to feel bad."

"Now I'm feeling bad. I'm getting pissed. I don't like you thinking about yourself this way. Hey? I'll never leave you."

The car stops. We're at the top of the tower now. We're both breathing really fast. He's looking at me, and he isn't turning away. "Just don't tell anybody about it, all right? My processing thing. Please?"

"This is forever, you and me. I promise." Somebody fires a gun next to my ear, and we're dropping—

—dropping down into a sandbag trench. "I promise, Céce," Anthony says. "I promise I won't die." He reloads his rifle and fires at a satellite.

Boo runs from me when I say "Stay."

My grandfather comes home from his night shift. Seventy-three, and he still has to work. He drives a forklift. He makes us breakfast and sings folksongs to us. He sings in the shower too, when he isn't honking to blow the forklift soot from his nose. He dies there while we take turns yelling at him through the door to stop using all the hot water.

Vic is all alone in his little apartment over the restaurant, doing the crossword.

I'm taking the gifted and talented test. Three minutes before time is up, I'm not even halfway into the first section.

My mother sips beer at the kitchen table, staring into nothingness.

Marcy cruises Facebook in a daze.

Mack and me are up on the roof, inside the hutch. We're lying back on his sleeping bag, looking through the hatchway for satellites. The sun rises, peaks, falls. I want him to kiss me, to crush me, but he won't even look at me. I ask him if he wants me to give him a blow job, and he rolls away. I'm alone now. The shadows swell across the hutch walls like fast-growing bruises.

The shadows are long on the visiting room floor. The room is empty. "Miss?"

I'm sweating. I'm looking at the wall clock. I'm seeing the time. Still, I ask, "How long was I asleep?"

"You have to leave now. The hours are over. You have to get that last bus. Call ahead next time, okay? Give him some time to get ready."

"Ready for what?"

"Call first. You'll see."

I hurry from the parking lot, out onto the avenue. The bus is anywhere but here. The cabs are gone with the visiting hours. So be it. I start walking. *Ka-klick ka-klick*, my spikes—Ma's—nail the pavement. I'm tripping all over myself in these cheap heels. The toilet paper jammed into the toes is flat now, and you can see the shoes are two sizes too big. I look like an idiot, and I am. I'm a fool. Weeds creep tall through fractured sidewalks. No one plays ball or jumps rope or rides a bicycle or even strolls. The streets are barren up here, except for a stray dog that reminds me less of Boo and more of the one that bit me. It's tracking me. I cut through an industrial park where sad-eyed men whistle at me from their tractor-trailers and double-flash their high beams.

THE FORTY-EIGHTH DAY, CONTINUED . . .
(Wednesday, July 29, afternoon)

MACK:

I almost go down to see her. Twice. To tell her to go away. To be mean to her. To make her hate me.

I can't.

I can't do anything but hunker in my cot and remember . . .

. . . the Freefall.

We kiss just as we start to drop. She squeezes my hand so hard she's going to break bones. It hurts something beautiful. She's screaming and laughing, her eyes shut hard. But I can't close my eyes to blink even. I can't stop looking at her like this. Her hair flying, coppery bands. It was dark chestnut when I met her back in June, but it's lightened the littlest bit in all the sun we've been having. I'm turned inside out after telling her my secret. But she'll never tell.

The Freefall whooshes to an almost stop. We slow sink the rest of the way, maybe another twenty feet. She puts her hands inside my shirt and draws little circles into my ribs with her fingertips. I can't stop looking at this beautiful girl. Her mom made us wear sunblock, and it smells like oranges.

We float toward where we have to get off the ride. The sun flickers between the stanchions. When she gets out of the car, the sun is low on her, and her shadow is long. Just one of those days, you're lucky if you get five of them in your life: middle of July but low 70s, feels cooler with the north wind being so dry. Way up there an airplane glints. She takes my hand, and we stitch fingers and she kisses me . . .

The kid in the next cot pukes on himself. The stink is worse in the heat. Has to be a hundred ten in here. I'm greasy. I wake humped up and hard and to the sound of the fellas laughing at me. Somebody throws a cup of piss at me and runs off, and that just makes me miss her so bad.

There's a million reasons I love her, but they all come

down to one: She was good, and she let me be around her, and when I was with her, I was good too.

Come chow time, I'm eating by myself at a table not too far from the guards. That kid who was falling out of his chair, he comes up to me. "Anybody sitting here?"

"You see anybody sitting there?" I push my grub around with my spoon. You better turn it in after chow or you get sent to solitary. I wouldn't mind. It would be quiet.

Dude sits. "Hot out." He's got a bruise at his eye and a split lip.

"Fell down, huh?"

"Don't hurt much."

"I bet." I almost ask him what he did to land here, but then I don't want to know. This is dumb, but in my mind I have it that he's the good brother of that Bible story.

"Name's Boston."

"Mack."

We eat for a good while, just spoons clinking on our plates, and then I say, "Why they call you Boston? On account you hate the Yankees, right?"

"I'm from Boston."

I poke at my peas. "Boston a nice city?"

"Haven't been in a while. Moved when I was a kid. But yeah, it was nice."

"I never been to Vermont."

"Boston is in Massachusetts."

"Like I said."

"Huh?"

"Ain't Massachusetts part of Vermont?" Back to saying

ain't. No reason to keep trying to better the way I talk now.

"Massachusetts is part of Massachusetts," he says.

"You sure?"

"Sorry."

I know I'm right, but I let it go. No need to embarrass the poor kid. "Nothing to be sorry about."

After a while he says, "They got good pizza in Boston. They put pineapple on it over there."

"I'm still eating here. You trying to make me sick?"

"You got to try it. Serious. Off the hook."

"That's like putting apples on a pizza."

"I don't think I would like that," he says.

"That's what I'm saying."

That short guard with the mustache, he's watching me again. I make slit eyes at him, and this time he doesn't look away. He nods once, like hey, and now I look away.

They let us outside the tent for an hour to get the breeze that's not here. Some play hoop in the half-light of the dome's shadow. I follow the jets into the airport and try not to think about it all. Her. Boo. Larry. I'm getting less mad at him each day that slows by, and more mad at me. He must've had the sadness in him too, to do what he did. Where does that come from, what we did?

Two kids shuffle past, big one in front, little in back to hold up big's jeans, because we aren't allowed to wear belts. They're out of the glare now, the two, and I see the little kid in back is Boston. The big boy is Blue. I angle over. "You ain't got to hold up his pants," I say.

"Yeah he do," Blue says.

I pull Boston away. His hand leaves Blue's pants, and they fall. Everybody laughs all screechy. Except for Boston and Blue. Except for me.

The hissing.

Blue's boys circle up on me and Boston. This other dude pinches Boston's cheek. "Look at that peach fuzz on him. Mold on fruit. Head looks like left-back melon."

"Hands behind your backs," comes deep and easy from behind me. The mustached guard points one index finger at Blue, the other at me. "Put ten feet between you."

Blue nods in my direction. "Punk made me drop my pants."

"You were playing slave master," guard says. He points that Blue and his posse should peel off left.

Boston breathes like he's got the asthma. I nudge him and we split to the right.

"Hold up," guard says. Then, to Boston: "You all right?"

Boston chews his lips.

I catch myself imitating his posture, slumped shoulders, wilted spine. I been him, hitched up onto some bruiser's pants and towed around like all God's lameness.

"Son, you don't have to hold up anybody's pants but your own," guard says. "Don't do it anymore. I'll put in a word with the tent guards, make sure you're all right. Go wait by the desk, watch TV with the nice lady guard there. I'll be in shortly. Go on inside now. It'll be all right."

Boston and me head for the right-side entrance till I hear, "You, *wait*." Good dog training voice on him, this guard. "What is your interest in that boy?"

"I got no interest in him," I say.

"You're watching out for him. I see you."

"That's a crime?"

"Hey, look me in the eye. Now, why are you looking after that kid?"

I shrug. "Guess he needs looking after."

The guard nods. He frowns, squints. "You know what's going to happen to you if you keep playing defender? You let me worry about Boston there. No harm will come to him while I'm around."

"And when you ain't?"

Guard nods. "Look, watch out for yourself. No need to go looking for trouble."

"Not looking for anything at all."

"You're looking to get yourself a buck-fifty or worse if you keep messing with that crew," guard says. "For your information, a buck-fifty is—"

"A hundrit fifty stitch cut or in other words, half a smiley." Hun*drit*. Sound like my old man. "Look, man, this ain't my first bid, all right? I ain't afraid of *nobody*."

"You should be. You know who your biggest enemy is? You." He jerks his chin like I should move along now, and I do.

With school out, the tent TVs run all day into night, different channels and loud. I head to chapel. Guard escorts me down the long hall, past the men's jail. Dark green jumpers, they wear. Violent offenders. Those boys got no problem tuning you up. I'll be with them soon, when I turn eighteen. Hopefully I'll be dead by then.

Nice and quiet in the chapel. You can sleep pretty good for an hour or so without anybody messing with you. Regular old room with one-piece chairs and a sagging shelf on the front wall where they hang a cross or don't, depending on which religion is using the room. "God comes to people in different ways," the chapel trusty says with a smile.

"Yeah huh? Sometimes he don't come at all."

(Two days later, Friday, July 31,
morning of the fiftieth day . . .)

The third time I go to chapel, Boston tags along. "Mind?"

"If you got to pray, you got to pray," I say.

He does, boy. Knows all the prayers by heart. Holy roller. Sings fine too.

"You got a gift there," I say.

"We all do."

"Sure," I say.

"When I'm singing, I feel everything is right."

"I used to forget all the bad stuff when I was with my dogs sometimes. Training them. I don't know why."

"You don't need to know why," he says. "You just got to know training dogs is your gift."

"I never went to school for it or anything."

"Don't matter. Just trying to do it. That's all that matters."

"Boston, man? You're a little crazy."

"You know that song 'Amazing Grace'?"

"My moms told me a slave trader wrote that one."

"Nah, serious?" he says. "I guess it don't matter anyhow."

"Sure it matters."

"Did he quit trading and ask God's forgiveness before he

died? Because that's what the song is about. You can do bad stuff, but if you're sorry, you're square with God."

"Nah, nah, man. You can't take back the bad stuff just because you don't want to go to hell."

"You can't take it back, and you still owe your debt to folks you wronged, and you pay it with a full heart, but being sorry for it helps you pay back that debt. I learned that in Bible study."

"I'm not one for churching music anyhow," I say.

"I'm-a teach it to you."

"Nah, it's all right."

But he's already into the singing of it. Long, slow notes.

That night, after lights-out, I play the song in my mind to block out the snickering from the dudes around me, and I dream of Céce and Boo . . .

We're at the west side shore with Boo at sunset. An old man and old lady are scanning the low-tide silt with their electric wands. "They're always here," I say.

"That's us in sixty years," she says.

"Fine by me." I scratch Boo's neck, and she buries her head under my arm.

(The next afternoon, Saturday, August 1, the fifty-first day . . .)

I'm just getting to know him, and Boston gets released, of course. He gives me a paper scrap with his number on it. "That's my moms's house. For when you get out. You can come live with us. She's a little mean, but she cooks pretty good."

"I'm not getting out anytime soon, man."

"I guess I knew that," he says.

He nods, I nod. "Well, good luck," I say.

"Yo Mack," Boston says. "Thanks."

"You better get along now. That nosy guard's waving you to the desk."

"Call me sometime," he says. "I would like to know you're doing all right."

"You don't need to worry about me, tell you what."

"Call me just the same," he says.

"You bet."

We both know I'll never call.

Blue and his pals catcall as Boston goes, and then they turn to me like they haven't eaten in a week and I'm the last chicken wing in the bucket.

The guard who always watches me is off tonight. I go to the preacher's sermon. As she leaves, I say, "Ma'am, if you happen to have an extra Bible on you, I would be grateful."

"Child, take mine," she says.

I hold it close to my heart, and as I turn I slip the little hardback book into my jeans where they bag.

(The next morning, Sunday, August 2,
the fifty-second day . . .)

At breakfast I ask for extra pats of butter.

"How many, baby?" says the woman who doles the food.

"Many as you can spare, ma'am. You all bake the most

delicious rolls. Man can survive on bread alone, if it's yours."

"You're too cute for your own good." She loads me up.

I'm eating. Blue and his gang sit at my table, real tight on me, shoulder to shoulder. Bad shine working their eyes, open too wide. "Need somebody to hold up my pants," Blue says.

I swing not at him but his boy. I slash across the inside of the elbow, where the blood is rich. Last night I rubbed the Bible cover on the cement floor and ground it down to a knife edge.

For just a second, Blue is stunned at the sight of so much blood, but a second is all I need. I slam his head onto the edge of the table. It makes a *bock* sound. I slam it down again, but by now I only hear the hissing.

The others are trying to snatch me, but my arms are slick with butter. They can't stop me. I can't stop me.

The guards are on me with the stun shield. I'm swallowing a wasp hive. A guard flattens me. "You are one greasy child."

A bright blink of daylight whitens everything out. I'm losing myself even, in the swirl of screaming guards, howling kids, flying food, trays pounding tables, everything dimming, getting far, far away.

Maybe Céce's right. Maybe I am smart after all. Smart about stuff like surviving anyway, for whatever that's worth. I'm going to solitary for sure now, and I'll be safe for a while. I wonder what the intake folks did with that peace medal Tony gave me.

THE FIFTY-SECOND DAY, CONTINUED . . .
(Sunday, August 2, night)

CÉCE:

The Too is dead in August. Vic gives us the night off. Ma braids, unbraids, and rebraids my hair. We're both not watching whatever's on TV. She's regular Bud tonight, I'm hanging with my friend Sara Lee, I forget how many slices, but I had to unbutton my shorts. I'm washing it down with Slim-Fast. I have about a billion cans left over, because I was all about getting myself a bangin' new body for my supposed boyfriend.

The test is in a few days. I have my study guide in my lap. I'm not looking at it. I'm not looking at anything really. I say what I've been thinking every few minutes since he went away: "I don't get it. What did I do?"

Ma says what she's been saying: nothing. She pretends she isn't about to cry. She pretends to smile. The woman refuses to acknowledge the reality that is perfectly obvious to me and everybody else I know:

Everything.

Fucking.

Sucks.

"Bet he calls in the next five minutes." She's talking about Anthony. Sunday is our one shot at contact with him. Sometimes his sergeant gives them call time, sometimes he doesn't. It's 9:48 p.m. Lights-out for him is 10:00 p.m. He still doesn't know about Mack. I should write him about it.

No, I shouldn't. Writing them takes longer than speaking them, these words I don't want to hear myself say: Mack's gone. He brutally ended the life of another human being. Yes, there were extenuating circumstances, but Mack didn't hit him just once. He kept clubbing the victim after he was dead, according to all accounts.

I'm trying to understand how he could do this, but I can't. I say that I would have clawed Larry blind, but I wouldn't have. If I was the one who found Boo, I would have just fainted. Am I that much of a coward?

I think so. I know myself. Yes, I'm that much of a coward.

We're at the extremes, Mack and I. I'm forever running from conflict and he's trapped in it. He'd warned me he could wreck someone, but I never could have pictured this. How can someone so destructive be so creative, the way he was with those dogs, with my Boo? That's the real Mack. That's the one I still can't live without. I have to ask him what happened. I have to know what he was thinking. To help him not think that way anymore. I have to *talk* with him.

Carmella rubs her temples as she stares at the phone. "Working my ESP," she says. "The phone's gonna ring right . . . *now*. No, okay, wait, right . . . *now*."

"Ma? The ESP? That's *my* thing. You're supposed to play the skeptic on that one. It's the one time you're actually negative about something. Let's not lose that."

The war report comes on.

"Change the channel," Ma says.

The TV reporter interviews a friend of one of the dead soldiers, a local boy. *"Johnny was just cool, you know?"* the friend says. *"He was, like, the nicest dude I ever knew. He was just, I can't believe he's gone."* The reporter interviews the dead soldier's mother. She looks beat-up.

"Change it," Ma says. "I'm begging."

The woman on TV says the last time she talked to her son was months ago when he sent her a heart candy on Valentine's Day.

"Céce Vaccuccia!" Ma says.

"Can you not give me a heart attack?"

"Change. The flippin'. Channel."

"Are you lame all of a sudden? The remote's in your lap."

Her hands go to her mouth, her eyes widen. She points to the TV.

Dog food commercial.

I grab the remote and kill the TV. Ma rubs my back. She's bawling too, except she looks pretty when she cries. "Let's go to the shelter tomorrow," she says. "We'll get one that looks just like her."

"Never." I shake her off and head upstairs to study, but all I can think about is this: Why, when I went again Friday to visit him, did he refuse to see me?

I lie back on my bed, slip my hand into my shorts, close my eyes and remember . . .

No.

It just makes it worse. This sense of absence, a fast-forming cave. I can't believe he told me he loved me. Looked me in the eye, said it over and over. Worse, I can't believe I never got the chance to say it back.

We never knew each other. Not really. Not deeply.

But we did. We *did*.

"Hey," Ma says. She looks twice as drunk as she was ten

minutes ago, holding on to the door frame to keep herself on her feet.

"Carmella, could you knock?"

"You gonna go visit him again?"

"Should I?"

She scratches her head. "I don't know. I mean, maybe he's ready now."

"Ready for what?"

"I keep trying to . . ." She's falling asleep on her feet.

"Ma."

"Trying to figure out why he won't see you. He's ashamed? What else could it be? I mean, he's a good boy. He wouldn't just, you know—"

"Fuck me then forget me?"

She gulps. She fakes that smile. "He would never do that to my baby." She slides down the door frame and dozes. "Just gonna rest here for a secuh . . ."

I help her to bed.

"Howya doin', babe?"

"Can't remember ever feeling more awesome, Ma."

Heinous snoring. Chain saw on a pipe. I take off her crappy worn-out waitress shoes and study her ruined feet, ruined arches blown out after twenty-five years of serving people. My feet will be exactly like this when I'm her age.

I call Marcy, pour my heart out. "Is that all I was to him, a drill-and-ditch?"

"*Céce, do you think my makeup makes my eyes look a little too close together?*"

"I don't know what happened. He was so cool, so nice, so compassionate."

"Oh Cheech, you sweet, slightly-chubby-but-only-in-the-totally-cutest-way fool. That's how they all *act, in the beginning."*

"Then how are we supposed to know, you know, Marce? What should we be looking for in a man?"

"I want somebody who's exactly like me, but with a penis."

(The next afternoon, Monday, August 3,
the fifty-third day . . .)

He's been coming every day, the guy who used to sell drugs to Mack in the alley behind the Too. He waits for Mack for a minute, and then he goes. Today will be different. Today I'm waiting in the alley. The dude sees me, holds up.

"Hey," I say.

He doesn't say anything. Close up, his smiley scars are thicker than I thought.

"Dog Man's locked up," I say.

He nods, frowns.

"I'll have whatever he was having." I'm holding out a ten. Of course, as soon as he pulls a bag, I am so out of here. If I'm going to prison, it's to visit Mack. Except I'm probably not going to visit Mack anymore.

The guy pulls a bag. I step back, but he's too quick with the hand slap. In half a second, he's got the ten and he's on his way, leaving me with the bag in my hand.

Cashews, no salt. The airplane snack size the bodega down the street sells for a quarter. I rip open the bag, and guess what's in there.

Cashews.

I follow Cashew Man. He walks fast. If he notices me, he doesn't care I'm tailing him. He jogs into the bodega, and a minute later he's back out with a plastic bag filled with what?

I follow him downhill to the highway. He lives beneath the overpass in a refrigerator box. He empties his bag.

Half a dozen cans of cat food. He pulls the Purina tabs, and the cats come to him on a run. Cashew Man pets the cats and laughs their names.

1.a. Mack Morse isn't a liar.

2.b. Mack Morse told me he loves me.

3.c. Therefore, Mack Morse loves me.

THE FIFTY–THIRD DAY, CONTINUED . . .

(Monday, August 3, night)

MACK:

Solitary confinement is eight long by five wide. I thought that would've been plenty. Tiny toilet bowl, cold water sink the size of a tissue box, steel shelf for a bed. Nothing to do in here but sit and think about how stupid I am.

They have cameras. I was just taking off my T-shirt because it was hot, but they took it anyway. My socks and sneaker laces too. Put me in paper slippers. Thin plastic mattress has mesh weaved into it so you can't rip the cover into strips.

If you do figure out a noose, you kneel on the bed, loop one end around your neck, the other around your feet.

Tighten the line against your spine and knot it. Tuck your fists into your waistband so you can't pull them out in case you get scared and change your mind—and you will, I figure. All that's left is you pitch yourself forward headfirst into that narrow slot of concrete between the bed and the wall.

"Lights-out," one guard says to another. Dark so pure it's either endless emptiness or filled with every wicked thing. Panting on the back of my neck? How many hours have passed? Or are we into days now?

In that darkness, a flicker:

She goes tiptoe to hit me with a surprise kiss. Her hands on my chest. She pulls back to look at me and smile. Her teeth aren't perfect, and that just makes them more perfect. Crooked with a little space between the front two. Yeah.

(The next morning, Tuesday, August 4, the fifty-fourth day . . .)

The lights come on. They give me five minutes for my eyes to adjust.

The assistant warden sits outside the cell. Ex-military for sure. Straight back. He talks through the barred slot. "You're going to kill somebody someday."

"I already killed somebody."

"Somebody else then," he says.

"Maybe I will, then."

"Big-time gangbanger, huh? Gonna get the T-drop tat, big man?"

You ink it on the outside corner of your eye, a teardrop, black Bic pen cooked with a smuggled lighter. Means you killed a man. I don't want any black tears.

"What do I do with you?" the AW says. "Look at me. You're special."

"Hell you talking about?"

"Sergeant Washington told me you looked after that boy."

"He that short guard with the thin mustache?"

"You see my problem here, right?" AW says. "I can't keep you in the tent and I can't keep you in isolation more than sixty days. After a sixty bid the outside monitors file for you to be remanded to the tent, and you have to go back once that happens. They think you need to socialize."

"'Magine that."

"Macario?"

"*What,* man?"

"I don't know what to do with you."

"You ain't got to do nothing with me. Whatever happens, happens."

The warden scratches his goatee. "You get yourself right, you could be something incredible. You could be useful. Hey, look at me when I talk to you."

"Warden, maybe you ain't heard, I'm about to bid two-five to life. I am *done.*"

"Son?" he says. "Think about what we can do with you. I need ideas. I hate waste." He leaves, and I'm like, that dude is serious crazy.

They give me an hour break from solitary each day. The swelter won't die, new records day and night. Sergeant Washington leads me toward the exercise field, baked dirt circling brown weeds, mowed scattershot. We halt in the tent shade. He gives me a piece of Juicy Fruit. A guard giving a prisoner gum or anything else is illegal. He's got another thing coming if he thinks he's getting anything back from me. He studies his fingernails, trimmed, clean. "I put you at fifteen. That about right?"

"Be sixteen soon."

"Happens to fifteen-year-olds."

"If they ain't killed first." The sweetness in this gum, man. I'm almost someplace else for a few seconds . . .

Me and Céce sharing Bazooka.

No. Can't think about her out here or anywhere. I have decided: She has no place on this island, not even in my mind.

Washington studies the guard tower. "I'm fifty-two. On the job here twenty-seven years."

"All right?"

"You tell anybody I gave you gum, I'm done. I'm three years from pension and a timeshare on the water."

"Then why you give me the gum?"

"Why you think?"

"You're bored," I say.

"Yeah?"

"You a lonely old man, got nobody else to talk to."

"You have me all figured out, huh?"

"You're an easy read."

"That right?" he says.

"Regret that you give me the gum now, huh?"

"Not at all." He nods toward the exercise field. "Let's move."

165

We sit the bleachers. They're griddle hot. I look out to the bay. "Bet it's cooler out on the water," I say.

"It's cooler anywhere else. You hang tough now, son."

I study this guard. What's he want from me?

Behind me: yipping. A German shepherd on the other side of the chain-link fence.

"Where'd that little fella come from?" I say.

"Seems more like a wolf, you ask me. K-9 training facility."

"Seeing Eye dogs?"

"Police," he says.

"Didn't know they did that here. Who trains them?"

"Who do you think?"

"Yeah, huh? How you get that gig?"

"Behaving," he says.

The dog barks at me, switches his tail.

"Mind I say hello?"

"He looks like he wants to eat you."

I crouch to meet the dog at eye level. I put my fingers through the chain link to stroke the underside of the dog's muzzle. The dog licks my fingers.

I try to find the sergeant's eyes in his outline blocking out the sun. "Sir?"

"You can call me Wash."

I nod and get back to petting the dog.

"What was it then, what you were going to say?"

"Forget."

"When it comes back to you then," he says.

The dog rolls over for a belly scratch, but I can't squeeze my hand through the chain link. I remember what I wanted to say, but by now the time to say it has passed.

The radio blips. Wash draws it from his belt, nice and easy, clicks, "Go ahead."

"Your friend there has a visitor."

THE FIFTY-FOURTH DAY, CONTINUED . . .
(Tuesday, August 4, dinner shift)

CÉCE:

I'm late for work. The bus from the visitor center got a flat, then I missed the city bus, had to hoof it to the train, which promptly stopped in the tunnel for forty-five minutes. I slip in semi-petrified dog crap just outside the Too, take off my sneaker, and hobble into the restaurant. I thought August was supposed to be slow. We're slammed.

Marcy: "Why you wearing only one shoe?"

Me: "Did Cashew Man come today?"

Marcy: "Nope."

Me: "Figured. Where's my ten bucks?"

Marcy: "In my pocket."

Me: "Can you take the money *out* of your pocket and put it in my *hand*?"

Ma: "Did he come down?"

Me: "Noper."

Ma slams her tray to the bar counter. "That sonuvabitch."

Me: "Easy Ma."

Ma: "No. He can't treat my baby that way."

Marcy: "Right?"

Ma: "I've been biting my tongue, hoping he'd come

around, but this isn't right, what he's doing to you."

Marcy: "What he *did* to her too."

Ma: "I mean, okay, the first time you visit it's a surprise, he's freaked out, you can sort of understand. The *second* time you go, though? Well, maybe he was *really* sick. But three times? Not even a word with you, half a stinking minute to thank you for going to that god-awful place to see him?"

Marcy: "Go, Mella."

Ma: "Who the flip does he think he is?"

Marcy: "Punk-ass."

Ma: "We all reached out to him."

Marcy, eyeing me: "Some more than others."

Ma: "And he can't muster the decency to come down and at least say hello?"

Marcy: "Or good-bye?"

Ma: "You were a *virgin,* for Christ's sake!"

Total. Silence. In the restaurant. Everybody is gawking at me.

I nod, hop into the bathroom, sit on the toilet with my shitty shoe and lament existence, not just mine but everybody's. I don't know one person I'd rather be, and I don't want to be me anymore either. I'm beginning to think about it: death by cheesecake.

Ma comes into the stall, arms folded. She paces in the tiny two-foot space. She taps her foot. "Time to move on, babe."

"I *can't.* I'll die if I don't see him again."

"You won't *die.* He was the first guy you slept with. I know it feels like he was the love of your life, but it always feels that way, with every guy you're with."

"We told each other things," I say, pointing my poop sneaker at her. "We shared our *secrets*. We trusted each other with the most important things in our lives."

Ma rolls her eyes. "You gotta put him out of your mind, Céce."

"Ma, what are you doing? I need your fake optimism right now. I need you to advocate his point of view. If *you* quit on him? You who catch cockroaches with yogurt containers and set them free in the garden? If you give up on Mack, then I'm done."

"Then you're done."

"Mom, please, why won't he see me?"

"I don't know, okay? Men are weird, Céce. They would be so much easier to understand if they were like women."

"Come with me next time. Get on the phone with him and make him come down."

"I can't make him do that," she says.

"Please. It hurts so bad. Tell me what I need to do to make him *see* me."

"I don't *know* what you should do." Total girl-spin scenario: My crying gets her crying, last thing I need. "Your brother too."

"What'd *he* do now?"

"He can't call me?" she says.

"He can't if his sergeant won't let him."

"I need to hear him."

"You're hearing from him. He's sending you postcards every other day."

"That's not the same thing. I need to *hear* him. I need to hear his voice."

Marcy leans into the bathroom. "Um, Vaccuccia women, we have thirty hungry tables out there, I have twenty-nine brain cells. A little help?" She does a double take on her reflection and puts down her tray to fix her hair.

(The next day, Wednesday, August 5, morning of the fifty-fifth day . . .)

"You have your pencils?" Vic says. He's cooking me breakfast.

I have no appetite. What I do have is a tension headache. *Mack* was supposed to be here to massage my shoulders, to chill me out. That was the plan.

"I have my pencils."

"How many?"

"Sixty-two thousand."

"They're number two? They have to be number two."

I show him. He nods. "Puissant," he says.

"Potent," I say.

Vic smiles and raises his eyebrows and taps his temple. "See?" he says. "See?"

I wink and nod and tap my temple. Have not a *clue* what he's talking about.

I walk to the test. *Mack* was supposed to walk with me.

I whale on the multiple choice. I'm buying Vic a new Vic-mobile. Every single word he quizzed me on is on this thing. I finish fifteen minutes early.

They hand out the blue books. The proctor writes on

the board: PLEASE TELL US ABOUT ONE OF YOUR GIFTS AND/OR TALENTS AND GOALS.

They list the essay subject on the website. They even tell you to prepare your answer. Why can't we just *bring it in*?

My essay is supposed to be about being other-centric— my *gift*. Vic practically wrote it for me. I cried the first time I read it. I had no idea I was such a wonderful person. He made me look nicer and more pathetic than a missionary nun with late-stage cancer. I have it memorized. It's supposed to be 500 words, max. I wrote it ten times for practice. The last three times it was 491 words. Basically Vic used waiting tables as a metaphor for life: service with a smile. Hard work. Making people happy, reaching out to your fellow human beings with warmth and all that crap. It's the kind of essay that if you lie sincerely enough, it makes up for slightly better than good-but-not-great grades, and you get into a better school than you deserve. I start to write it, but something happens. I cross out what I wrote, and I write:

Mack is beautiful trouble. The time we went to Cindi Nappi's party, we were waiting for the train. This junkie was totally out of it, stepping the edge of the platform like a tightrope walker. Everybody screamed when he walked right off the platform. He hit the track pit hard, but he must have been really spun out, because he got right back up and into his tightrope act, on the track rail this time, the one right next to the rail that will electrocute you.

This other guy hopped down into the tracks. I turned to Mack to say That dude's psycho. *But Mack wasn't there. The psycho who hopped into the tracks was Mack.*

He tapped the junkie's shoulder. The man turned. He stared at Mack with strange eyes, somehow stunned and jaded at once. Mack was talking to him. The dude listened and nodded. Mack pointed to a spot between the rails. The dude stepped off the track rail to where Mack pointed. The weirdest thing? The dude was laughing quietly.

People helped Mack pull the junkie out. When Mack hopped back up to the platform, everybody clapped. Mack dropped his head to hide from them. He seemed mad. He grabbed my hand, and we hurried up the steps. I said, "What about the train?" He said, "Let's take the bus." I started to tell him he was a hero, but he cut me off. "Don't tell anybody about this, okay?"

"I don't understand," I said.

And then Mack said, "Talking about stuff like that ruins it."

We sat in the back of the bus and kissed so hard I got dizzy because I kept forgetting to breathe. I couldn't stand it when his lips weren't touching mine. All I could think was that someday one of us would die first, and I hoped it was me, because how do you keep going without a man like that in your life? Ma wants me to move on? To what?

I know he still loves me. I know he's a good person.

I'm going there again. I'll keep going until he comes down to see me. I'll call him first. I'll keep calling until he comes to the phone. I can wait for him. By the time I'm thirty, maybe he'll be out. Or if it's a twenty-five-year sentence, I'll be Ma's age. I'll work hard and save money and buy us that nice little house he wanted. Everything will be ready for us by the time he gets out. Everybody tells me I can't think this way. Marcy gives me another month before I'm with some other guy. She says once you have sex, you have to keep getting it. But I can't imagine being *with anybody else. Ever. I'm supposed to be with Mack. I feel it, and I have ESP.*

I count the words: 477. Nice. I rip the essay in half and toss it out the window into the hot wind with the rest of the test I spent the last year studying for, and I am so out of here.

Ma will be not at all surprised but extremely thrilled to hear Anthony is number one in his platoon. She will be very pissed that his special privileges limit him to twenty minutes of Skype time at 8:00 p.m., smack in the middle of Carmella Vaccuccia's Wednesday night shift.

"You don't need it anyway," Anthony says.

"You're right, Ant. C-team status in Ultimate Frisbee Club and a year and a half of Brownies in a hand-me-down uniform—I'm sure to get into Princeton."

"Two pieces of advice: Take it again in the fall. Don't throw it out the window. Done. How's Mack?"

I rehearsed the lie in the mirror until I actually believed it: He's just *great*, I'm just *great*, everything is just *great*. "Well, Ant, Mack is just . . ."

"What happened? Cheech, we have seventeen minutes."

I tell him.

He's motionless, eyes downcast, stays like this for maybe a full minute. He clears his throat and nods. *"It's gonna be okay."*

"It's *not*."

"First things first: He loves you."

"You're an idiot."

"I'm a guy. He's trying to make it easier for you."

"And this is so easy."

"All he wants is for you to be happy. If he sees you, it just prolongs the inevitable."

"That we can't be together."

"Yes."

"No. I reject that."

"How do you think he feels, Cheech? He knows how long it takes you to get there, what you have to go through to get inside. To be inside, seeing him struggling. I wouldn't want you or Ma to go through that for me."

"But you would at least come down to tell us that."

"I hope I would, but I'm not looking at being locked up for the next two decades."

"Ma's gonna flip when she finds out you're taking his side."

"No sides here. I'm dying for the both of you. Seriously, it sucks. Look, I'm not telling you to stop going. I don't think he'll sit with you, but you have to do what you're doing until the sting fades, you know?"

"Ant, I know that down deep you're probably furious at him—"

"In no way."

"Well, I just want you to know he never hurt me."

"Of course he didn't."

"I don't want you to feel bad about setting us up."

"I don't."

"You could feel a *little* bad, asshole!"

"I think this'll be a defining moment for you. You just have to go through it, kid. When you're ready to stop hurting, you'll move on. But that won't change the fact that you'll always have

a part of him with you. He made a terrible mistake, but he is an exceptional human being. He's a good person. I know you know that. You were lucky to spend time with him. And he was lucky to know you. That doesn't go away. It's okay to keep loving him. Hey, Céce, it's never easy, but it's always great."

"What is?"

I hear somebody on his end yell, *"Vaccuccia, twelve minutes."*

"Cheech, hang in, kid. And tell Ma I love her like a crazy person."

"We still have twelve minutes."

"I gotta call Mack." The Skype window *boinks,* and he's gone.

THE FIFTY-SIXTH DAY . . .

(Thursday, August 6, morning)

MACK:

The test was yesterday. I know she crushed it. A month or so from now, she'll be okay. She'll be busy with a new school, new friends. A new man. Good.

They gave me a message paper, hand-scripted. Takes me a bit and some to make it out. Says Tony Vaccuccia will try to call Mack Morse next Sunday 8:00 p.m.

Takes me even longer to scratch out that I hope Tony's doing good, that I'm sorry for everything, and he can't call me anymore. I have no idea if I spelled one word right. I can't send it, because I don't have a stamp. Maybe they give you one. I don't know. I never tried to send a letter from being locked up before. I don't have Tony's address either. How do I get it without asking Céce for it?

Wash has a pal in the K-9 training center. I pet the dogs and memorize their faces, close my eyes, let the being of each dog into me. The sun's warm through their hair. We play chase while Wash and the trainer hash. Wash nods with his lips bunched. "Mack, come here a second."

I jog over. "'Sup?"

Trainer says, "Can you write? I'm talking numbers, one to ten. That's all you have to know."

"Yeah, I can write one to ten. Can *you*?"

"I'm wondering if you would like to evaluate these dogs for me," he says.

"Say again?"

"You take the dogs to that isolation cage over there, one at a time, okay? You say 'sit,' and then 'up.' If the dog don't do it, I need you to note it."

"I can train them to sit, if you want."

The man gets an attitude with me. "No, no, *no*. They already been schooled. We just need to monitor them to see how much that learning is sticking. 'Sit' and 'up' them ten times in a row. Mark down how they do."

"All right, then."

"Good." Dude hands me his clipboard and a pencil wrapped fat with orange glow tape. "Dogs' names are on their collars. Thanks, little brother. You just made my lunch break an hour longer. They have that *Judge Judy* running back to back now most afternoons. I am addicted to it. You all excuse me, I'm gonna get back to the hutch before the next trial starts."

"Wash?"

"Yup?"

"I remember what I wanted to say. That time by the bleachers there."

"All right?"

"Thanks."

Wash shrugs, looks away to the guard tower, spits through a V-gap in his teeth. He's a real good spitter.

(The next morning, Friday, August 7,
the fifty-seventh day . . .)

Twenty German shepherds. Yesterday, they averaged a little better than fifty percent retention on the obedience training. But today they're worse. I chuck the clipboard and go to hands and knees. I show the dogs by example what *sit* and *up* mean.

Corner of my eye is Wash. He studies me acting like a dog.

I teach them *sit* by lifting their chin and pressing down on their backside. I feed them snuck breakfast bread bits for rewards. End of the second session, the sheps are up to eighty percent.

"You German?" Wash says.

(The next morning, Saturday, August 8,
the fifty-eighth day . . .)

End of the third session, every dog is a hundred percent solid on *sit* and *up*.

Guard comes over. "Morse, you got a phone call."

I eye Wash. He's squinting at me.

"Who is it?" I say.

"Didn't say," the other guard says.

"I know who it is anyhow," I say.

"Then why'd you ask?" guard says.

Wash walks me to a phone bank. I have to make myself do this. "'Lo?"

"Mack?"

"Please, don't call anymore, okay?"

"Please, *baby, I just wanted to tell you—*"

"Céce, I can't do this, okay? You can't come anymore either. I'm begging you. I gotta go." I hang up.

Wash walks me back to my solitary hitch. He doesn't ask me about my business. I want to tell him about her, but what's the point of spreading the pain?

I almost asked how she did on the test. Almost told her I've been so worried about her, that I was sorry. I almost told her a lot of things.

"Wash, you mind I call somebody? The detective offered me three free calls after I got arrested."

"And you didn't use them?"

"Not a one."

Wash frowns. "I would have to listen in on the call."

"That'd be fine. Not planning any break. Just want to drop a quick hi on Boston is all."

Wash nods. "You know how it is, though. Folks are different when they get out."

"Not Boston."

"Got to know him pretty good, did you? You only spent a few days with him, though, right?"

"Sometimes that's all you need." I hand him the paper scrap of Boston's number from my pocket. I'd nearly sweated the numbers to a fadeout. Wash hands me the receiver and picks up another to listen in.

Lady picks up. *"Bueno?"*

"Yes, ma'am, I'd like to speak with Boston?"

"Who?"

"Rafael, I mean. Sorry. Me and Bos, Rafael know each—"

She yells off, and the phone thunks like it got dropped, and then there's, *"Yo?"*

"Boston?"

"Yeah?"

"Mack."

"What?"

"It's Mack. Mack Morse?"

There's a little quiet, and then, *"Oh, yeah. Hey."*

"Yo Boston, how you doing, brother?"

"Good."

"Yeah, huh? I'm doing real good too. Yeah, man. You ain't gonna believe this, but I got me a job training *dogs,* yo. Ain't that crazy?"

"Cool-cool, listen, my moms don't like me on the phone."

"Sure-sure, I understand. I call you when she ain't around then."

"Mack? Like, good luck, you know?"

"Yeah. You too. Yo Boston, maybe I'll—"

Click.

I cradle the receiver. Wash cradles his.

"Moms don't like him on the phone."

"I heard."

"I'll try him another time, maybe."

"I expect we could work that out," Wash says.

"I'm real excited to see what your pal in K-9 thinks of the dogs now."

The K-9 trainer dude studies my chart. "They came a long way, huh? Aw, now, wait. You didn't train them did you?"

"Well."

"Son, please, do *not* train these dogs. Serious. This is a very specific program. I told you not to do that."

"Yeah, I know," I say. "I'm real sorry. I am."

Trainer flips through the evaluations. "Well, the paperwork don't lie. If these dogs are at a hundred percent obedience, I have to promote them to bomb detection drills and get them one step closer to the street." He leads the dogs away.

One dog turns back. She runs to me, rolls over at my feet, and whimpers for a belly scratch.

"Heya, *come*!" the trainer says.

"Wash," I say, "you know these dogs are being trained for the bomb hop?"

"I was thinking narcotics seizure. That's what they used to train them for. With the wars on, I suppose the bomb sniffing should have occurred to me."

"I heard they have robots to bomb sniff now, and I heard they do it better," I say.

"I think I heard that too."

I spit, because sometimes I just spit when I don't know what else to do. "You got a dog at home?"

"Two," he says. "You got some spit on your shirt there."

"Thanks. What kind, pits or rotties?"

"Mutts."

"The best."

"Yep," Wash says, and I say yep too. We watch the last dog hustle toward the kennels.

This other dude in solitary, I haven't seen his face, because they take us out at different times. He's a screamer. He was a pounder too, head on the door, till they put him in the burrito bag. They had to, because he kept yelling he was going to cut himself. Everybody used to tell him shut the fuck up, they were gonna kill him, but that just made him scream louder. He's screaming now. I can't tell where we are between sunset and sunrise. I sleep with my hands cupped over my ears. My dreams are staying vivid. She asked me once, *all quiet and sweet and even a little hesitant . . .*

"Do you want me to teach you words?"

I throw a chewed tennis ball deep, toward the fence. We're on the west side of the reservoir, where nobody goes. Pits aren't real great at fetch. They get the ball and then they want you to chase them.

It's just dawn and muggy. Me and Boo have been picking her up for morning walks. She's always waiting out on her stoop. She comes running as soon as she sees us.

"Words, huh? Not real sure I need to know fancy words."

"You don't." She has her study book with her. "Most of the ones in here are junk, but there are a few really good ones. Might be good to know them. For when you're in school."

I shrug. "I guess that'd be fine. If you teach me the good ones. Hit me."

"Execute," she says.

"Yeah, uh, I already know that one."

"Not like that. Anthony executed the mission and was ready for the next one."

"Execute means complete. Cool." It's nice, not feeling stupid for a minute. I throw the ball. Boo jets after it. "Yeah, that's a good one."

"I'm gonna kill myself," the kid in the burrito bag wails.

"Then do it already!"

(The next night, Sunday, August 9,
the fifty-ninth day . . .)

At 8:00 p.m. Tony calls. I want to hear his voice, to hear he's good, to tell him about the dogs. But we won't talk like that. He'll just yell at me. How he trusted me, and what did I go and do but break his sister's heart?

I'd rather pretend we're still friends. Better I remember him the last time I saw him, at the airport, that grin—

"Do you want to take the call or not?" guard says.

"Not."

(The next morning, Monday, August 10,
the sixtieth day . . .)

The next batch of dogs are sharp. Hundred percent memory retention.

I untrain them, again by example, teach them to run when they hear "Sit."

Wash frowns. "Don't think I don't know what you're doing."

By lunch the dogs are rolling around, digging holes in the training field. The K-9 trainer smiles as he thumbs through the dogs' evaluations, every one a failure. "These were A-list dogs, my friend."

"Paperwork don't lie."

"What you in here for?"

"Murder in the two."

"Me too," he says. "I had you figured for one of those wily types. The way you have the dogs fawning and falling all over you? I think you might do real well for yourself when you get out."

"The world will blow herself up before I get out of here."

"How old are you?"

I tell him, and he pats my shoulder and tells me in Spanish to take it easy, and I say him too, and he chuckles on his way back to the kennel building.

"Doesn't even seem mad," I say.

"He's a good man," Wash says. "I don't suppose he wants to be sending those dogs out into the world any more than you do. Tell you one thing, though."

"Tell it."

"That old man right there is a longtime inside lifer. He worked hard to become a trusty. If he loses this gig, he's back working in the shop, maybe the laundry. He has a little autonomy out here in the kennel runs. A little self-respect. Whether he's here or not, somebody is going to do this work. He has got to make sure these dogs perform." Wash eyes me. "You just geniused yourself out of a job."

THE SIXTY-FIRST DAY . . .

(Tuesday, August 11, morning)

CÉCE:

We're at Curves, arm curls. "You gonna take it again?" Marcy says.

"Nope. I'm more comfortable with people having low expectations of me."

"Good. I'm like, losing friends all over the place. What is wrong with people?"

"They don't like seeing embarrassing pictures of themselves on your Facebook page."

"What the flip do you know, Céce? You're like the laziest status updater in our grade. By the way, I'm getting a lot of friend requests with the snap of you and the murderer making out as my profile pic."

"Stop calling him that."

"Tell me you didn't go there again. Oh. My. God. You gotta move *on* already."

"Stop! Telling me! What to *do*."

"You don't have to get spastic about it."

"I wish I told him."

"Told him *what?*" she says.

"That I love him."

"Cheech, get yourself the black Chucks, put a safety pin through your eyebrow, and make every song on your Nano an emo ballad. Snap. Outofit. You're lucky he didn't kill you."

"He never would have hurt me."

"Right, because you're so not hurt now."

My biceps are burning. "I hate exercise."

"That's why they call it exercise, duh."

"*Wha?*"

"Let's go smoke a bowl."

"I was thinking more like let's hit the diner for cheesecake breakfast."

"Compromise: We hit the diner and smoke a bowl."

I go in for the takeout while she lights up behind the Dumpster. My one day off and I'm trapped in Marcy's sucky, depressing life. She drags me to the city pool. Bazillion little kids screaming, sounds like ninety-nine cats shredding each other. All the guys are getting up into this one girl's grill. She's wearing a shoelace for a top.

"*Hate* lying out," I say.

"Take off your towel," Marcy says. She's sweating in her long-sleeve T-shirt. "C'mon, advertise the globes, girl. Get the cutie-pies looking our way. Wait, that dude is *totally* mackin' on you."

"He's *leering* and he has a ball of socks tucked into his suit."

"Those are socks? Those *are* socks. Ew, here he comes."

"How you doin', Mami?"

"Gag," Marcy says.

He moves on to the next towel. "How you doin', Mami?"

"This sucks."

"Why you gotta be so *stank*, Cheech?"

"I don't want to be. I don't know what I want to be."

"Take off your towel."

"I'm gonna get a knish."

"If you lost like fifteen to seventeen pounds, you would be like twenty-second-prettiest in our grade. Serious. Wait, twenty-third. By the way, can you tell Carmella to stop trying to push her crappy cornbread on the customers? They chew it in front of her, and then when she turns away they spit it into their napkins. You gain ten pounds just looking at it, shit is like *all butter*. Serious, Céce, have you tasted it?"

"Marce, you ever feel like you're just kind of floating along?"

"All the time."

"Anthony is on his way to getting shot at, and we're poolside."

"Where you going now? You better not be going back to that prison. Céce Vaccuccia, wait up. Céce."

THE SIXTY-FIRST DAY, CONTINUED . . .
(Tuesday, August 11, afternoon)

MACK:

"You sure, son?" Wash says. "She came an awful long way again now, right?"

"Wash, if I go down there, you know what's gonna happen."

"I expect she'll say hi, you'll say hi, you take it from there."

"It'll be like cutting a healing wound. She's almost through it. Another month, she won't even remember me."

"How about you, though?" he says.

"How's that?"

"How you going to be in a month when she stops visiting?"

"I'm not goin' down there."

"Her mother's here too," Wash says.

"Bad to worse."

"Guard in the center says she brought some pretty interesting baking. Says they look like goblin squares, but that they taste just fine."

"They're snowmen. Christmas cornbread."

"In August?" Wash says.

"I know. No, sir. I have to stick to my plan."

Wash nods. "Okay. Then let's go see the AW."

"The AW?"

"We're looking to become part of a statewide program called You Can Teach an Old Dog New Tricks," the assistant warden says. "These Old Dog folks are interested in helping exceptional men and women segue to community-service-oriented careers after they finish their bids."

"What does *segue* mean?"

"Transition. Move on."

"Warden, I ain't segueing to anything anytime soon."

"Kid, I'm fifty. Trust me, time has a way of passing faster the older you get. Now, we're not even publicizing this yet, because we don't know if we're going to be accepted into the program. The program directors are giving us a trial run, and then they'll evaluate whether we're up to hosting the show. This is a one-shot deal. They're giving us one dog. That's it. We do right by this dog, we get more dogs, more chances for our people to be part of the program. On the other hand, if we blow this, they'll take the program someplace else. Lots of prisons want to be a part of this, so we have to be perfect. This is a highly competitive situation. They like the trainer to be at least thirty years old, but I have to go with my best chance for success this first time around. Mack?"

"Yessir."

"I'm thinking about offering you a chance to be our man. I'm personally accountable for this application. Should I stake my credibility on you? Sergeant Washington identified you as a possible excellent trainer. Wash has a good eye. I rely on his instinct. If I put you in on this thing, are you going to show Wash and me the respect we're showing you? You going to do a good job?"

"This is a trick, right?"

"You would train the dog to be a companion for a veteran," he says.

"Wounded?"

AW nods. "You would focus on housebreaking, teaching simple commands. Basically make the dog a good buddy for the vet."

"Sounds easy."

"Hold up. These are dogs rescued from the shelters. Broken animals aimed at broken soldiers."

"Trained by broken folks," I say.

He nods. "You're on point. I won't candy it for you. It'll be a challenge. So?"

"Warden, I killed a man."

"I know what you did, son."

I chew at my thumbnail. "I guess I could give it a shot."

"I don't have to tell you what happens if you mess up my deal."

"You don't and I won't."

"Let's get you in to meet the program director."

*(The next morning, Wednesday, August 12,
the sixty-second day . . .)*

"Mister *Morse*," the program director says. He's like forty-five or something. Another ramrod-up-the-ass-type dude. Except he hides his left hand in his right. Palsy struck, I figure.

"You can call me plain old Mack."

"I will call you Mister *Morse,* and you will call me Mister Thompkins. Here's how this works: You make one wrong move, you're out. You blow it, *I* blow it, see?"

"Yessir."

"I don't need to be out looking for a job in this economy."

"No sir."

"Mister *Morse,* I'm going to be frank: You're not making a good impression on me."

"How's that?"

"Looking away like that. You know what I think of a man

190

who can't look another man in the eye? I think he's either weak or a liar, or both. So which is it?"

"So which is it?" she says. "I'm too ugly to look at? Or are you hiding something from me?" Soft hands on my face. She turns my head so I have to look at her.

"You're too pretty to look at."

"Now that you're looking me in the eye, I almost have to believe you."

I force myself to look the man in the eye. "Sorry, sir."

"Don't be sorry. Be better." He sighs, rubs the back of his head, glares at me like I'm the cause of his headache. "This is not like training a Seeing Eye dog, you understand?"

"That's real good, because I only know how to train a dog to be a human dog."

"What is that supposed to mean and why are you pinching the inside of your wrist like that?"

If Céce was here right now, she'd hold my hand to keep me from doing it.

"Basically you want to housebreak the animal. This is by far the most important thing. We can't be passing out dogs who are not disciplined. You have to get the animal to eliminate on a regular schedule, in a certain area. You will teach him not to jump or beg. Sit, stay, give paw, leave it, heel, simple commands. I will give you a list and specific training manuals. Now, I'm told you have a learning disab—"

"I can read. Mostly. Just takes me some time, and I got plenty of that now. So you don't have to sweat me about—"

"*Hey.* Do. Not. Interrupt me. I was going to say, before you so rudely cut me off, that the manuals are largely pictures anyway." He eyes me hard. "The pay is forty-five cents an hour. Will that be a problem?"

Getting paid to play with a pit bull? "I think I could work with that, forty-five an hour."

"Indeed. Mister *Morse,* all we want to do is make the animal a well-behaved friend. Good company to cheer up the sick person, okay? A dedicated, faithful companion. Do you think you can handle that and will you *stop* pinching your wrist? I find it very disturbing." Bad eyes on me.

The hissing.

I swallow hard, stare a little past him to avoid his eyes. "I think I can do that, sir."

"Mister Morse, look at me. Do you *want* to do the job? Or have I just wasted a lot of my time on an opportunist?"

"How's that?"

"I know your type. You act all one way to get the gig, and then you slack off. Look at how you're sitting, slumped over like that. Like you're hiding something. Sit up straight—"

"Why you got to disrespect me? What I done to you? I'm calling you sir, and you treat me like I'm dirt? Why?"

"Stop. Pinching. Your wrist."

"I'm trying to."

"Don't try. Do."

"You yellin' at me ain't helping me."

"Right here, right now, I'm not here to help you. You're here to help me. And if I determine that you can't help me, then we have nothing to talk about."

The static. Electric snowstorm. I sit up and force myself to match his stare. Got to hold it. I need this gig. I need something good so bad.

Thompkins frowns. "If you last two days, it'll be a miracle." He pushes a pen and a paper filled with small print across the table at me. "Sign there."

"What's it say?"

"In the event of complications, no lawsuits will be filed."

"Complications like?"

"Death."

"I would never kill a dog."

"I meant if the animal kills you." He nods to his assistant, this skinny lady with pocks on her cheeks. She looks like she might have seen a day or two in the joint herself and done some street living to get there. "Let's have him meet the animal," Thompkins says.

The assistant leads us down the hall into an empty sickbay room. Trembling in the corner is the biggest, dopiest-looking blue-nose pit bull. His head is fairly the size of a basketball. He's scarred, half an ear gone. His eyes, though. My God. His eyes are worlds, gold brown. He knocked over an apple juice carton left open on the table. Except where's the carton? Wait, is that apple juice on the tabletop, or pee?

"What do you want to name him?" Thompkins says.

"Boo."

"Speak up. And stand up straight."

"*Boo.*"

"That's what I thought you said. *Boo.* An auspicious beginning."

"Boo, come."

The dog runs to me all wiggly and dopey. He bumps his head into the table and knocks himself over on the way. To hell with my dog-greeting rules. I crouch and open my arms wide to the dog. He rolls right up and hides his head in my armpit. His tail stump whirls so fast it shakes his whole body and mine too.

This dog is a creampuff. This is gonna be cake.

The Old Dogs, New Tricks folks need a day to set up where me and Boo are going to be living, the top floor of this old jail they're not using anymore because it needs revelations, or however you say it. It all starts tomorrow.

I can't sleep. Wash, putting his neck out for me.

I bet Wash has a nice little house, aboveground pool in back, grandkids in water wings splashing at his dogs. I bet his wife is the kind of woman who holds your hand at night, the two of you falling asleep like that, fingers locked, like that night . . .

. . . I tell her I love her. In the alley, the rain. Fingers locked. I tell her over and over, but she never says it back.

(The next morning, Thursday, August 13, the sixty-third day . . .)

We have six weeks. We'll be together, 24-7. We get two hours a day out in the field next to the garbage dump to exercise. Boo has to wear a tracking collar. Me too, on my ankle.

Training center is made of cells with their walls knocked down. Table is made of safety plastic, the kind on playgrounds, won't crack, no shanks. Same with the chairs. Supposed to pass for a kitchen. Shelf-bed for me and a plastic crate for Boo to bed in. Nothing else. Bad light in here. Place is a creepy old hole. Boo doesn't seem to mind. He's all eyes on me. Tail spins every time I look at him. The caged rooftop off the back doubles for the yard Boo will live in if he passes training. If he doesn't pass he's going back to Animal Control, where probably he will be put to sleep, because who wants a fierce-looking street mutt that failed training? If he goes, I do too, out of the program and back into the tent.

I say, "Sit."

Boo jumps to kiss me. He knocks me flat.

Thompkins's eyes say he has as much doubts about Boo as he has about me.

"He's just saying hello," I say.

"Tell that to the paralyzed vet he knocks out of a wheelchair," Thompkins says. "Chain him to the ring in the wall. Sit."

"Sit." I lift Boo from under the snout and push down on his backside.

"Not him. You."

I sit up straight in the chair, force myself to look Thompkins in the eye.

Thompkins eyes me a long time. Boo yips. He wants to play.

"Mister *Morse,* the guards see you on the surveillance monitors but they are told not to interfere with training, unless they think you might be injured."

"Boo won't bite."

"You can know an animal for years and it might still turn on you. That is an ugly truth, but true nonetheless."

"Most truth is ugly when you get all the way down to—"

"Don't talk. Listen. I have five sites and fourteen dog

trainers to mind. I won't be here but once a week, twice max. Mister *Morse,* stop turning away your eyes."

I look at him, and he's shaking his head. I want to tell him that even though I'm a killer, I'm other things too. I don't know what exactly.

He points to the manuals lined up on the counter. "Follow the protocols in order. Page one shows you how to teach the dog to sit. Even the slowest dog should be able to learn sit within the first day or so. Any other result is an indication that something is wrong not with the trainee but the trainer."

I eye Boo. He spins his tail.

Thompkins stands up. Stern face. Slings his left arm behind his back to hide it and offers his right hand. He's got a stronger handshake than I'd have thought.

"I won't let you down, sir."

He frowns. He leaves.

I let Boo off the leash. He jumps onto the table and sprays it with pee. Six weeks to train this dog? I eye the clock like I have six minutes.

"Morse?" guard calls. "You got a visitor."

THE SIXTY-THIRD DAY, CONTINUED . . .

(Thursday, August 13, morning)

CÉCE:

You can't give the prisoners anything directly. Any gift of food and the like goes to the guards before you even get close to the visitor center. They X-ray the package and deliver it later—if the person you're visiting chooses to accept the gift. He's got a lime cornbread coming his way, Carmella's Citrus Surprise.

The guard says he's coming. I lick my lips and check my hair, using the scratched metal on the front of the pay phone for a mirror. I decide my hair's a mess and needs a ponytail when he marches up to me.

He seems taller. He's definitely thinner. His hair is a little longer. Those dark eyes. He's even more beautiful than I remembered.

The sudden heat in my stomach makes me woozy. I whisper his name as he reaches out to me to take my face in his hands and kiss me.

No, not kiss me. He grabs me by the shoulders. He grabs hard.

"Hold up there," the guard says.

Mack doesn't hear him. "First and last: I don't ever want to see you again."

I shake no. "What?"

"You deaf?"

I'm laughing and trembling. My teeth chatter. "I don't get it. This isn't funny, baby—"

"Who the fuck you callin' baby?"

"Mack—"

"Don't *touch* me, girl. Just get along now. Serious. Go."

"But you love me. I know you do."

"Don't you get it? I told you that to get you to fuck me."

"Shoulders to the wall, son." The guard crosses toward us.

"We had us some fun, all right?" Mack says, ignoring the guard. "Let it go. Hey, I'm lookin' you in the eye right now, right? I don't love you." He goes.

I follow. "So you expect me to believe I was what, just—"

"What was around. You think I'm playin' with you, girl? You're gettin' to know the *real* me now, all right?"

"Mack, don't do this. Please. I never got to say it to you."

"Fuck you talkin' about?"

"I never got to tell you I—"

"Will you get on out? Goddamn, man. Just git!" He pushes me away.

Wait, he just *shoved* me. Oh my god.

The guard pulls his baton, but Mack's done with me, turning and quick-stepping for the door.

I run toward him, but the guard holds me off. He rips me off my feet and swings me back toward the exit, and I'm screaming over my shoulder the whole time, "Go ahead and run then! You're a coward, Mack Morse. Fucking *ass*hole! All I wanted to do was say . . . I hate you! I *hate* you."

Everybody's staring at me. They're looking at me the way I look at them, with pity. With *Thank God that's not me.* Except it *is* me this time. It's my turn to be torn in half.

Carmella's at the bar, folding napkins and getting mascara on them as she uses them to dab her eyes. She's watching Lifetime, the weekly mother-with-cancer tearjerker. Mother-daughter scene, mother on her deathbed.

I roll my eyes, tap myself a soda, realize it's Sprite, gag, spit it out. Back to Pepsi.

"You're not even gonna cry for me when I die," Carmella says.

"Would that make you happy, Ma, if I cried?"

"Very."

"Then I'll cry, Ma. I'll cry until my eyes fall out of my head and I have to walk around with a stick."

"Thank you, babe."

"You got it, babe." I head into the walk-in for my cheese-cake. Knocking. "Come in."

Vic sits next to me on the cheese wheel. "Howya doin'?"

"Any better would be illegal."

"Lemme have a piece of that cake," Vic says. "He didn't come down again?"

"He did. Except it wasn't him. He sent some punk who looked exactly like him."

Vic nods slowly. "I think it's time I go talk to him."

"Good luck."

"Oh, he'll talk to me."

"Don't, Vic. Seriously."

"I know what I know."

"Promise me you'll leave him alone?"

"Go check in on Marcy. She's been in the bathroom for a while. I knocked twice. The first time she said she was fine she sounded like she was sobbing. Second time I believe you could say she was *keening*."

"*Keening.*"

"I'd send your mother, but she's keening at the bar."

I head into the bathroom. Marcy is keening all right, staring at herself in the mirror.

"Marce?"

"They call me Lefty. They posted it on my page, Céce. That dick Brendan? He flippin' *tweeted* it. *Knew* I shouldn't have gotten naked with him." She rolls up her sleeves and holds out her arms. The left doesn't extend the whole way. The shoulder is rolled forward and her hand hangs at an odd angle. After all those childhood surgeries, it's not quite right. And the scars. "Does it really look that bad, Céce? Does it?"

Now I'm keening.

THE SIXTY-FOURTH DAY . . .

(Friday, August 14, afternoon)

MACK:

I'm on the floor. Boo is conked on top of me. I trained him from sunrise—or tried to. He just thinks this is some big old party, being locked up. He won't do a thing I tell him. *Sit* means tackle and kiss.

When Céce left yesterday, I barely made it out of the room. I slumped in the hallway, sure the fat man was standing on my chest. They got me into a chair and wheeled me to sickbay. Nothing was wrong with me, the medic said.

She won't come anymore. Not after that. I don't know how I made myself shove her like that.

I hope she gets another dog.

Boo wakes and slobbers me, and I shove him off. He starts sniffing around in circles. I drag his fat butt outside. The rain makes a mess of the papers I laid out on the caged rooftop in a ten-foot by ten-foot square, just like Thompkins's manual said. Let it be a hundred by a hundred, Boo isn't setting a paw on it.

"Boo, we don't housebreak you, you know we're both dead, right?"

He knocks me flat to kiss me. I claw him off and wrestle him. He spins his big old butt up in my face, his little tail stump wiggling, and sprays me with a serious wet fart. I let go of him to wave off the stink, and he breaks for the table-top. Ten seconds later there's pee all over it.

After I clean up the mess, I get back to where I left off in the training manual, page two. I thumb the rest of it. Garbage. I pitch it and call for the guard.

"What's up?" he says.

"You won't be seeing Boo or me for the next little while or so."

"Yeah, huh? Where y'all headed?"

"The can."

"Course you are."

"Once we go in, we ain't—aren't coming out till Boo does his business."

"I see." He doesn't. "How long you expect that will be?"

"I bet about an hour."

"I never heard of housebreaking a dog in that way," he says.

"You got dogs?"

"Cats."

"There you go then."

Guard shrugs. "Well, Wash told me you know what you're doing. Just the same, I am going to have to write this down in my report."

"You do what you have to do."

"You just remember, we have an overhead camera in there," he says. "It's blurred to give you privacy, but we can tell if you get to thinking about hanging up."

"Appreciate the warning."

Guard twitches a little smile. Nervous type, dot your *i*'s, cross your *i*'s, but he's all right. Boo jumps up and licks the guard through the bars, and the guard jumps back. "I don't know why they picked this dog," he says. "My opinion, they stuck you with a lemon. He seems plumb loco to me."

"He's a little creampuff."

"That head," the guard says. "I don't know if it has a bit of brains in it. Look at it. It's a boulder all right."

Boo tackles me to lick me.

Guard nods. "Good luck with that little creampuff."

I stock up on dog biscuits, extra-salty peanut butter, Cheerios and boloney, and march my Boo into the bath-room and shut us in.

Two hours later I'm sitting on the bathroom floor with this giant Boo curled in my lap. He whimpers.

"Sooner you pee, sooner we get out of here."

He drops his monster head into my hands and looks at me with those huge brown eyes. His tail stump whirls.

I'm training him to spot pee in the shower, a big old crumbly tile step-in stall. I put newspapers around the drain. I use the Money section because rich folks can stand some pissing on for once.

I trained many a dog to pee in the rain drain up in the hutch. When they were sick and injured, they didn't have the strength to make it down to the street. Winter too. Gets subzero out there, a dog will burn his paws on the sidewalk. Road salt isn't good for them either. Dog needs a fallback plan. All else fails, he has the drain.

I dip a dog biscuit into extra-salty peanut butter.

Boo tries to snatch the cookie. I make him sit and give paw and push back on his forehead to make him take the cookie real polite. He inhales it, laps at his nose to get at the salty peanut butter covering it. Now I set down his water bowl. He drains it dry, whimpers, and digs at the door to be let out to pee on his tabletop.

I get on all fours and sniff the floor like a dog looking for a choice spot to pee. When I get to the drain, I wag my butt like, *Hey, this here's the* perfect *spot to pee.* I circle the drain, unzip my fly, and pee into the drain.

Boo cocks his head and sinks to the floor and groans.

Comes a knocking.

Boo just wags his tail and cocks his head at the door. Pits make rotten watchdogs. They love people too much.

Guard says through the door, "I see you on the camera. Like I said, it's blurry, but . . . I know this sounds batty, but from a top view, it looks like you are acting like a dog, making water over that shower drain."

"That would be correct."

Stretch of quiet, then: "You all right?"

"I'm just fine," I say.

"Mind-wise, I'm saying. How you doing?"

"Real real great, thank you. How *you* doing?"

More silence, then: "Why you getting all dog-like and making water over the shower when you got a perfectly fine toilet right there?"

"Nothing at all to worry about. This is just part of the normal training."

"Well, all right then," the guard says, but I can tell by his voice he thinks I'm some flavor of mental.

THE SIXTY-FOURTH DAY, CONTINUED . . .
(Friday, August 14, dinner shift)

CÉCE:

This new guy is refilling the bar ice. "Hey, Céce."

"Oh, yeah, hey Bobby." He goes to my school, year ahead of me. I don't know him except from Marcy. They're in marching band together. Marcy's like second cymbals, and I think he plays the tuba or whatever. "Didn't recognize you with the buzz cut."

"My mother left."

"Huh?"

"She joined an ashram out in Washington State. She forced us to wear our hair long. The minute she left, my brother pulled out the clipper."

"No, hey, it looks good."

He shrugs. "It's a lot better for the summer anyway."

"Marcy get you the job?"

"Saw the sign in the window. I feel really bad. After Mister Apruzese hired me, Marcy quit."

"You're kidding."

"Right before lunch started. Your mother was pulling double duty. I don't know what I did to make Marcy so mad."

"I'm sure you didn't do anything. I better call her. Sorry about your mom."

He shrugs. "What are you gonna do? You gotta keep going, right?"

Somebody just punched me in the throat. He's shorter and nowhere near as nicely shaped, but for a moment there he looked just like him, sad and strong at the same time.

There's a hurricane in the background. *"What! Talk louder! I'm in the shower!"*

The girl showers with her phone? "I said, why did you quit!"

"I can't look him in the eye! Bobby! He was one of my FB #1's! He saw the post! The Lefty thing!"

"So, what, you're never leaving your house again?"

"I'm gonna go to the east side, move in with my sister! Start over, you know?"

"Regina's gonna let you live with her after the epoxy on her Maxi episode?"

"Not Regina! Nancy said I could sleep in her craft room!"

"Marce, you can *not* live with Nancy! Nancy tweets more than you do! I see two anorexic Napolitano girls on their phones, billions of largely untouched, festering take-out Chinese cartons all over the house! Death by Twitter! This is not good, Marcy! Come live with me and the Mella! You'll have the whole basement apartment to yourself! You can smoke all the pot you want down there, and Ma will never know!"

"It's really tempting, but I gotta get away from, like, here!

Céce, I gotta go! Maybe I'll see you around the mall or some-thing, okay?" Click.

Everybody's disappearing.

I swing the dough to the pizza refrigerator. I stop midway, look over Vic's shoulder, at his computer. He's frowning as he reads to himself. The war. It's intensifying again. The U.S. is in the middle of launching a major offensive.

My mother comes in with rainbow-colored hair. "How-yas doin'?"

Vic taps his mouse pad, and the crossword comes up to cover the news. "Good, Carmella. Good. I love your hair, sweetheart."

Work is slamming with a waiting line going out the door. Bobby tries to help, but he's kind of klutzy and drops a lot of stuff. Ma's tables are calling me over. "Where's our food?"

Ma's back in the kitchen. She's chewing gum like a cow on crack. The kitchen stinks of Bubblicious Savage Sour Apple. She keeps picking up the wrong plates.

Vic works the stoves. "Carmella, howya doin', hon?"

"Awesome," she says. "What's up?"

Serving Ma's tables and mine, I look like I walked in from a rainstorm, just what you want from your waitress, sweat rolling off her beak into your eggplant parmigiana.

Then it hits me. The gum. I check the dining room. She's not there, not in the bar, not in the kitchen. I catch her com-ing out of the walk-in with some grated. Behind the cheese wheel, there it is, the glass, Ma's bright pink lipstick on the rim. I dip my finger and lick it.

You have to get really right up in someone's face to smell vodka on them, especially when they're chewing Savage Sour. I get right up into her face. She's adding a bill—trying to. I grab her arm and whisper, "Ma, go home."

Bobby and Vic are looking at us. Bobby's confused. Vic just looks sad. "Céce, that's enough now," he says.

"What's your problem, Céce?" Her face is red.

I hiss through clamped teeth, "You think we're idiots, Ma?"

"Back off, sister. I'm serious. You want me to call you out on your stuff in front of everybody? How many times you disappear a shift? You think Vic can't count how many slices he sells, how many he buys?"

"I'm entitled to one free meal."

"Half a cheesecake isn't a meal."

"Ma, you're sneaking vodka in the middle of your *shift*."

"How many times did you try to see Mack? Huh? Even after you knew he was blowing you off, you still went back. We all have our little things we need to do to get through, okay?"

"Just *go,* you stupid selfish drunk!"

The table chatter dies like when you turn off the TV in the middle of *America's Best Dance Crew.* I hear the ceiling fans shimmying, nothing else.

My mother gulps. Shakes her head. Her face turns red, then gray. "The cornbread," she whispers.

"The cornbread?"

"They don't like it." She holds up a breadbasket. The Parmesan sticks and white rolls are gone, but the slightly burned loaf of Carmella's Crazy Confection remains untouched. No, one piece has a nibble missing. I warned her that folks might not be too jacked up to munch on cornbread whose second main ingredient is sourballs. Decorative icing in the shape of snowmen that are often mistaken for goblins? What does she expect?

She pulls her checks out of her apron, gives them to me.

"Where you going now?" I say.

"Home. Isn't that what you told me to do?"

"Carmella, let me drive you," Vic says.

"No, Vic. Thanks. I'm sorry, everybody." She heads out, stops when sees the customers staring at her. She turns around and slips out the back, into the downpour.

The rain never lets up, and the people keep coming. Vic has to cook and serve. The bartender helps. Bobby is a little better by the end of the night, filling in at the stove when Vic is out on the floor. He cooks second staff meal too, and it's pretty good, but nothing like Mack's.

After we clean up, Vic hands Bobby his keys. "Drive yourselves home. Bring the car back tomorrow."

"I thought you had to be seventeen to drive at night?" I say.

"Hardship license," Bobby says.

"Cool. I mean sorry."

He drives slower than an old lady. Trips over the curb as he walks me to the door with his umbrella. What sixteen-year-old carries an umbrella?

"Thanks." I almost ask him in for a piece of cake, but I stop myself when I remember that boys don't like to come into my house.

"Night." He runs back to the car. He's chubby and he kind of waddles. I flash forward thirty years and see him in a recliner in front of the TV, eating ice cream. He looks happy.

I go to the kitchen for a Slim-Fast, click on the light to find Carmella Vaccuccia sitting on the stepstool, her shorts around her ankles. She's peeing.

"Um, whacha doing there, Carmella?"

"Isn't it obvious? Do you *mind*?"

"Ma, you're not in the bathroom." Right about now is when I would start yelling at her to go back to AA, that I'll go with her again, like me and Ant used to in the oh so good old days, but frankly, I don't have it in me anymore. If she wants to kill herself, I can't stop her.

"I'm just so worried about him."

"He's gonna be fine, Ma."

"Not Anthony. Mack."

I help her upstairs, make her drink three glasses of water with Alka-Seltzer, and I tuck her in. She won't let go of me. "You're magic," she whispers.

"You're nuts."

"You're doing it."

"Doing *what*?"

"You're making your way through." She strokes my face and kisses my eyes.

She shrugs. "It's always darkest before the dawn."

"That's a lie, Mel. It's a lot lighter just before dawn, and then the sun comes up and scorches you."

THE SIXTY-FIFTH DAY . . .

(Saturday, August 15, after midnight)

MACK:

We've been in the bathroom since noon. I'm panicking now. Boo paces, holding in his water. He will not go near that drain.

"Boo," she says. "Pee."

Boo circles the roof and squats over the rain drain and pees.

Céce lets out with a scream and that little snort that's in her laugh sometimes.

Knocking.

"Yep?"

"Mack, I'd like to talk with you a minute, if you can spare one," Wash says.

"Yessir. Course."

The door cracks open and Boo blows through the slot, fairly knocking over Wash. He lets a good half gallon go on that tabletop. When he's done, he hops down to me, sits nice and gives me his paw.

Wash clears his throat. "How's the paper training coming?"

"Working out a few kinks, but we're gettin' there." I get

to cleaning up the mess. Can't get Wash to stop helping me. He's in his street clothes, hair like he got woken up with a late-night phone call, like Tony's that night he came to save me and my pittie girl out by the highway. Wash's wife has got to hate me. Tony must hate me more.

Boo grabs the paper towels from my hand to get me to chase him.

"Now, I'm not criticizing you, okay?" Wash says. "I'm just a bit concerned about you holing up in the bathroom with that Boo there for so long."

"Wash, trust me, this is the only way to get this variety of dog to spot pee."

"Spot pee?"

I explain it to him.

He listens real close. When I'm done, he nods. "Well then, I am satisfied that you know what you are doing."

"I won't let you down."

"I know you won't. Let's have a little sit-down." He pours from a Sprite bottle into two cups. "Son, you don't have to do this, you know."

"Oh, I want to do it all right."

"It's a lot of pressure—"

"No pressure, Wash. I love it. Gonna be fine."

"I feel I might have put you in a jam, you know?"

"Sir?"

"Your young lady friend there. Got to be hard on you. You have a lot going on, trying to work that out. Now you have the dog here. Are you sure this Boo here is trainable?"

"Positive." I look at Boo. On my look, he jumps me and knocks me out of my chair and pastes me with slobber. I tell him "Sit," and he sits on my chest, all ninety pounds of him. I brush his coat with forked fingers. It calms him down. "Wash, could I ask you something along the lines of a question?"

"Go ahead, son."

"Your wife," I say. "What color is her hair?"

He blinks a couple, and then he sips his soda. "Well, she dyes it blond-ish."

I nod. "You ever see those folks who comb the beaches with those metal detectors? This couple I saw, they would go to the shore every night."

"How'd they make out?"

"They'd find bottle caps and rusty nails, like that, but never anything good."

"Hm."

"Sorry," I say. "Not sure why I told you that."

"Well, let's figure it out. Why'd you tell me that?"

"I guess I was just thinking, like, when you tell your wife a secret, and you have no doubt that she'll keep it forever, that's kind of like finding buried treasure, right?"

"I believe it is," Wash says. "I believe it is exactly that."

"How many kids you all got, Wash?"

"Three. I'm sorry, two. My oldest died in the war. Just last year."

"I see."

"He was a chopper pilot. Twenty-eight years old. His craft went down secondary to equipment failure."

"I'm real sorry, Wash. Sorry I made you talk about it too. Him, I mean."

"You didn't make me, and I don't mind talking about

him, so don't you trouble yourself. His name was Ezekiel."

"I like that name a ton."

"We nicked him Zeke."

I nod. "I have a friend training to go over there. Army. He's got to be into his seventh week of basic by now. Probably the best dude I ever knew."

"How's he making out down there?"

"Dunno."

Wash nods.

We sip our Sprites and you can tell there's nothing left to say, so I say, "Maybe I ought to get back to work."

"All right then."

"Wash?"

"Yup?"

"Thanks for worrying about me."

"I'm not worried, and you shouldn't be either. I'm a hundred percent certain you are going to do well by Boo here. Now, you go and train your dog as you see fit."

I feed Boo more peanut butter. He drains a bowl of water. He scratches at the door to get at his tabletop. I do my thing, act like a dog, pee into the drain, and Boo just slumps flat and groans. We fall asleep curled into each other. I wake up to Boo licking my eyes.

I wonder what I would do if she came to visit one last time.

Boo whimpers to be let out of the bathroom.

THE SIXTY-FIFTH DAY, CONTINUED . . .
(Saturday, August 15, morning)

CÉCE:

I dust off my bike and hit the road. Steamy rain escorts me to the VA hospital, uphill all the way. I lock my bike to the handicap rail that zigzags to the main entrance. Not that anyone would steal the piece of crap. Anthony put it together from junk parts. I have a sissy bar.

"I want to volunteer."

"Need to beef up the résumé for those college apps, right?" Nurse Nasty says.

"Truth?"

"If it's available."

"I want to be a good person."

"You're not now?" she says.

"No. Now I'm a self-centered mope."

"Interesting. What are your skills, besides moping?"

"I'm good at making pizza. Maybe I could teach a class?"

"Or maybe you could wheel the veterans out to the garden and sit with them and read the paper to the blind ones."

"Cool. I don't mean *cool.*" I take the application to the waiting room and turn to this guy sitting at the end of the row of chairs. "'Scuse me, you got a pen?"

He's not in a chair but a wheelchair. In a hospital gown. "Is it winter yet?" he says. He's staring out the window, at the lush trees snapping around in the hot wind.

I have to get out of here.

Some lady in a wheelchair yells at me for locking my bike to the handicap ramp.

I pedal to the animal shelter, or halfway there, until my pedal breaks. I walk the godforsaken bike the rest of the way, uphill, wondering if I should just leave it on a corner for somebody to take, except who would take a bike that was garbage even when it had two working pedals? I open the shelter door, and it's hotter inside than out on the street. Barking and crying. And the stink. They make me watch this ten-minute video and hand me a pooper-scooper. All pit bulls here. Scraggly, as Mack would say. Eyes open too wide, ears back but not soft, pinned flat. They have seven days to be adopted. Most won't be.

One kind of looks like Boo, but she's wild. I take her out for a walk, and she nearly pulls me into speeding traffic. I try to do all the things he showed me, get her to walk behind me, to heel, but I'm no Mack Morse. I just don't have the gift. Any dog I get will have to come trained, except who can afford a dog trainer?

I try to dream it every night, dream *him,* but it feels more and more like a movie I think I've seen before. Somebody else's story. I still remember his eyes, though. The way he looked at me that last night, when we were together in the alley, the rain smashing us. He looked into my eyes for such a long time, not saying a word. I kept saying "What? What are you looking at?" And he just had that sad smile, and he was shaking his head, and he kept looking.

I bring the dog into the shelter by the back alley. This

dude is dragging garbage bags to the Dumpster. Ten or so. "They're triple-bagged," he says.

"What?" I say.

"You look like you're worried they'll spill out."

I press the leash into the man's hand and I run. My brother is about to head overseas and wade through carnage, and I can't find the courage to work at an animal shelter. I suck. On the upside, somebody stole my bike.

I hike home. If riding from home to the VA to the shelter was uphill the whole way, how is that when I backtrack the exact route home, it's all still uphill? And how do you ride a bike and hike for two hours, sweat the whole time, don't eat or drink anything, and you still gain a pound? My ass is killing me.

I head down to the highway to bring Cashew Man a PBJ sandwich and an eight-pack of Costco tuna for the cats, but he isn't here anymore.

THE SIXTY-FIFTH DAY, CONTINUED . . .
(Saturday, August 15, afternoon)

MACK:

After twenty-some hours cooped together in the bathroom, me and Boo know each other pretty good. He sits fine now, gives double paw, goes to his belly for cookies, then for a scratch under his jaw, then just a sweet word. What I cannot get this dog to do is pee anywhere but on top of that table.

"Boo."

He cocks his head, puts his nose under my elbow, and flips up my arm for me to pet him.

"Where you from, boy? What've you seen?"

He licks my Adam's apple.

I massage the scars around his torn-up ear. "You lived a thing or two, huh? How you stay so happy, man? How you forget the bad stuff?"

He cocks his head the other way and puts his huge paw on my chest. He trembles from tail wagging, has to be three hundred switches a minute.

"How you make friends so fast and deep, man? I'd tell you that you ought to be careful about that, but it would ruin you. Hurts, though. Get ready." Then I stop talking, because talking too much to a dog only confuses him.

Why'd I let myself fall in love with her when I knew we never should be together? Why'd I let her love me back? She never said the words, but she wore that stickpin every change of shirt. Still, would have been beautiful to hear her say it.

Boo looks from my right eye to my left and back, and I swear he's reading my mind. He nudges my chin with his nose.

"What you want, boy? You want a cookie?" I dunk one in peanut butter, and he takes it nice and polite and tosses it to the side.

"What's up, boy? You want to go out and tag your table again, right?" I open the door to swing him out to the caged-in porch, but this time he won't leave the bathroom. He sits on my foot and looks up at me.

I crouch close to him to look into his eyes, but I can't read him. "I don't know what you want, boy."

He wiggles himself into me so I have to hug him, and when I do, he rests his head at my neck and sighs. I swear this dog is the easy side of God. When I stroke his shoulders, he sighs happiness, and I believe this is what he wants me to know: That this right here, this minute of him and me being lumped up on a prison bathroom floor is all we need, and more than anything we could ever want. That's when I hear, "Mister *Morse*."

Thompkins points for me to sit. Wash sits next to me. Boo jumps up into my lap to lick my ears.

"The animal is not supposed to be in the chair," Thompkins says.

"Down."

Boo pops down to wrestle my sneaker. I claw him till he goes over for a belly scratch, farting up a peanut butter cloud, tell you what.

Thompkins stares at me. Frowns. Left hand hidden in his right. "What's this *spot* peeing business? Hey, don't turn away from me."

And here it comes, the hissing.

"The training manuals very specifically tell you how to paper train the animal. The pictures show you how to do it. I could not have made it simpler. Did you study the manual, the part about laying out a ten by ten foot square of newspaper?"

"Boo won't go on paper, sir."

"After you *feed* him, he will have to *eliminate*. You walk him to the *paper*—"

"He holds it in."

Thompkins squints. "The guard told me you are trying

to get the animal to eliminate in the shower drain. He says you are trying to show the animal by example, acting like a dog as you do."

"Mister Thompkins," Wash says. "This young man is special. He understands these dogs in ways you and I can't. Give him another chance."

Thompkins eyes Boo, then me. "If the dog is not eliminating on the paper, then where is he eliminating?"

By now Boo's sniffing the table.

"I'm cleaning it up real good," I say.

"Mister *Morse*, I asked you a question. You are *evading* it, and there you go again, pinching your wrist."

Boo trots around the table.

"Boo, come," I say.

But he's up on the table and letting loose, splattering me, Wash, and Thompkins. When he finishes he crawls into my lap and yawns and nuzzles his way to sleep.

"Mister Thompkins—"

He silences me with a wave of his hand. He grabs some paper towels and wipes his arms, careful to hide his left hand. He makes a note into his book and packs up his case. "Gentlemen, I have worked very hard to develop this program. Nowhere in the protocol books I gave Mister Morse does it say the boy and the animal should be hiding out in a bathroom for twenty-odd hours. Nor is there anything in the books about training the dog to eliminate on top of a *table*."

"Listen," Wash says. "If you boot this kid from the program, he's going back into the tent. This is a very sensitive young man."

"They're *all* sensitive, Sergeant."

"Agreed, but this fellow has a hard time *hiding* his sensitivity. He has a contract out on him. Then again, I suppose you don't know about the tent, do you, Mister Thompkins?"

"Actually, Sergeant, I do. And I am genuinely sorry for Mister Morse's predicament. But what you and Mister Morse need to understand is that I have to deliver these dogs to our veterans. I don't know if you are aware of it, but there is a war on."

"I am aware of that fact, sir." Wash frowns that one away. "Give the boy another couple of days."

"We would only be delaying the inevitable."

"Give him till tomorrow."

Thompkins heads for the cell door. "To process the termination paperwork will take that long anyway. Will you please inform the assistant warden he will be hearing from me tomorrow morning?" The guard opens the cage door and lets the man out.

"Son?" Wash says. "Seems to me you have until tomorrow morning to get that dog housebroken. Can you do it?"

The building trembles. I look out the window. An older, noisier 747 just clears the dome. Boo is playing chase with a big black fly.

Another guard comes to the bars. "Morse. Visitor."

"He reminds me of you," I say.

"Yeah?" Vic says.

"He's real cool, but he's sneaky. Wash isn't afraid to bend the rules a little."

"Sounds like a great man. Potent, this Old Dogs thing. You found your calling."

"Had to get locked up to do it."

"You'll be out sooner than you think," Vic says.

"So I been told."

"By people who aren't locked up, right? When you get out, you come see me. I'll help you get that dog training company started. You'll make us millionaires."

I study him: pushing seventy. He isn't in great shape at all. Twenty-five years from now? "I appreciate that, man. Thank you." My lips are trembling.

"Hey?" he says. "What's up?"

"Things aren't looking great right now."

"They never do, till they're great," he says. "You watch: You're gonna be okay."

He thinks I'm upset because I'm locked up. Better to let him think it's that. He can't help me with the fact Thompkins is about to fire me. "Tell me more about Tony."

"He says he wants you to know he's there for you."

I look away. "Tell him I said thank you."

Vic nods for a while. "I need a favor."

"Anything, man."

"Just for a few minutes, I need you to let Céce sit with you."

"Anything but that."

"This is a matter of honor. Hers. Yours. One last visit. You need to do this."

"Vic, ten minutes ago, when they said I had a visitor, I was ready to cartwheel down here. But now I got my senses back. I can't see her. She's almost through it. The forgetting.

Why stir up all the feelings again when her and me can never be together?"

"Because you need to say good-bye," he says. "I don't tell somebody to do something unless I'm one hundred percent sure it's—"

"Look, man, I have to get back to my dog."

"You're gonna see her, kid, whether you like it or not."

"Damn, man, my plate's full, okay? I appreciate you coming down here, but just leave it alone, all right?" I fish my pocket for that letter I wrote, and I push it across the table to Vic. "For Tony."

"Kid, there's three ways to do things: the wrong way, the right way, and my way. Wrong way: Make her hate you. Right way: Be a gentleman and sit with her for ten minutes, let her say what she needs to say."

"And your way?"

"You don't want to know."

I kick back out of my chair and slam it into the table, and I'm so gone.

THE SIXTY-FIFTH DAY, CONTINUED . . .

(Saturday, August 15, just before dinner shift)

CÉCE:

Bobby drops a tray of glasses. "Yup, yes, yet again," he says. Five minutes later, he spills ice all over the kitchen floor. "I am so sorry about that. It's an age-old problem."

If you're a certified klutz, why would you seek employment in a restaurant, which is pretty much about carrying stuff from one place to another without spilling it? He's an excellent cheesecake pal, though. We go into the walk-in and eat and we don't care that we're licking our fingers in front of each other. A minute later Ma's in with us, because the air conditioner is broken again. She's sipping iced coffee, hungover but sober for half a day and still promising to stay that way. A minute later Vic comes in, and he's huffing and sweating.

"What happened to you?" Ma says.

"Car broke down again. Get this: The tow truck crapped out. *He* had to get a tow. And when he dropped the Olds at the gas station, it started."

"You just have to hit it really hard with a cinderblock," Ma says. "Passenger side, front quarter panel. It restarts like maybe thirty-five percent of the time. I left the brick in the trunk."

"Good to know."

"You need help unloading the stuff?" I say.

"What stuff?" Vic says.

"The Costco crap."

"Yeah, no, it was too crowded. I'll go tomorrow. Hand me a piece of cake there, kid."

Bobby reaches for the box and knocks over a bucket of mushrooms soaking in wine. "Yup, yes, yet again. I am so sorry about that."

The new waitress cracks the door.

"Grab a spot of Parmesan wheel, Jeannie," Ma says.

"Um, Carmella, I . . ." She opens the door, and this older

guy is standing there. He's in a U.S. Army uniform. The nametag. Anthony's recruiter. He searches our faces and decides my mother is the person he's looking for. "Mrs. Vaccuccia?"

"No," Ma says. "Please, no."

And then I hear myself saying, "The hell are you doing here? He's still in boot camp. It isn't time yet."

My big brother, my mother's only son, Anthony James Vaccuccia, was "seriously injured." Part of his face was burned in the explosion, though that wound is supposedly minor. Also burned were two fingers on his right hand, the one that launched how many touchdowns I can't remember. Those burns were so bad, the fingers had to be amputated, along with his legs, which were pulverized. Shrapnel lacerated his larynx, but doctors are hopeful that surgery will restore part of my brother's voice box.

No roadside bomb in some faraway land. No grenade. No sniper fire aimed at a Humvee gas tank. An insanely random accident. No one to blame, except Anthony.

My brother and his platoon were leaving their barracks for a workout. A maintenance vehicle crashed into the barracks. The old man behind the wheel was having a heart attack. Anthony being Anthony went to help the old man. The truck was on fire, but Anthony couldn't—no, wouldn't—leave the man. The truck door jammed in the crash. Anthony was climbing into the truck to kick out the door when the fire lit up a propane tank.

I did not see this coming. I can only conclude, definitively, that ESP is a crock of shit.

✕ ✕ ✕ ✕ ✕ ✕

Vic closes the restaurant for the night and drives us home—after Ma smashes the engine with the cinderblock. Vic takes the long way, for some reason, all the way around the reservoir. We're riding for a while, nobody saying anything, until Ma says, "You guys mind I put on the radio?"

"Course not, sweetheart," Vic says.

Ma rolls the ancient dial to the community college station for Punk Hour. DJ sounds like he's huffing lighter fluid. Between the commercials a song occasionally comes on, this really old hard-edged music, The Clash, Iggy Pop, The Ramones. The station fades to crackles every time Vic makes a turn, and Ma constantly retunes the dial. She starts singing along with this band called Suicide. The song's called "Dream Baby Dream," and the singer keeps telling us that our dreams will keep us free. Sure they will.

I reach over the seat and click off the radio. "How can you stand it, Ma?"

"It makes me feel good," she says. And that's all anybody says until we pull up to the house and Vic pats our arms and nods. "It's all gonna be okay."

"How you figure that?" I say.

"I just know it." Vic's face is pocked and gray and fragile in the shade-side light. We go into the kitchen. Vic makes coffee.

Anthony is unconscious in post-op recovery, but apparently he's stable. We can't go down and see him yet, because they might have to move him to another hospital. Do I even *want* to go down and see him? Will I recognize him?

I head upstairs for a shower, but it doesn't make me feel

any better. I just sit there in my towel, on the floor of the upstairs bathroom, the same floor Grumpy died on. I flip through what I was flipping through while on the toilet this morning, when my life only sucked: a magazine, *Bark,* for dog lovers. It came in the mail yesterday, from Anthony. He picked it up at the PX for Mack. Could I leave it with him next time I visited?

No, I can't. Mack gets what he wants: He's dead.

His absence leaves me with plenty of shoulders to cry on, plenty of people to tell me everything will be okay, but no one to believe. He did exactly what he promised he'd never do: He left me stranded.

I'm looking out the bathroom window. It's still light out, but the streetlights are on, and the gnats are swarming.

THE SIXTY–SIXTH DAY . . .

(Sunday, August 16, just after midnight)

MACK:

The gnats are chewing at us. But if I close the window, we'll roast.

Thirty-odd hours in the bathroom. We're staring at each other. Boo licks my face with his extra-long tongue. It hangs out of his mouth three inches when he sleeps.

He pees on the side of the toilet. I'm mopping up the mess with newspaper when I suddenly understand what he needs.

I'm an idiot. How could it take me this long to figure it out?

I take the wet paper and lay it around the shower drain and lead Boo into the stall. He smells his mark in the paper and starts to pee on it.

I give this blessed dog a quarter pound of boloney dunked in peanut butter. I'm howling and hugging him. We're running around the training center.

I get him full of water again. "Boo, pee."

He gives me paw.

"Nuh-uh. *Pee.*" I lead him into the stall. He smells him-self in the newspaper and lets loose over the drain again, and again I feed him boloney and praise. "*Good* pee. *Good* Boo."

I take the dirty papers and set them out on the roof, and Boo nails them there too. For a slice of boloney, this dog will climb a tree to spray a newspaper hung in its top.

Wash is in the door frame. He was ripped from deep sleep again, but he's grinning. Has a phone to his ear. "Yessir, I have good news. No, I said *good* news."

(Monday, August 17,
morning of the sixty-seventh day . . .)

Four days since I told her I never loved her. She hasn't come back. It's done. If I didn't have Boo with me right now, I don't know.

Thompkins stands tall to watch, arms folded with his lame hand tucked into his armpit. Wash watches from the door.

"Boo, sit," I say.

Boo sits.

"Boo, pee."

Boo puts up his paw.

"Boo, I want *pee.*"

Boo trots to the shower stall, lets loose over the drain, comes back out with a spinning tail for his baloney reward and a "Good boy" from me.

Thompkins scowls. "Can you make him go outside?"

I lay out a paper on the roof. "Boo, *pee*."

Boo trots to the paper, lifts his leg, pees what dribble he's got left.

"Mister T., this dog is housebroke."

"I still don't understand the reasoning behind getting the animal to eliminate in the shower drain."

"Sir, a dog needs options. You take him outside, he knows it's cool to make water outside. But if he's stuck alone in the house or with a paralyzed veteran who can't let him out—"

"He won't be *put* with anybody who can't let him out, as I *told* you. How many times must I say this? He is not a medical aid animal. He is a companion. The veteran may be physically disabled, but in order to qualify for the animal he or she at minimum will need to be able to provide for the animal's basic needs, for example, letting the animal out to eliminate and for the last time *stop, pinching,* your *wrist.*"

Blizzard of radio static now. Roof cage hot. Day hazy gray. Heat lightning inside me. I see myself going crazy on Thompkins. My hands are getting tight to do it. I step toward him.

Boo cuts me off. He sits between me and the man. He nudges me for petting. Leans into my leg. Big eyes. Tongue hanging out his mouth. This bait dog from the fight pits. A dog that lived terror and came out the other side with his heart still open.

I can't forsake this dog.

The radio static fades, and the world comes back with sounds of a hot summer day, men working a tar rig out behind the tent, an airplane climbing.

I hold my head up and look the man in the eye. "Mister

Thompkins, due respect. These vets, sometimes they need to drink at night. You know, to keep from getting scared and sad, right? So, let's say the poor vet passes out drunk. As a fallback, Boo can go into the bathroom, *eliminate* over a drain, where you can rinse away the mess. Better there than on a carpet or a bed, right?"

Thompkins looks at me for a long time. He makes a note in his book. He leaves.

Boo fetches his chewed-up Frisbee.

"Think Thompkins is gonna have to fire me, Wash?"

"I think he's gonna have to rewrite his training manual."

"I don't know what that dude wants from me."

"I expect he's just one of those people who don't know how to give praise. Son, deep inside, he sees you are doing just fine. He would have pulled you from the job by now if he thought otherwise. As much pressure as you feel to come through for him, he has that much pressure to come through for his people."

"The vets."

"I believe so. No, I wouldn't ever expect a word of praise from Mister Thompkins. His praise is his silence, and he gave you that. Hey?"

"Yessir?"

"How you doing?"

I look at my boy Boo chasing his Frisbee. He isn't on a caged-in rooftop. The incinerator stacks, low-flying jumbo jets, sun-faded concrete, and the razor wire—all fade away. Boo's running through a field of wild grass. "Wash, I'm doing just fine."

THE SEVENTY-FIRST DAY . . .
(Friday, August 21, just after lunch shift)

CÉCE:

Ma's at the bar. She sips her coffee. Sober a week. She and Vic pretend to do the crossword.

Last night the doctor called to tell us the second surgery on Anthony's larynx went well. He can't talk just yet, but in a few days he'll probably be well enough to have visitors. We can come down and see him next week, what's left of him.

Ma's phone blips with an e-mail. She checks the sender, pushes the phone toward me. "I can't."

To: crazy4cornbread@sallgood.com

From: ajcooch@hipmail.net

Subject: Yo

I can't either. I give the phone to Vic.

Vic clears his throat. "'Ma, Cheech, Vic, it's all good. We're gonna get through this. I'm doing great. One request: Don't come down here, okay? You'll only get freaked out. I'll be home soon and we'll figure out this whole thing then. Do me a favor, keep sending that cornbread to the guys, okay? They love it and they sure could use it. Rehab is going great.

I'll see you in a month or so. Love you all like a madman. Chin up, folks. xox Ant.'"

Vic frowns, clicks the e-mail closed. "Well," he says. He puts his hand on Ma's shoulder.

Ma nods. "Well," she says.

"You know," Vic says, "I really think you ladies should get a dog."

"Please?" Ma says to me.

"No," I say.

"Yeah, a rescue," Vic says. "Just think about it, I'm saying. You know, *mull* it."

"Abso*lutel*y not," I say.

"Oh absolutely," Vic says. "One of those vet buddy dogs for Anthony, maybe a pit bull."

"A *pit* bull?" I say. "Are you insane?"

"Almost certainly," he says. "Kid, you need to do this."

"I don't and I *can't*," I say.

"Sure you can. You just do it. Perhaps I'll make some inquiries."

"Will you *stop*?" I say.

"Never," Vic says.

"Céce"

"*No*, Ma."

(Saturday, August 22,
3:00 a.m. of the seventy-second day . . .)

I'm in Ma's bed. She's not. I check the bathroom. No. Downstairs, probably cruising petfinder.com again. "Mel?" Not in the den. Kitchen? Nope. She dumped all the alcohol in the house after that last binge. Maybe she went out to a bar?

The basement.

The downstairs pantry, where we keep all the Costco crap. She's on the floor, an empty bottle of vodka at her side. She started in on a jug of cooking wine with a straw. She's slurring so softly, but I think she's saying, "Was that bad, what I did? You and Mack? Saying you. Could sleep down. Here? Was that wrong?" Her eyes flutter and she passes out. I'm shaking her and screaming her name, but she won't wake up. I call Vic. He calls an ambulance.

They pump her stomach. The doctor says, "The good news is, based on what you're telling me, your mother isn't so much the paradigmatic alcoholic as a self-medicating addict who engages in heavy episodic drinking."

"What a relief, Doc. Really, thanks so much." I head back into her room.

Ma's asleep, Vic's at his iPad. "You gotta keep going," he says.

"Do you, though?"

"The answer to the Vaccuccia family's situation is a dog."

"Vic, say it again, and I'll get the Hammerhead to sucker you into another game of cards."

"Céce," Ma says, except it comes out "She-she," because she has an oxygen mask over her mouth. She's still out of it. She waves me to her bed and works up a smile. "Ah ah ee."

"Huh? I can't hear you with the mask."

"Ah ah ee."

"Anthony? Anthony *what?*"

She shakes her head, frustrated. "Ah *ah* ee."

"I can't under*stand* you."

"Easy, ladies," Vic says.

She's crying. "Ah *ah* ee. Ah. *Ah*. Ee."

"Goddamn it, Ma—"

"She's sorry, Céce," Vic says. "She's saying *I'm sorry.*"

*(Five days later, Thursday, August 27,
morning of the seventy-seventh day . . .)*

Anthony e-mails me a video: His face, throat and hand are bandaged. He's balancing on the back wheels of his chair. His hospital buddies cheer him on. The video is pixilated and dark, and you only see him from the side, but I don't see any feet on those foot holders. I see no calves. No knees. When he left home, he was taller than Mack, and Mack is six one. Was six one.

The video zooms to a close-up. Anthony rasps, *"Don't worry, kid. It's all good. Love ya like a crazy person."*

Ma calls up from the kitchen, "Ready, babe?" We're going to market with her cornbread, the flea market.

I can't show her this video.

Bobby is at the curb with the Vic-mobile. Ma's flipping him a few bucks to help us out. He wears old-man glasses. "I lost one of my contacts. I think it might be behind my eye." He drives forty miles an hour in the fifty-five zone.

Steamy rain. The flea market is empty. We're pretty much the only car in the lot. We're sitting in the Vic-mobile. We have the back open with the lamest hand-painted poster:

C&C CORNBREAD. YUMMY. Hail pounds the windshield. Cue balls. Ma is knitting a hat for Anthony.

"It's August, Ma."

"Not forever."

"But fuchsia and yellow stripes?"

"Only yarn I had."

Bobby's glasses are fogged up. He's reading zombie Manga. His mouth is open a little, and his tongue kind of sticks out. I'm studying my belly button lint.

Rapping on the window. The one moron who bought a loaf. "This bread sucks."

"I'm very open to suggestions on how to improve it," Ma says.

"Next batch should not smell like hand soap and burned ketchup and be softer than the bow of an icebreaker. You should advertise it as a weapon."

"We have several other varieties," Bobby says.

"Get a load of this kid. *Several.* Like seven ain't good enough. You don't fool me, champ. What are you, three dollars an hour at the car wash, right? 'Vacuum the seats for you, sir?' Gimme my money back."

I trade him five dirty wilted dollars for the loaf, minus one very big bite. "Well, we sold negative one loaves."

"Better than selling zero," Bobby says.

I squint at Bobby. Ma pinches his cheek. "Let's wrap it up and head back."

Me and Bobby pack the bread into the boxes. Bobby knocks over a box: cornbread puddles. "Yup, yes, uh-huh . . ."

We drop the stinking bread off at the VA, but they don't want it. The soup kitchen will take it only after Ma makes a forty-dollar donation. We drop off Ma at this support group for mothers of wounded soldiers, and then Bobby drives me home.

"You take the G and T, Bob?"

"Yeah, I think I did okay on the multiple choice, but my essay was ass. I'll probably take it again. Maybe I'll write something metaphorical about the tuba. Problem is, I'm not that good. Really the only thing I'm good at is watching movies. I like food-related activities too. Do you mind if I tell you something about your brother?"

"Absolutely. I mean, no, I don't mind."

"He remembered my name every time he saw me in the hall."

"He remembers everybody's."

"Yeah, but he was the quarterback and I was in the band." He takes out his old-man umbrella and waddles around to my side, slipping just once on the way. He walks me to my stoop.

"Wanna come in for some ice-cream sandwiches?"

"Definitely."

"Seriously?"

"What kind?" he says.

"Carvel, Skinny Brown Cow, and this tofu-type thing."

"Tofutti?"

"No, a Tofutti knockoff. I forget the name of it."

"Doesn't matter. I'm relatively certain I'll like it."

"The tofu might be rotten. I bought it like three years ago."

"Let's check it out. The preservatives they use these days are excellent. You'd be surprised how that stuff keeps."

We go in.

"Do you mind if I scroll through your DVR SAVED list?"

"Scroll away."

I'm getting the ice cream. He calls to me, "*Biggest Loser* season finale? *Loved* it."

"We can watch it again."

"Do you have two computers?" he says. "We can totally do a World of Warcraft team-and-slay."

"I'm more an EverQuest girl."

"Me too!" he says.

"God, I haven't logged in since June." Since I started hanging with Mack.

"Can I see your DVDs? Oh no you didn't. *The Outsiders* deluxe edition? I might have to Mac the Ripper this. I totally wore mine out."

"Exactly how high up is it on your favorites, might I ask?"

"Are you serious? On my list of coming-of-age novel-to-screen adaptations featuring one or more Brat Pack actors, it comes in at number *three*."

"Holy shit."

"I know. And it ranks even higher on my list of flicks featuring Matt Dillon when his hair was parted in the middle—number *two* in fact, second only to—"

"*My Bodyguard.*"

"Sorry, the correct answer is *Rumble Fish.*"

"*Rumble Fish*," I say, nodding. "Of course."

"Has anybody ever told you that you slightly resemble Cherry Valance?"

I try not blush as I throw off a "Like, maybe once, sort of." Yeah, right after the hair-frying episode and hunting fifty stores for the same exact baby blue bow-tie sweater she was wearing, and I asked Anthony, "Do I look like Cherry from *The Outsiders*?" And he said, "You look exactly like you're *trying* to look like Cherry." I rack my brain for a return compliment, but the only thing coming to me is, has anybody ever told Bobby that he greatly resembles Kermit the Frog?

We hang and eat and he drops and spills stuff and apologizes. We play slap cards while we watch the gang fight scene from *The Outsiders* and then *Polar Express* for the seven hundredth time—he has the DVD too. He says stuff out of the blue, like, "Some people think that if cats grew thumbs before we did, *we'd* be *their* pets."

"That's actually rather interesting." I pretend I don't want to cry. It's happening: I still think about him, worry about him, still love him when I'm not hating him, but I'm starting not to miss him so much anymore.

I reach under the couch for the Wii controls and I hear clinking. So this is where she's been hiding her empties. I'll wait till Anthony comes home to bring this up. It's all good, huh? Then you handle her.

THE EIGHTY-FIRST DAY . . .

(Monday, August 31, morning)

MACK:

"Mister *Morse*."

"Mister Thompkins."

"Please reconsider."

"I can't do it. I get nervous."

"May I remind you that Old Dogs is a privately funded program. Publicity is critically important. We do not get many interview requests, and I am loath to let this opportunity pass us by."

"I'm not real comfortable with folks knowing stuff about me."

"Your comfort is not the primary concern here. If you don't do the interview, you will be in breach of our signed agreement. I will have no choice but to terminate your contract and remand the dog to Animal Control. We've put too much time and money into Boo to restart him with another trainer. Your choice, Mister Morse."

"What if I mess up?"

"Excuse me?"

"The AW told me he was hoping to get some of the other

fellas training here too. But if I blow the interview, you won't bring the program here, to the island."

"Will you do the interview, or not?"

(The next morning, Tuesday, September 1,
the eighty-second day . . .)

The dude they match me up with is all right. He's in one of those alternative to incarceration programs where they try to get you a job based on what you like, go figure.

"What I really want to do is be a sports reporter," he says. "Free tickets to the games, like that. Meantime, I have to do this kind of shit."

"All right, then." Me and Boo take him down to the junk field to show him how we play soccer. "Which it's called tackle soccer with Boo. He was a rotten fetcher at first, till I got the peanut butter working. You bring me back that ball, you're swimmin' in Skippy. He got it quick after that."

"Mm," dude says, writing it down. Kind of cool, him writing down what I'm saying, like I'm a famous type of celebrity or something.

I kick the ball way deep into the field, over the junk heap. Boo runs for it and doesn't come back.

"C'mon," I say to my reporter. We hustle over the junk heap. Boo's on his belly, whimpering.

"What's he doing?" reporter says.

"See, about two weeks ago, we were out here, and he happened on this dead mouse in that exact spot. He real gentle nudged it with his nose to try to wake it up. He was fairly crying, I swear, the moaning he was doing. I pulled him off the mouse, but the next day, he cut straight through the field to this same spot, looking for that mouse, which it must have been carried off by a crow or such, right?"

"Mm," kid grunts, writing it down.

"Every day he does the same thing."

"Mm." Man, he scribbles fast. "Dog's in love with a dead mouse. Potent."

"My friend says that word all the time."

"He a writer?"

"He reads a bunch."

"Then he's an inside-the-head variety of writer," dude says. "If you want to be a writer of any sort, you got to know *potent*."

"Well, all right then."

"Mm."

"Leave it," I say to Boo.

He's whimpering and looking back over his shoulder at where the mouse died as I lead him away. He follows me lockstep, no leash.

Guard who's watching us says, "I don't know how you did it. I was sure that there dog was untrainable. Wash is right. You're some kind of magic."

I play it like it's no big deal, but really I'm tingling with self-respect for myself, and self-respect for Boo too. I kind of look out of the side of my eyes to make sure the dude wrote down that the guard said I was magic, but I can't make out his scratch. "You happen to catch that last little part there, with the guard?"

"I did."

"All right, then."

We walk the kid to where his escort will take him to the bus. The first razor-wire gate rolls open, and he steps into the slot, and the gate closes. We wait for the second gate to open before we say good-bye, because then he can leave fast. You don't want to take a long time saying good-bye when you're locked up.

"What name you want for your fake name?" dude says.

"Fake name?"

"They won't let me use a real one."

"I don't care about it if you use my real name." I was kind of hoping Céce would see it somehow.

"I know, but it's the rules. Something about being a juvenile and stuff, you can't let out the dude's ID."

"Like it matters when you're locked up."

"I know. How 'bout Ed?" dude says.

"*Ed*? You serious?"

"Fredo then. Fredo's a cool name."

"Fredo's all right. How 'bout Zeke? Yeah, let's do 'er Zeke."

"All right then, Zeke buddy." He writes it in there. "I'll call the dog Cosmos, if that's all right, on account he is one of the biggest pits I've ever seen."

"Cosmos. I like that."

"Yeah. I like using imagery and that kinda shit when I write, you know? Gives you more of the *feel* for the dog's *soul,* see?"

"Mm."

"*Mm.*"

"No pictures then, huh? For this here article?"

"Nope."

"Not even of Boo?"

"No names, pictures, or videos. No identifying geographical markers."

"Anybody gonna look at this thing?"

"I know. Prob'ly not. It's like for this lame-ass animal shelter website or whatever. They're doing an online newsletter type of thing to raise money for your program, I think. But hey, I do a good job on this one, and maybe I get something better next time around. You gotta have hope, right buddy?"

"You do. You got to have hope."

The second gate rolls open.

"Mack, buddy, thanks, all right? Y'all helped me a bunch."

"Good luck to you, man."

"Yeah, man. Luck back. Hey?"

"Yup?"

"Peace. Y'all stay cool now."

"Yeah. Y'all stay free."

Me and Boo watch him disappear. I crouch and headlock Boo and scratch him up real good behind his ears. "Been three weeks since she last visited, Boo. I think she's on her way, bud. On her way to peace of mind."

THE NINETIETH DAY . . .
(Wednesday, September 9, after dinner shift)

CÉCE:

"Howya doin'?" Vic says.

"School started this week," I say. In addition to weekends, I'm working Wednesday nights during the school year to save money for the college I won't get into.

"I know. So howya doin'?"

"I just said, *school* started. Must I translate?"

"Good news is, I've been looking into the dog thing," Vic says.

"Oh god."

"Yeah."

"No."

"I hit the salad bar with a few of my buddies from the VFW a couple of nights back. They're co-sponsoring an application for a dog for Anthony."

"VFW," I say. "*Foreign* wars. Anthony never made it overseas."

"Kid, they all know your brother. They know what he gave up for that old man in the truck. They love him. Everybody does. We'll probably have a dog within the month."

"Vic—"

"*Hey.* Stop. I'm sorry you had a bit of a rough summer. I am. And it's okay to be in a bad mood. But it's not okay to be in a bad mood around other people."

"What are you *talking* about? A bit of a rough summer? You have no idea what I've endured these past weeks."

"Céce, look, I'm sixty-eight years old. I know what you've endured. The time for enduring is over. Now it's time to be happy. This dog thing: You need to do it. For your mother, kid. For your brother. And you have nothing to worry about here. They come one hundred percent trained, the dogs."

"You're *sure?*"

"Specifically for injured soldiers too," Vic says. "They train them in the jails."

"The jails."

"The prisoners are the trainers."

"Prisoners."

"Good for the prisoner, the dog, the vet. Everybody wins."

"Backtrack. Prisoners like Mack?"

"They want the older guys doing it. Here." He taps the website onto his iPad.

Old Dogs, New Tricks: We look to rehabilitate dogs while giving veterans companionship and prisoners hope. Trainers generally are at least thirty years of age with significant offenses on their records, with the average age being fifty-one. By taking part in the program, older participants often are able to reduce their sentences, achieve early parole, and, upon release, segue to community-service-oriented positions that will sustain them both financially and spiritually in their senior years. Many trainers find post-prison employment at Old Dogs, New Tricks. Dogs are trained individually and to accommodate each veteran's needs. Trainers visit the prospective adopters' homes with the dogs to incorporate special needs into training.

"So the prisoner is coming to my house?"

"Absolutely," Vic says. "Probably sometime in the next few days, the vet who filed the application tells me."

"Okay *wait*. Again, I know it's a ridiculous long shot, but Mack is ridiculously gifted—"

"Check the list of training sites there," Vic says, shaking his head no. "You'll see that, unfortunately, the island hasn't been approved as an official site yet."

"It says 'application pending.'"

"Exactly," Vic says, "which is why I'm having all my buddies from the VFW write letters of support to get it there. A few years from now, Mack comes of age, they'll hire him. Won't be long after that when he'll be running the show, just you watch."

"Why do you keep investing in him?"

"Investing?"

"Your hope. You taught him to cook. You were willing to send him to school. You trusted him, and then he goes and—"

"Nah, now look, none of that. Horrible things happen. They do. But you move on stronger. This Old Dogs thing is a great program. In the future, Mack can be a big part of it. He *needs* to be a part of it. Look at the testimonials link there."

I'm studying the site. All these older inmates say Old Dogs,

New Tricks saved their lives. I'm starting to soften. And I'm too drained to fight Vic anymore. "You're unrelenting."

"Indefatigable even," he says.

"How'd you find out about this thing anyway?"

"Remember that kid Cameron who used to work over at the original Vic's a few years back, used to do delivery at the Too once in a while? Maybe you were too young, but your mother will remember him. Good kid. Anyway, he's in this alternative to prison program, and for his parole, he asked me to be one of his sponsors. He's trying to be a journalist. I turned him onto this site looking for animal rescue stories. He tapped a few of his contacts from the old days, went out and dug up the Old Dogs story, and they published it. Here, click that link, the one that says *A Spin With Cosmos*. It's a potent little piece." He heads off with his crossword.

The link redirects me to this animal rescue website that Vic was pushing on Ma a few weeks back. A side banner asks readers to send in interesting animal rescue stories. *A Spin With Cosmos* is featured on the front page of the group's newsletter:

> *Zeke made a mistake. Cosmos was a throwaway. They live in a small but clean room, and they are each other's everything. Bars and razor wire surround them, but when they are together, they are free. "This dog has taken me places I didn't dare dream," Zeke says, throwing a knotted stick into a mound of chopped branches. We are in the prison's grounds maintenance yard. Recent storms felled many trees. We watch as Cosmos digs through the*

*branches for the one his trainer threw. "I used to
lock into the past," Zeke says. "I used to fear the
future. But Cosmos has taken me into living in this
minute. I never thought I'd get here. He just wants
to be happy, and you can't stop him from doing that.
That's his job, having a gas with himself. He doesn't
care where he is or who he's with—he even loves the
guards. You can't be sad around him. He won't let
you. I know what peace looks like now."*

*Cosmos retrieves the very stick Zeke threw and sits
on his trainer's feet. "Pit bulls like to do that," Zeke
says. I wonder if the dog is guarding Zeke. "No,"
Zeke says. "He just has to be touching something
alive all the time. I've trained him not to jump up,
so anything above the knees is off limits, unless I
squat and call him to me. Then he's allowed to curl
into me. It can be a hundred degrees out, and he will
still try to climb inside my shirt." Zeke and Cosmos
demonstrate. "If you take the time to train a dog,
he'll teach you what you are and where you can go.
How you can be calm and strong at the same time.
This Cosmos is special, though. He catches houseflies
with his mouth and brings them outside and spits
them to set them free." Zeke buries his head in the
dog's neck. He turns away and runs with the dog.*

Then there's this bit about Cosmos being in love with a
mouse, and my ESP is making a comeback. It's tickling hard:
I think we're going to get a really good dog. Yeah, I *feel* it.

THE NINETY-FIRST DAY . . .

(Thursday, September 10, morning)

MACK:

"Mister Morse, you will recall I told you publicity is most important to our program."

"I do recall that, Mister Thompkins."

"That was a statement, not a question. Eye contact please. Good. A member of a prominent VFW organization read your interview. On behalf of the membership, he has applied for a dog, specifically the Cosmos mentioned in the article. This is an exceptionally strong submission. Sixty-one letters from veterans accompanied the application. The recommendations are unanimous in their praise for the wounded soldier. We are grateful for the opportunity to work with enthusiastic sponsors, and I personally would very much—*very much*, Mister Morse—like to work with this group again. It's extremely important that this site visit go smoothly."

"What visit?"

"You will assess the living situation, the physical plant, its layout, for special needs and considerations. You will tailor the remaining training time you have with the animal accordingly. I'm saying you'll have to go to the *house*, Mister Morse."

That's what I thought he was saying. A field trip? A day in the free air, no bars or barbed wire? "Well, I guess if I have to."

"Indeed," Thompkins says. "You will be cuffed and shackled from the moment you step from this cell to the moment you return. You will be blind on the way over and back. You will have no contact with these folks after the visit. You are not to give them your name, nor are you to ask for theirs. Understood?"

"Yessir."

I look to Boo. Dopey tongue sticking out, tail whirling on my look. "Mister T., does this mean Boo passed training?"

"Not yet, but he would not be placed, *tentatively*, if we did not suspect that he *might* pass."

"That mean I'm a suspect for passing too?"

"I can be nothing less than honest with you. Some of your training methods are entirely unorthodox and certainly not in the manual my team and I worked so very hard to develop. You are under review. We'll see how you do with the site visit."

"Whatever the vet needs, I'm sure I can make it happen."

He crosses his arms and nods toward the chair. "Sit."

Me and Boo sit.

Thompkins takes off his glasses, rubs his tired eyes, and hides his left hand under his right arm. "Boo's prospective adopter was wounded in an explosion. He—"

"Car bomb, right?"

"Something like that, and Mister Morse at this stage of our association, do I really need to remind you not to interrupt me?"

"Sorry."

"May I continue, then? *Thank* you. The soldier lost his legs. Boo can't be knocking him out of the wheelchair."

"He doesn't pounce anymore. I trained it out of him."

"Did you train him to respond to whisper commands? The young man's voice box is partially compromised secondary to shrapnel. There's a chapter in the manual—"

"Boo, down," I whisper.

Boo flops over to offer up his big fat belly for a scratch.

Thompkins frowns.

"I interrupted you again, Mister T. I'm toast, right?"

Thompkins looks at me for a long time. I have to say one thing about him: He never rolls his eyes at me. He glares straight on. "Look, these site visits are almost always emotional for the family. You have to be strong. You must remain calm. Your job is to keep your focus on what you can control, and that is the dog. After that, your job is finished." He leaves.

"Boo, we found you a home, boy. You're gettin' there, bud. You're almost free."

(Two days later, Saturday, September 12,
late morning of the ninety-third day . . .)

Me and Boo huddle in the backseat of the beat-up Department of Corrections van. I'm in a bright orange jumper, cuffs at my ankles and wrists. The shackle chain threads a ring on the floor. Handcuff chains tie into a chain belt around my waist.

Wash signed up this other guard to be the driver. I seen him around. He never says much, but he's all right. Him and Wash go back pretty far, Wash told me. They're both wearing guns today. Wash readies the hood. "Sorry, son."

"I understand, Wash."

Boo's asleep and snoring in my lap before we're two turns into the ride. I give up trying to figure north, south, east, west after the fifth turn. Sun flickers through the gauzy mesh hood. The windows are open, the breeze soft. I smell cheap perfume, crackling chewing gum, cinnamon, vanilla incense, pizza, chicken gyro smoking on a cart vendor's grill. I hear birds. A street preacher rages. Trucks bang over potholes, bass beat booms, talk radio, planes, sirens, a car door shuts, a dribbling basketball, a sneaker squeak, the ball rattles the rim, a skateboard scrapes a rail, a jackhammer far off, shopping bags rustle, pigeons fuss, flapping wings. The elevated train rumbles, then a long squeal of brakes. A trash picker's cart clicks over sidewalk cracks. Bottle glass tinkles. The clinks ripple out and melt into the bricks of buildings. Somebody drops his keys.

"Pizza smells pretty good, huh, Wash?"

"It does."

"I hope they have lots of hydrants."

"Hydrants you say?"

"On Boo's new block. Dogs need their hydrants."

"Yes they do." Wash chuckles and I chuckle too, because I copy people like that sometimes, I don't know why.

"Wash, you ever had pineapple on a pizza?"

"Nope."

"Me either, but I heard it's pretty good, though."

"Doesn't sound too good."

"Boston told me he had it all the time. He was like, 'You got to try it, you got to try it. Don't judge it before you eat it.'"

"Hmph," Wash says.

"Yeah," I say.

Boo licks my hood and whimpers.

"Easy, boy. We're gonna be there real soon."

"I had macaroni and meat sauce on a pizza once," Wash says. "Was pretty good."

"Yeah, I had it once too. Was pretty good, like you just said a few seconds ago."

"Mack?"

"Yessir?"

"Don't be nervous about this. I'm sure everything is going to work out just fine."

"Yessir."

"That's right," Wash says. "Now, when we get there, I'll walk you to the front door. Then we'll get that hood off you, let you see some free world."

"Amen."

THE NINETY-THIRD DAY, CONTINUED . . .
(Saturday, September 12, noon)

CÉCE:

"Ma, you *seriously* don't need to give the guy cornbread."

"Will you re*lax*?" Carmella says.

"All we need: The dude strokes out on your Jalapeño Halleluiah."

"Where the flip is Vic? Try his cell again."

"Just did. Straight to voicemail."

A green van idles in our driveway. The engine cuts out. Two guys in the front. One of them gets out, looks up and down the block. Grills cover the back windows.

"Don't smile, Ma. You have lipstick on your teeth."

"Well, can you wipe it *off*?"

"You had to pick the sluttiest red in your arsenal? This guy's a criminal."

The van driver smiles at us as he climbs the porch steps. He tries not to do a double take on Carmella's hair, Day-Glo Sun. "Ladies, would you mind if I do a quick walk-through?" He checks the rooms, for what he doesn't say. He asks Ma to unplug the phones as we go through the rooms "—to minimize the possibility of distraction."

"You think he might try to do something bad while we turn to answer the phone or whatever?" I'm seeing a montage of all my there's-a-convict-in-your-house movies.

"Not at all. Please don't worry about that. It's just that we have less than two hours, and we want to keep everybody focused on the site assessment."

"Oh."

"If you could turn off your cellular devices too, I would appreciate it."

"But we're expecting somebody else," Ma says.

"This is the application sponsor, Victor Apruzese?" the driver says. "And you've tried calling him? Then I suggest you leave word on his voicemail that your phones need to be off." He explains the rules to us: Don't touch the prisoner—like who would want to? Keep arm's length from him at all times. Don't ask his name, don't give him yours. If he asks personal questions, don't answer. Keep your conversation about the dog. "Now, when he comes out of that van, he'll be wearing a hood."

"That's horrible," Ma says.

"We'll take it off as soon as we get him inside." The guard tells us to wait in the vestibule, and he heads back to the van.

First out is the dog.

Oh. My. God.

Ma and I claw each other's arms. "He's so *cute*."

"Huge."

"Look at that *tongue*."

"Look how fat!"

"How pretty."

"That *tail*."

"Those eyes."

The giant one-eared pit bull sits and waits, looking into the van. The other guard helps the prisoner out. Tall thin dude in a baggy orange jumper. That hood. A white mesh sack with patches over the eyes. Ghostly. The guard has him by the arm and coaches him as he turns him toward the house. Toward us. Shackles clink on the driveway. The driver has the dog on a leash, but he doesn't need it. The dog walks behind the prisoner. The shorter guard helps the dude up the porch steps into the house. "All right," the guard says, and the prisoner stops. The dog peeks from behind the prisoner's legs to look at me and cock his head. That tongue hanging out of his mouth. When I smile, his tails whirls.

"Ladies, my name is Sergeant Washington." He indicates the prisoner with a nod. "My friend here would like to have a look around your house. Would that be all right?"

"Please," Ma says.

"Hold still now, son. Close your eyes and open them slowly, till they adjust to the light." Sergeant Washington takes off the hood.

Suddenly the house is freezing. And dark. Airless. I think I'm breathing, but I can't be. My lips and fingers are numb. I half fall into the couch. I know where all the heat went now: into my stomach. It's cooking something up down there, making squishing noises—loud—as it twists. I'm going to cough blood.

Ma yells at Sergeant Washington, "What the flip is this? You think this is funny? Seriously, why are you doing this?"

The sergeant squints at her, then at Mack. Mack's mouth is moving, but I can't hear him. He's talking to *me*, though. I read his lips, and he keeps saying, "Céce."

"You come heavy," I say.

"What?" he says.

"You're finally inside my house, and you come in chains."

"I'll kill him," Ma says. "Victor Apruzese is a dead man."

"Let's all settle down," Sergeant Washington says. He's calm. The other guard is too, but they're resting their hands on their gun butts. "Now," the sergeant says, "nice and easy, what all's going on here?" His eyes dart from Ma to me to the other guard to the kitchen door to Mack. "Son, how do you know these folks?" He turns to Ma. "Ma'am, are you the one who makes the goblin breads?"

"They're snowmen," I whisper, my eyes on Mack, his eyes on mine.

Ma explains how Vic must have duped us. As she talks, Mack and I stare. His face is hard, tight lips, jaw clenched. Two tears, his, spike the carpet. "Tony?" he says. "But he's still training, no?" His eyes drop to my chest.

The stickpin. I still wear it every day.

I'm a fool. I'll never be more embarrassed in my life. Letting him see that I still love him, even after he treated me like I was weeks-old garbage our last visit—or what I thought was to be our last visit. But this is the one. This is the final time I'll be with him. I'm sure of it now. The chains on his arms and legs. I can't bear to see him like this.

"The dog?" I say. "What's his name?"

Mack looks down at his feet.

If he did, I'll never forgive him. I make a clicking sound, my tongue against the inside of my teeth, the way he taught me. The dog looks my way. "Boo," I say.

The dog comes to me. He rolls into my feet and over onto his back for me to scratch his stomach. But I don't. The new Boo does a wiggle worm dance for me. I back away.

"How could you?" I say. "How could you do that to her? To me?"

"I did it *for* her," he says. "For *you*. Céce, please." He's stepping toward me, reaching out to me, his arms stunted by the chains and the guards' pushing them down. They're pushing Mack back into the wall, trying to calm him. He's crying out to me. I almost can't hear him. Now I'm the one drowning in white noise, the whoosh of a UPS truck flying by the house. He yells from where they have him pinned to the door frame, as I back away, "Céce, hold up, just for a second! I gotta tell you something!"

No, I can't hear it, not again, no matter how nicely he says it, the truth he needs me to know so we can move on, what he tried to tell me in the visiting room: that we can't love each other anymore.

My legs are shaky as they hurry me through the hall, to the front door, out onto the porch, toward the street.

"Céce?" Ma says. "Céce!"

I'm running to the corner, pulling the stickpin from my shirt, throwing it, pulling my phone, waiting for it to boot up. *Hurry*—dialing—*before I change my mind*. Ringing. "Bobby, you wanna go to the movies?"

THE NINETY-THIRD DAY, CONTINUED . . .
(Saturday, September 12, ten past noon)

MACK:

"Wash, I swear I didn't know—"

"I know you didn't," Wash says. "Let's everybody just stay calm now. It'll be all right."

"What do you want to do here, Wash?" driver says.

Wash sizes up Mrs. Carmella. She's got her arms crossed, and she's tapping her foot fast. She's glaring at me. "I think we're okay here, Jack," Wash says. "Why don't you go on out to the front porch and wait to see if this Vic gentleman shows up." Wash backs up a bit to the kitchen doorway, turns half away, pretends to check his phone.

I force myself to look Mrs. Carmella in the eye. "I'm sorry, ma'am."

"You ought to be. Do you know how worried sick we've been about you? Do you know what you put her through? Not even a *word* from you. That poor girl, laying her heart out for you, going all the way over there? You were *awful* to her, Mack. You were mean to my daughter."

Boo leans into my leg. His tail whirls, shaking him, shaking me. "I had to be mean to her."

"No. Hey, look at me. No. You didn't have to hurt her like that. You could have explained it to her. You could have let it wind down slowly. You should have given her the time to take it in, that you two had to let go."

"It would have hurt too much, the slow fade."

"You're not giving her enough credit. She's a smart girl. A strong woman."

"Not her. Me. It would have hurt me too much." I know I'm right too. Seeing her just then? Her soft brown eyes? Sucking her lips to hide their shivering? I saw my lips on hers.

The stickpin. Still wearing it after all this time.

How many times have I fallen asleep to the memory of us, and there she was right in front of me, and I didn't even get to hold her hand, to tell her what I need her to know?

If I'd touched her, even for a second, I would have started it all over again, the lie that someday we can be together.

Boo nudges my hand. He just has to show me he's a whirly-tail Boo.

"I meant I was sorry about Tony, ma'am. Can I just peek in on him and say hi?"

Tony's name gets her misty and madder. "He's still down south, in rehab. The two of you. What's wrong with you? Throwing everything away, for what?"

Boo crosses to her and leans into her leg and looks up at her with that dopey tongue sticking out of his mouth. His tail is spinning so fast you almost can't see it. She bends to cuddle him. She squeezes him. "Look at his eyes," she says. He licks her head like it's ice cream.

"I'm sorry, ma'am. I'm sorry about everything."

"Let's get you some cornbread," she says, or I think that's what she said. I can't really focus on anything but the door. Damn me, but after all that pushing her away, I pray she comes back.

The weeks of seeing her only in my mind, the details of her fading.

That little gold fleck in her left eye—I can't ever forget that. I have to burn it into me to carry me through the nights. I need to look into her eyes, just for a minute, to kiss her one last time, no matter what it costs us.

THE NINETY-THIRD DAY, CONTINUED . . .
(Saturday, September 12, an hour and a half later)

CÉCE:

Me and Bobby have a seat between us. In the empty seat are two jumbo buckets of popcorn. I'm eating, not tasting; watching, not seeing. Popcorn shrapnel speckles Bobby's gut. He spills his soda bucket. "Yup. Yup. There I go again. Sorry about—"

"It's *fine*."

I just had to pick a comedy. I should have picked the

tearjerker, for cover. The last person I want to talk with about Mack is Bobby. I don't know how I'm not losing it in front of him. Fortunately, he's really into the movie. His tongue is sticking out of his mouth.

I can't see the screen. My eyes are blurry with the memory of Mack in my living room and the movie I want to see: The guards fade away. Carmella fades away. Mack's chains fade, and now it's just the two of us—the three of us. The new dog. The new Boo. We run. We escape. We're together, forever.

Maybe they'll give us one last minute alone together. How could they not?

He was supposed to be at the house from noon to two, and then they were taking him back.

"Bobby?"

"Uh-huh?"

"Don't tell me what time it is."

He checks his phone. "It's one forty."

"Don't let me leave this seat, Bob."

He stands up to make room for me to get out. "You look like you have to puke," he says.

I'm heading for the aisle. "Trip me."

He trips himself as he waddles after me with a near-empty popcorn bucket. "Here, barf into this."

I'm running through the lobby. Out the door. Into the warm afternoon breeze. Once I ran a mile in eight minutes. Twenty pounds ago. I'm sprinting for the bus, pulling away . . . gone, but I'm still hauling. My lungs are like, *Are you insane?*

I flag down an unmarked cab, the only kind that comes

around here, but the drivers are fast. Twenty minutes. I'm going to make it. I can be there for him—

"—here for you," he says. "Céce, you can tell me anything and everything."

"Not everything. Not this."

"Yes, this." We're in the hutch, just after being together for the first time. It's July 19, and I'm shivering.

"When I was nine. When that dog bit me in the alley that time. When it bit me in the face? I wasn't alone."

"All right?" he says. "Who—"

"Marcy. Marcy was with me. She said we shouldn't cut through the alley. That the old man who lived in that house had a pellet gun, and he was crazy enough to use it. He'd shot Marcy's sister for cutting through his yard. One of the pellets was still in her ass fat. I laughed. I thought that was funny for some reason. Like it was something that happened in a cartoon, not in real life. The radio said the temperature was a hundred and two but felt like a hundred and sixteen with the humidity. It was either cut through Pellet Man's yard and be home in the air-conditioning in three minutes, or go all the way around the block and be home in ten. I can't believe I was so stupid. All for seven minutes."

"I would've done the same," Mack says.

"No. You would never do what I did that day. The guy didn't even seem to be home. No car in the driveway, shades drawn, outdoor light left on from the night before. So I hop the fence. Marcy's calling me an idiot and telling me to come back. I'm laughing at her, telling her to have fun melting as she hikes around the block. I fill the dog's water bowl, go to kiss its head, the dog latches on and won't let go. Marcy hops the fence. She's jerking on the dog's collar—"

"And the dog spun on her and latched on to her arm," Mack says. "A dog tied up like that? He's cornered. If he thinks he's under attack and he can't run, he has to fight. That's why you grab the back legs and lift them high. Marcy was done for the minute she grabbed the dog's collar. You didn't break her arm."

"Break it? It was destroyed. Do you know how many surgeries she had? The rods and pins—"

"It's not your fault."

"It is my fault. It went on and on. The dog won't let go of Marcy's arm. Marcy's screaming for help, and what do I do? I leave her there. Now the idea that Pellet Man is going to shoot me doesn't seem so far-fetched. And in my mind he's not shooting pellets, but slugs. I hopped the fence and ran, Mack. Covering my ears to block out her screams. After she warns me not to cut through, she hops the fence to save me, and I left her there."

"You couldn't have pulled the dog off her."

"I could have run for help. Instead I ran because I was afraid I was going to get in trouble, for trespassing, for getting bitten in the face, for getting Marcy bitten. I hid in somebody's hedge and just froze there. The police came ten minutes later, and then the ambulance got there ten minutes after that. Ten minutes of being with that dog. And all the while I'm in that hedge, sucking the blood through the cuts in my lips until I threw up."

"Céce."

"She never made me feel bad about it, either. She talked about it like it was something that just happened to her, not something I caused."

"You were nine years old."

"I deserted her."

"No," he says. "You're a friend to her."

"Some friend."

"You take care of her. Getting her the job at the Too. Being on the phone with her all the time, listening to her, hanging with her."

"Out of guilt."

"You're a friend *to her. To me. That's gold."*

Gold so bright I see it after I close my eyes. The sun. I feel it falling. I'm running out of time. The cab has moved a quarter mile in the last ten minutes. The traffic on the highway stretches as far as I can see. "If you get off the highway and take the side streets it'll be faster, I think."

"More mileage, though," the cab driver says. "It'll be cheaper to stay on the highway."

"Please, the side streets, hurry. How fast can you get me to my drop-off?"

The driver revs into the service lane, toward the exit ramp. "If the streets are clear, five minutes."

I'll make it with time to spare. I'll be in his arms, telling him what I need to tell him, face-to-face. Looking into his eyes as I say what he never gave me the chance to say.

THE NINETY-THIRD DAY, CONTINUED . . .

(Saturday, September 12, 1:45p.m.)

MACK:

Mrs. V. is holding my hand. She has to sit close to me. The chains that run from my wrists to the chain around my waist are short. I'm happy she's friends with me again, but I wish it was Céce's hand in mine.

I don't blame her for not coming back. I was weak, wanting that last kiss with her. It's better this way, that the last time we touched was that long kiss in the rain, at her front door, the night before everything changed, when we had hopes, when we felt safe with each other, keeping each other's secrets.

I'm in the basement apartment, where Tony will be. I'm sitting at his desk. Boo lays his giant head in Mrs. Carmella's lap for petting. She cradles him. Wash is in the corner, talking soft into his phone.

It's quiet down here. You can't hear the traffic too much. On the side of the house Vic built a ramp that leads up to the street for when Tony and Boo go walking. Wheeling. We practiced with Mrs. Carmella playing Tony in the wheelchair. Boo followed behind, except when he got to a narrow hallway. Then he went onto his belly and crawled under the wheelchair. I can train him out of that, no problem. Couple of other things I need to do to get him ready to live in this house, but I can knock them out in the time we have left together. Eight days ought to be enough time.

Eight days.

"Mrs. Carmella, I saw the utility shower when I peeked into the laundry closet off the hall there. I trained Boo to make water over the grate. You rinse it down right after."

"You trained him to pee in the *drain*?"

"It's like a cat box. For when folks are out of the house and Boo is alone. Or if Tony's having a tough time getting outside to, like, walk Boo."

266

"The burns," she says. "Apparently they're worse at night. He'll be on painkillers. For a bit." Boo nudges at Mrs. Carmella and gives her his big brown eyes. "That tail," she says. And then to me: "Show me."

We take Boo to the drain. "Boo, pee."

He cocks his head and gives paw.

"Pee."

Gives other paw.

Mrs. Carmella touches Boo's muzzle, points to the drain. "Boo, pee."

Boo trots in, makes water over the drain, and hops out for his cookie reward. Cuffed, I have a hard time getting it out of my chest pocket. Mrs. Carmella helps me and leaves one of her hands on my heart while she gives Boo the cookie.

"Amazing," she says.

"You have a special dog here, ma'am."

"Mack, look at me. You're amazing." She's reaching out to me.

I look past her to Wash. He pretends to be studying his fingernail beds. He gives me a quick look and a nod that it's okay.

In me is this feeling of lightness. It's a one-way hug with my hands chained, but she's hugging me fierce. Her arms are strong from years of carrying trays full of food.

"Mack, all those times we invited you to come in, you never wanted to?"

"I wanted to."

"Why didn't you?"

I close my eyes and remember the walk-through with Boo. The pictures on the walls, on top of the TV, in windowsills and on tables. So many pictures. The faces. The Grumpy that Céce was always talking about. He's not grumpy at all, smiling in every picture. Pictures of Tony and Mrs. Carmella and Céce and sometimes Vic and plenty of Marcy too. I swear Céce looks so pretty in every picture. They're in different places, the family. Snowy places. Beach places. But they're always together no matter where they are. There's a feeling of forever in those pictures, on these walls, in this house. Especially the kitchen. The pictures cover every inch of the kitchen walls—

"The kitchen walls were empty," I tell Céce. The wind is hard through the hutch windows. It's July 19, but she's cold, and I draw her close to me. "All the walls in the apartment were the same, just bare. Curb junk furniture. We were always moving every time the old man's work ran out. He was at work that night, though. Bar back at a roadhouse, I think. It was my birthday. Lucky seven. By then I was in the special classes, and around the schools they were starting to call me retard. The doctor told my folks I'd likely always be behind. That even if I improved some, this wasn't something that had a cure. That it was gonna be a long hard haul for me, and for them too.

"My mother pulled a couple of Scooter Pies from the package. She got them free from the motel snack bar. She was a maid there. She set the pies out and candled one. She said, 'Macky, that time in town, in the alley there. That scraggly pit bull. Why'd y'all name it Boo?' 'Because he was a surprise,' I said. And she's nodding at me, and she's smiling, but she's sad, I don't know why. She says, 'That was real smart of you, Macky. That is beautiful.' She lit the candle. 'Macky, sometimes I think I have

to go away from your father. How would you feel about that?' I didn't know what to feel about that, tell you what. 'We don't love each other anymore,' she said. 'He's content that that's the way it is. That love fades and you just got to stick with each other anyway, because what else are you gon' do? But there has to be more, don't you think?' I didn't know what to think. She never talked much and never this way and I felt like she was a stranger at the table. 'If we go,' she said, 'it'll be hard on you. I feel God is calling me to do something big, Macky. Something special, so that we'll have everything we need later on. We'll have enough money left over to give it away to folks like us. But that kind of money don't come cheap. We'll be moving around a bunch. You would be alone a lot and your heart would hurt all the time and what ever would we do about your reading problem? Now, Macky, don't look away like that. I need you to look at me. Macky, what do you want to do? Be with me or your father?' I hugged at her so hard and said, 'I don't want you to go.' 'That's not an option,' she said. 'I have to go. I know this is tough, but you have to choose: me or him.' 'Please,' I said. 'Just stay.'

"And she sighed and we hugged for who knows how long, and she's rocking me and humming the happy birthday song but real slow when the old man comes in. And he is mad, tell you what. And drunk. He gets to slapping her around and calling her a whore. 'He's bragging about it all over town,' the old man says. 'Telling everybody that you and him are getting ready to head north together.' And Mom doesn't deny it. She says, 'What do you expect? He's sweet and kind, and you're just cold all through you. You don't love me. You don't love anybody, not even yourself.' And then the old man just lit into her. He hit her like it was ten seconds left in the fifteenth round, and he was fighting for his life. And then, mid-swing, he stops. He turns to me. 'Go to your room,' he says. Mom's kicking and clawing at him, drawing blood, and he's pushing her off. 'Cario!' he says. 'Go to your fuckin' room, I said! Now!'

"I ran into my little room there and shut the door and dove into my mattress and put the pillow over my head, but I could still hear it. The banging around. The old man screaming she ripped his ear. Mom's yelling to me through the wall, 'Macky, run! Get help! He's killing me!' But I didn't. I couldn't. The old man is saying, 'Crying out to that boy? You think he's gonna put it on the line for you?'

"There's all this slamming into the wall. Sheetrock breaking. And I was afraid to go out there. Afraid to see it. To hear it. I turned on my little radio Mom got me for my birthday. I rolled that tuning dial back and forth and found nothing but static. We were so far out from the cities, you couldn't get a station. It was all I had, so I rolled the volume all the way up and held the radio to my head to deafen myself with the hissing.

Cops came sometime later, I don't know how long it was. They locked up the old man and Mom went to the hospital, and I stayed at some lady's house for the next day or so. Mom didn't press charges—she never did—and two nights later, we were all around the kitchen table, and the old man was crying and apologizing to Mom and me, and he was just sure he was drunker than he'd ever been, and it would never happen again, and couldn't we all just stay together? And Mom stroked his hair and said it would be all right, we would see. The way she was looking at me . . . I don't know. Sad, sure, but a little disap-

pointed too. I don't think she meant to think it or wanted to or even knew she was thinking it, but I could read her clear: She thought I let her down.

"We finished dinner, the old man read me a baseball story, and I fell asleep, and when I woke up, my father was reading the letter she left, and she was gone for good.

"I feel real bad for her, Céce. I bet she isn't even alive anymore. And I still can't help loving her like crazy. Thanking her for a couple of sweet memories. How she taught me the way of dogs." I'm lying back on the sleeping bag, but inside I feel myself falling over.

"I'll never leave you," Céce says. And the way she holds me, I believe her. How she quiets the static as I'm rolling into her, her arms crossing my back.

"Why, sweetheart?" Mrs. Carmella says. "Why wouldn't you come into the house?"

"I'm here now, ma'am."

I have Boo too, leaning into my thigh and shuddering me with his tail wagging. Big old dopey head cocked and that slack tongue.

"Son?" Wash says. "I'm afraid it's time to go."

We hear the upstairs door swing in hard. Her feet pound across the floor overhead on a fast run, down the stairs.

My heart is running so full I feel it in my eyes, the lids twitching, the light dialing up, everything turning hot gold. I turn to the stairs and fight the shackles to hold out my arms for her.

Mister Vic almost runs me down.

"You're a dead man," Mrs. Carmella says.

"Could you pick up your goddamn phone?" Vic says.

"Could you check your voicemail?"

"This is Vic?" Wash says.

"This is Vic," the other guard says, coming downstairs.

"I called you like sixty times from the cop's phone," Vic says. "Oil tanker jackknifed on the interstate. Half-mile-long fire. The Vic-mobile is no more. Consumed in the swell of angry traffic. The engine simply died in a hideous puff of smoke. In my blindness, I coasted into a little fender bender with this Mercedes SUV, no damage to the fancier vehicle, mind you, *nil.* Okay, perhaps a mere nick to the rear bumper, yet the driver has to be a spaz, everything must be *documented.* No faith in humanity, this driver. Waiting two hours for a tow truck, missing out on the playing out of my machinations. It has been an afternoon, I must say. My phone, my car, everything's breaking down. I couldn't even flag a fake cab to pick me up."

"Have you seen yourself, you sweaty mess?" Mrs. Carmella says. "Your comb-over isn't combed over. You look like you ran out of the barbershop halfway through the haircut. You look crazy."

"I am crazy. Howyas doin'?"

"We're hangin' in. I don't know whether I want to kick you or kiss you, Victor."

"Ey, I know what I know. Will you look at this dog! Where the hell is Céce?"

THE NINETY—THIRD DAY, CONTINUED . . .

(Saturday, September 12, 1:58pm)

CÉCE:

The highway traffic is spilling into the side streets. I reach over the seat, slap my money into the driver's hand, and I jump out the door. The driver screams I gave him too much. I run down the main drag, past the CVS, past where we saw our first satellite together, along the route we used to walk Boo. People think I'm insane, sprinting in one Croc. I lost the other when I jumped out of the cab because the strap on that one never stayed up.

Turning the corner to my street.

Down the block: a green van in the driveway. Backing out.

I scream for them to wait, but they don't hear me. Don't see me. They're pulling away, toward the traffic light, turning yellow. The van speeds up to make the light and then stops as the light turns red.

I'm screaming his name. Screaming *please.* Screaming *wait.* Stay. I'm close. The light turns green. The van turns. I'm too breathless to scream now, but I'm going to catch up to the van. Fifty feet and gaining. I kick a crack in the sidewalk and trip just like I did that first night he walked me home. Except this time he isn't here to catch me. To keep me from skidding over the pebbly concrete, skinning my hands and knees.

The van accelerates through loosening traffic, toward the west side freeway, until it turns another corner, out of sight.

I wasn't even going to tell him I love him. I know he doesn't want to hear it. All I wanted to do was say good-bye.

THE NINETY-THIRD DAY, CONTINUED . . .
(Saturday, September 12, 2:05pm)

MACK:

Mrs. Carmella gave me a hat she knitted. It's pink and yellow stripes. Maybe I'll give it to one of the lady guards. But for now, I pull it low over my eyes to block out the world on the way back. Wash doesn't bother with the hood. I know where I was, where I am. I don't think about where I'm going.

Tell you what, I'm shot. Boo's shot too, belly up and snoring in my lap.

I just don't know. Tony. Why did he do that? What is he going to do now? Boo feels me sinking, and he wakes and wags me through the feeling. The feeling like the good guy can't win.

I keep going back and forth. My brain knows this is the way it has to be, with Céce and me. That she was right to run. But my heart knows that's all wrong. That even if the price of one last kiss with her was Wash having to shoot me, it would've been worth it.

I wonder if it's possible to forget her. To forget that night we were at the shore, watching that old couple hunt for treasure they must have known wasn't there. Here I'm fifteen already, and I don't know a damned anything. I just don't know.

Halfway into the ride back, Wash tells the driver to pull over there for a minute. He comes back fifteen minutes later with a pizza box.

The van turns gentle here then there and eases me into a nice, halfway sleep. Must be twenty minutes later, Wash has the driver pull over a second time. The engine cuts out. I lift the hat off my eyes.

We're at the waterside, in the visitor parking lot ahead of the jail's checkpoint trailer and the guard tower. The parking lot is full of folks sleeping in cars, waiting for visiting hours to start up again tonight. Lots of folks waiting for the bus, ladies mostly. The parking lot is dirty, pint bottles, spent rubbers. Fast-food wrappers tumbleweed.

The driver checks my shackles and helps me down the rocks to the water. Wash leads Boo. We settle on a flat rock. Wash's radio starts up. He clicks it off. He opens the pizza box. Pineapple pizza, man.

Wash shrugs, hands out slices. I pull off some cheese, give it to Boo. And here we are: three dudes and a dog, eating pineapple pizza. Tell you what? It is *good*.

THE NINETY-EIGHTH DAY . . .

(Thursday, September 17, afternoon)

CÉCE:

Anthony comes home in a rainstorm. Vic and me go to the airport to pick him up. The accordion tunnel reaches out to the plane.

"Dazzling feeling, fear," Vic says.

"What?" I say.

Vic shrugs.

The guys start coming off the plane. Tears, laughing, kissing, but no Anthony. Down the tunnel is this guy in a wheelchair. He's turned away from us, talking to the pilot. He shakes the pilot's hand. I can read the pilot's lips, I think. "What's he saying? 'Thank you for your service'?"

"Sacrifice," Vic says. 'Thank you for your sacrifice.'"

The wheelchair spins around, and there's that smile. He rolls fast at us. I scream and laugh his name, everybody laughs. I practically knock him out of his chair when I hug him.

"Welcome home, kid," Vic says.

I pretend I'm thrilled, and I am, but more I'm in shock.

Again and again I watched that video he sent, so I would be ready. But now, here, Anthony in the flesh, I can really see it: He's a mess. The burns on his face aren't *minor*. The stumps where his fingers were. He's in a wheelchair, and he's never getting out of it. His legs are gone.

Ma waits at the door. It's dark in the vestibule but I can see her by the dull glow of her teeth as we're heading up the driveway. She's leaning against the door frame. Anthony coughs out, "Yo."

"Yo," she says.

My brother wheelies up the ramp. The two of them are out on the porch. Each says the other looks great. I've never seen Ma this happy, and I wonder if she's like me, pretending.

"So tell me about this dog," Anthony says.

She does. ". . . and then Boo pees right into it, I swear."

Anthony rasps a hoot. "Mack Morse, man. Love that kid."

He does a backward wheelie into his room, and we laugh. Ma yells at him to be careful.

I go to the backyard to cut some tomatoes for dinner. On my way back up the ramp to the kitchen, I hear murmuring from the basement. I look through the window.

He's on the floor. He fell out of his chair as he was taking off his shirt—one sleeve is still on. He talks softly to himself. His head is down. He sits himself up on the floor, leaning himself against the bed. He wipes his eyes and catches his breath and pulls himself onto the bed and into a clean T-shirt.

(Three days later, Sunday, September 20,
night of the hundred and first day . . .)

He's coming tomorrow night, the new dog.

The new Boo.

After the green van disappeared that day, I limped up the block, my toe bleeding, to where I threw the stickpin. Of course it was still there in the curb sand, because at that point it was nothing more than soft grimy metal and cracked glue where the fake jewels used to be.

I carefully wrap it in tissue paper and put it away in the shoebox in the back of my closet where I keep all my really special stuff like old pictures I don't look at anymore. I tuck it next to the letter he sent the day after he and the dog came to the house. I take the letter out for one last read:

> *Dear Céce,*
>
> *Just so you don't think I got smart all of a sudden in here, I'm dictating this to my friend Wash. I wanted to tell you what I think you already know: that I never meant those things I said the day you came to visit me. The day I pushed you away. I think you know I meant the exact opposite of what I said. That instead of pushing you off, all I wanted to do was hold you.*
>
> *I know you are going to take great care of Boo. He's going to be great to you too. He's a Boo, all right. He's a treasure like she was. Céce, you and the Boos are with me until I die, okay? I'll never forget you. You*

are going to be awesome, in your life, I mean. Your
future. When I think of you living a beautiful life,
I'm happy. All I have to do is close my eyes, and I'm
with you, and I'm free.
Good-bye, Céce. Thank you for being my friend.
Sincerely yours,
Mack Morse

And then, at the bottom, he handwrote:

I koodint this say inin frun t uv Wahsh,
but I wil yoo luv youyoo aw-ll ways.

I fold the letter and tuck it into the box. I put the lid on
the box and wrap tape around it and put it away for good.

THE HUNDRED & SECOND DAY...
(Monday, September 21, a clear morning)

MACK:

Me and Boo are spooning in the bed. He's snoring to shake the world, his bad breath all up in my face, and I can't let him go. His tail, man. He wags it in his sleep.

They're taking him to the vet first, to get him all checked out, but he'll be with them tonight, the Vaccuccias. By about dinnertime, Wash said. His first dinner inside a real home.

I wonder if he'll remember me. Better he doesn't. Nothing cuts you worse than a slow fade. I wake him up, and he strips my foot of its sock and gets me to chase him. We go out to the rooftop. The sky's clean blue on the other side of the cage. We play Frisbee wrestling till Thompkins and Wash show with Thompkins's assistant, the nice woman who came that first day. I put on my tough face and clip the leash to Boo's harness. I point to the door. "Go on now, Boo. *Go.*"

Boo cocks his head, gives his paw.

I tell him again, and he gives me his other paw, and then I remember, I never taught him that command, go. I make my face hard. *"Git."*

Boo cocks his head.

Thompkins's assistant takes the leash, gives it a gentle tug. Boo looks over his shoulder at me while the assistant leads him out. When the dog hits the door he trots off, tail whirling. He doesn't look back.

Thompkins hurries out after the assistant. Wash hangs back for a sec. "You all right?" he says.

"Psh, yeah, man. This ain't nothing. I'm cool."

"You want me to get you a nice cold Sprite?"

"Nah, thanks, I'm not so thirsty, Wash."

Wash nods and follows after Thompkins.

I wait till I hear the barred door crank shut, and everything is quiet. I slump down the wall and cop a squat in the corner, and I can't think of anything to do but hurt.

That nervous guard peeks in. "Morse?"

"Uh-huh?"

"You got a visitor."

LATE MORNING
OF THE LAST DAY...

CÉCE:

He looks terrible. He looks beautiful. His hair is longer still. He sits at the table. He keeps his hands on the tabletop, kind of toward me, to let me take them in mine if I want, but I keep my hands under the table. I can't touch him. Not yet. I'll crumble if I do. His eyes drop to my chest, to where the stickpin used to be. "Guards made you take it off, huh?"

"It was off before I came."

He nods and he's about to say something, but he doesn't. And then he clears his throat and fakes a smile and says, "I'm real happy to see you, Céce," as he puts his hands under the table.

"I knew he was leaving you today," I say. "The dog. Boo, I mean. I thought you could use a little comforting."

"Nah, I'm all right," he says. "I mean, I'm glad you came. Thank you for taking him."

"He'll be delivered to the house around dinnertime."

"I heard."

"Anything special I should keep in mind? About his food, I mean?"

"That dog'll eat any damned thing. Just no ch—"

"Chocolate or raisins, I know, you told me how many times."

"Or grapes."

"Mack?"

"Yup?"

"Thank you. For Boo, I mean."

He nods, and in a blink his eyes are wet, and he has to look away, and I can't kill him like this anymore. I have to tell him what I need to tell him, and then I have to force myself to go. I take his hand and pull him close to me and hold him tight, and I whisper it: "I'll love you too, always." And then I leave him, and I don't look back.

The night is weirdly hot, summer's last bang. With everybody going nuts with their air conditioners, the power goes out, and a blackout shuts down the west side. Vic has to close the Too. He loads up the new Vic-mobile, a totally smashed-in tan van from like 1978, with the perishables and brings them over to the house. We eat as much as we can and play slap cards, but pretty soon it's too hot to stay inside, and we head out to the porch to wait for them to bring Anthony's dog. Our dog. With the traffic lights all messed up, Boo arrives late, just after sunset. He runs up the porch steps to us like he has known us forever.

We go up to the reservoir with flashlights like we used to do when we were kids whenever they had those rolling brownouts. The clouds are blowing off and the breeze starts up. Ma pushes Anthony's chair, and Boo walks alongside perfectly, slightly behind the chair. My brother hasn't stopped grinning since they dropped off the dog. He says "Boo," and Boo swings around the wheelchair and leans into what's left of Anthony's lap. His tail spins and his tongue sticks out of his mouth. When Anthony bends to kiss him, Boo laps at Anthony's lips.

Vic walks alongside Ma. "Pretty sure I'm gonna get a loan to open a new restaurant," he says.

"Vic's Too Too?" Anthony says.

"Tony's," Vic says. "I'll need somebody to manage it. Don't argue with me about this. I know what I know. You can bring the dog to work with you every day, and we'll feed him meatballs. We'll have the fattest pit bull on the west side."

When they start talking about Mack I fade back a little with Bobby.

Up ahead, they run into two girls Anthony knows from school. The one looks away, pretending to be on her phone, stealing peeks where Anthony's legs should be. But the other girl has her hand on his shoulder, and they're laughing, and I think she might be crushing on him. Boo goes belly up for scratching and does his wiggle worm thing, and this *third* girl comes over. "Oh my god, he's so cute. Can I pet him?"

"You'll hurt his feelings if you don't," Anthony says.

"Dog is a total chick magnet," Bobby says. "Céce, have you ever considered that there weren't any dogs in *The Outsiders,* at least none featured prominently?"

"Actually, Bobby, I have not."

"This might be the movie's only flaw. If there *had* been a dog, perhaps one owned by Dallas Winston, I wonder if the outcome would have been less horrific, particularly for Matt Dillon."

"Hm," I say to be polite.

Far off, a section of the city lights up. My phone beeps with a text from AT&T, one they better not charge me for. Did I know I could pay my bill anytime online by going to att.com?

I was hoping it was Marcy. I reached out to her with a Facebook post last week and then again yesterday. I haven't heard back, but I'll keep trying.

This is a nice spot here, this reservoir. This part of the city is still without power, and the stars are insane.

They offer the G and T next month. Maybe I'll take it again. Maybe I won't. I'm sure of this though: My gift is that I can take a fair amount of crap and keep going. What else am I gonna do? I'm thinking ESP isn't real after all, but I still have the strangest feeling. I guess you could call it hope. I hold Bobby's hand. He looks into my eyes. "Look," he says, pointing to the sky.

I look up, and I see a satellite.

THE LAST NIGHT . . .

MACK:

The place stinks of diesel with all the backup generators running. I wish they would turn them off and let it be dark, because I bet the stars would look as true as they did the time me and my folks lived at this real cool campsite in west Texas.

I have my brown paper bag packed with my underwears and socks for tomorrow morning, ready to head back to the tent. I heard Blue got transferred, so I figure I'll be all right for a while. This bed in here was too soft anyways, and I have a backache. Yeah, I'll be okay.

I lie back on the floor and shut my eyes and picture Boo free, up at the reservoir, the ball fields at night when they can let him run. I bet they have him up there tonight, even. He's hanging with Carmella and the Tone, and then, when it's time, Céce leads them all home.

After a while I open my eyes and it's nothing but the bars over the window. Metal and stone and grime-struck glass.

And Thompkins.

He's standing tall over me. Arms crossed. Looking down on me.

I sit up and make my face tough. I'd stand, but my legs are boneless. It's hard not to hear her saying those words over and over in my mind, words that will stay with me and make the hurt permanent, *I'll love you too, always.* I needed to hear them, but it's a blessed curse owning them now. Treasure keeping is the longest haul.

"The dog was delivered to the family," Thompkins says. "All appeared to be going quite well when I left."

I nod. "Real happy to hear that, sir. Thank you for coming in to tell me. You didn't have to do that."

"Indeed." He sits next to me on the floor, our backs against the wall. I notice, him close to me, he isn't hiding his hand anymore. He's got a faded, home-inked gang tattoo between his thumb and index finger, the kind burnt into a man with a Bic and a flick in the joint. "Not for nothin', you did a beautiful thing," Thompkins says.

"Not for nothin' back, I appreciate y'all giving me the chance."

"Your work will help a young man transition to his new reality with a little more ease. Mack?"

"Yessir?"

"You have a gift."

Wash is watching from the door. His eyebrows are up, and I guess mine are too.

Thompkins nods, just once, gets back to the tough old Thompkins face. "Mister *Morse.*"

"Mister Thompkins."

"I have brought someone with me who is most interested in the program. You would help us a great deal if you would share your experience with her."

"Yessir. I won't fight you with the interviews anymore. I would like to do anything to help the program."

Thompkins nods to Wash. Wash looks out the door and nods, and a few seconds later the assistant lady brings in one crazy-looking pit bull. She's got these bugged eyes. Snout is crooked to the left. Lamed leg, probably car-struck, healed wrong. But it doesn't slow her down much. This dog is jumping wild.

"No downtime on this job," Thompkins says.

"Last thing I need is downtime, Mister T."

The dog drops belly up into my lap. Another basketball head, but this time on a skinny little body. "You're kind of runty, huh?" I nod to Wash and Thompkins. "I like this dog, man. She's a cupcake." Wiggling all over. She's got a bent rattail, beats the dust from the floor with it. Coats my face with slobber. I'm hearing a sound that surprises me. I haven't heard it come in this clear for as long as I can remember. I hear laughter. Mine.

Wash says, "What're you going to call this one?"

"Boo."

This Boo dog is just running circles around me, teasing me to play with her. I say, "Boo, stay."

Tell you what? She stays.

ACKNOWLEDGMENTS
(with a disclaimer about dog training, sort of, mixed in)

Thank you to my agent Kirby Kim, who put this fable on the road from dream to print. Thanks too to Shaun Dolan, Nicole Sohl, Ian Dalrymple, and Derek Zasky.

Thank you to my friends at Penguin and Dial, Regina, Jasmin, Lori and Deborah, Liz, Alisha, Jess, Marie, Steve, Scottie, Donne, Mary, Julianne, and Samantha. (Nan, Rob, and Emily, while you've moved on, you're always in my thoughts.) Heather, you went above and beyond, drinking penny-poisoned milk. Lauri, thank you for making time to read and to give such awesome notes. Kathy, draft after draft, your notes excited, heartened and inspired—you are the best. Kate, thank you for the title, your fearlessness and generosity, your laugh, and most of all your notes, every one a thrill. Your compassion and patience are unending, your wisdom and sense of humor infinite.

While working on this story, I received encouragement and friendship from the wonderful writers Scott Smith, Barry Lyga, Sarah Campbell, Jeff Jackson, T. Stores, Jay Kumar, Phil Gwynne, Scot Gardner, Coe Booth, Shawn Coyne, Jack Sussek, Rita Williams-Garcia, and the nicest man in publishing, David Levithan.

Thank you to the librarians, teachers, booksellers, and literacy and human rights advocates that have given me opportunities to connect with their students and readers. I'm particularly grateful to Molly Krichten, Julianne Wernersbach of Book Revue, Lainie Castle and the ALA's Great Stories Program, Pete and Molly Rosenquist and the Doylestown Bookshop, Richie Partington, James Falletti, Marie Hansen, Debra, Geri, Chrystal, Patricia, Nafisah and the Bloomfield High School Book Club, Angela Carstensen, Judy Card, Ann Branton, Nancy Opalko and the Mississippi Librarians Association, the wonderful folks at Voice of Youth Advocates, Michael Dodes and the Samuel Gompers staff, the International Reading Association's Children's Literature and Reading Special Interest Group, Anne Lotito Schuh and the Crossroads family, Jessica, Ma'lis and Literacy For Incarcerated Teens, the Texas Library Association, Penny, Michael, Anne, Bridie and Team Text, Jo, Chris, Micaela and Behind The Book, the Junior Library Guild, the Chicago Public Library's Great Kids Initiative, the Pennsylvania School Librarians Association, Mark, Jack and Follett Library Resources, the Kentucky Reading Association, the Amelia Bloomer Project and the Feminist Task Force of the ALA's Social Responsibilities Round Table, the Simon Wiesenthal Center for Tolerance and Human Dignity, the Georgia Library Media Association, Becky and the Anderson's Bookstores team, and, most especially, the glorious Sheila Hennessey, guardian angel, moon-hanger, and guiding star.

By the way, if you're thinking about adopting a pit bull, you're in luck: Every year more than a million pits go into shelters, so you'll have your pick. But do your research. Pits need a ton of exercise, mental stimulation, and socialization. If you can afford the time, you'll never have a better friend. Much of Mack's training methodology is mine (including "spot-peeing"), but there are so many different and great ways to work with dogs. Read every training book your library can get you, DVR the dog shows, talk to trainers and dog owners, check to see if your local shelter or rescue group offers free classes, and I suspect you'll end up borrowing a little from here, a little from there. My experience has been that every dog is a special case, and keeping an open mind when it comes to incorporating various training techniques will save you and your pal a lot of heartache.

Old Dogs, New Tricks is imagined, but gifted people in prisons across the US are training dogs for our veterans. Check them out online. I bet they would be grateful for your interest. To those serving here stateside and overseas, particularly Lou and Omar: Thank you for your sacrifice.

Thank you to my wife, who for the past fourteen years has allowed me to keep an ever-changing pack of goofballs. They come and go, but Risa stays.

PAUL'S PACK

Paul's cupcake of a pit bull, Ray-Ray, the inspiration behind Boo. (And yes, he can spot pee.)

Ray-Ray and fuzzball Eddie, who thinks he's the alpha dog of the house.

Learning stay

TURN THE PAGE
FOR A PREVIEW OF
PAUL GRIFFIN'S NEXT NOVEL

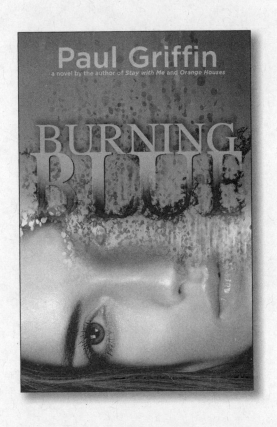

ONE

I was at the cemetery when it happened. I didn't even know Nicole at the time. Well, I knew *of* her. Everybody did. She'd won a high-profile beauty competition the year before, the under-sixteen division. She had been on the front page of a lot of newspapers. People in the pageant world were saying she was sure to win Miss New Jersey. I had seen her in the halls and hungered for her from afar like every other dude at the Hollows, but we hadn't talked. Not yet. Still, that afternoon, that moment, when that first molecule pierced her skin, was the beginning of our connection, one that led me into a darkness that was as twisted as it was sublime.

The water brought us together. The storm. The sky was horrific, a dark, dirty green. According to maps.google, Pinemont Cemetery and Brandywine Hollows High School are 4.11 miles apart, but Nicole and I were bound by the rain. It was something that day, so strange, too hard to be liquid, too cold for the second Thursday of September. It smashed my mother's gravestone, a nothing-special marker the size of a high-tops shoebox. The first burst of downpour ricocheted upward at my eyes and stung my face like a sucker punch. I'd cut my last two classes to clock an extra hour on my shift

1

card after my boss texted that a lot of people had called in sick. I often stopped by the cemetery on my way to work. I loved the quiet, but with that rain I didn't linger. I was chasing down the bus, dodging the spray the wheels drew from a lake-like puddle the exact moment Nicole was hit.

She was with Dave Bendix, our wrestling team captain and thought by many, me included, to be one of the nicest guys in school. He was definitely the most popular. This was just before last period. They were messing around in a cutout in the lockers past the C-wing water fountain, by the windows that overlooked the creek. They had been together maybe five months. Nicole would tell me later that up to this point Dave was a sweetheart and a total gent, but that afternoon he was jacked up on too many Red Bulls or whatever, desperate. He wouldn't let her go. He kept saying, "One last kiss." The first bell had rung, and the last few stragglers were moping toward their classes.

Dave was playing safecracker, circling Nicole's belly button with his fingertips. She had to get to AP chem. Mr. Sabbatini, chairman of our science program, was looking for a reason to ruin her. He'd dreamed of being the next big pharm sellout and ended up at the Hollows. The man reeked of bitterness and schnapps. He loved to knock down anybody who looked like she was going to one-up him. You're late to his class, you get docked in a very big way: thirty points off the midterm. Nicole had already been late once, thanks to another impromptu make-out session with Dave.

The second bell rang. The hallway was empty. Nicole wriggled out of Dave's hug and ran for the circle that connects A, B and C wings.

Whatever your concept of gorgeous, Nicole Castro trumped it. Tall, thin but not too, round in all the right places, long chestnut hair. More than that?

Her face.

Her lips, full, pouty, except back then she was always smiling. High cheekbones. No need for makeup, not a blemish to cover. It was unassailable, her splendor. Almost unassailable.

She hooked left for B-wing. She turned back briefly to airmail a kiss off the tip of her index finger to Dave, but he wasn't there anymore. She sagged for a second and then spun away for Mr. Sabbatini's class. She was halfway into her turn when it happened. Life as she knew it: gone. Took maybe half a second.

The last thing she saw was the squirt bottle coming up toward her face. A squeeze machine wrapped in orange foam, the lightning bolt.

Sent moments after the attack:

Subject: The new Nicole
Date: Thursday, September 9, 2:13 PM
To: Assistant Principal Nadine Marks
N.Marks@brandywine_hollows_hs.nj.edu
From: Arachnomorph@unknowable_origin.net

Now she's beautiful.

The first person to hear her scream was Dave Bendix. Not that Nicole could see him with her eyes clamped shut. When one gets hit, the other reflexively closes down to protect what's left of your vision. Trying to wipe off the acid made the situation worse. She burned her hands. Interestingly, Dave had the presence of mind not to touch Nicole, even before she stopped screaming long enough to weep, "It burns!"

I don't know that I would have been that smart. I probably would have been like most everybody else in that situation. You find somebody writhing on the floor, covering her face and screaming, you instinctively try to peel her hands away to see what the problem is. Not Dave, though. He told Nicole to stop rubbing her eye, that she was only going to spread the burn.

From what I heard, the classrooms emptied into the halls. Everybody had to see what all the screaming was about. Nicole managed to get out that someone had squirted something into her face. Everybody was asking "Who?" Only Mr.

Sager, one of our custodians, realized that right now the primary question was "What? What did he squirt?"

Nicole didn't know, but whatever it was, it was still burning. She begged, "Please, get it off, I can't *see*."

Mr. Sager wrapped his hand in a rag towel and pried away Nicole's hands. He told a girl with a water bottle to douse the burn. Everybody with a water bottle did the same. Nicole couldn't breathe. The water filled her mouth and throat. She was choking on it when Mr. Sager told them to stop. In his statement to the police, Mr. Sager reported that Dave Bendix slid down the wall and said, "I'm sorry, Nic. I'm so sorry."

TWO

The following is from Nicole's journal:

The prep room is cold green curtains. A window tinted violet, the color of my eyes, what's left of them.

"Multiple grafts," the surgeon says. "A degree of paralysis is certain, Nicole. But you were fortunate."

"*For*tunate?" Mom says.

"The rule of nines. We use it to describe burn coverage. The front of each leg is nine percent of your skin's total surface area. Same with the back. The front of your torso: eighteen percent, the back too. Each arm is nine percent. And then your head is nine percent. You've burned somewhere between a quarter and a third of the left side of your face."

Mom: "*She* didn't burn anything, Doctor."

Doc: "I'm just saying that if you break it down, the burn covers less than one percent of her body."

Mom: "It was her face. It was Nicole."

Doc: "It could have been much worse."

Mom: "Her face. Can you get her back to—"

Doc cuts her off: "No. You can't think that way. This is a life-altering event."

Me: "The other one percent?"

Doc: "Excuse me?"

Me: "The rule of nines. If you add up all those numbers, the body parts, you get ninety-nine percent. What's the other one percent?"

Doc: "That's what we use to describe the males' private parts."

Me: "One percent, huh? I'm sure they'd be thrilled."

Doc: "A sense of humor is important, Nicole. You're doing great."

Me: "The girls get nothing. The boys get the extra point. They're complete at one hundred percent. That's why women are stronger: We live with omission."

Mom (sobbing): "Can't you give her more morphine?"

Doc: "The left side of your face. I'm hopeful you'll still be able to blink. If you can't, we'll give you drops to keep your eye lubricated. If you can't cry, you'll go blind."

Me: "I'm sure I can cry, Doctor." I'm crying all right. "I can't see out of that eye anyway. I can't see. I can't see."

Mom: "Don't touch it, Nicole. Oh my god. Oh my baby."

Me: "What does it look like, Mom? How bad is it? Please. Tell me."

The doctor rolls me onto my side. With two tugs on the strings he unties my hospital gown to expose my left leg, and then he draws lines into the back of my hip with something.

Me: "Is that your fingernail? What are you doing?"

Doc: "I'm surveying the donor site, Nicole."

Me: "Please. No."

Doc: "I know this is horrible for you. Don't try to look, Nicole. If you have to, look at your mother. That's right, close your eye and hold Mom's hand. Hold it tight."

Close your *eye,* as in *one.*

"My other eye," I say. "Is it—"

Mom cuts me off: "Hush now, sweetie. It'll be all right."

Worst liar ever.

The surgeon's hands are cold and way too soft on my hip. I feel tapping and tugging and a vague sense my skin is being stretched beyond the limits of its elasticity. A minute later they're wheeling me down the hall for the surgery, the first of several, I'm told. The doors to the OR swing in. I see through a slit eyelid a nurse is checking the equipment. The scalpel flash reflects in the glass of one of the implement cabinets. Mom gasps. She nearly collapses as the OR doors swing shut on her.

Doc: "Do you like this music, Nicole?"

I didn't notice any music was playing. It's New Age, waves crashing, whale calls. "Got any Eminem?" I say.

Doc: "Atta girl."

My attempt to make the doctor laugh surprises me as much as it does him. Where is this bravery coming from? I feel bolder now that Mom isn't weeping over

8

me. Or maybe I feel worse. The situation is absurd. Have I really burned my face?

Anesthesiologist: "We're ready to go."

Surgeon: "Beautiful."

That word.

My first memories, going back to when I was four years old, maybe even three.

Beautiful.

My identity.

Oh Nicole, you're simply beautiful.

Not the real me.

Sixth-grade yearbook: MOST BEAUTIFUL: NICOLE CASTRO.

The fake me.

Ridiculous, how beautiful you are—just beautiful.

Just? Nothing else?

Isn't she just the most beautiful thing?

A thing.

What will it be like, not being *the word* any more?

The mask goes over my mouth. Dad, where are you? I'm afraid of the dark.

Anesthesiologist: "Count backward from one hundred, Nicole."

"One hundred, ninety-nuh . . ."

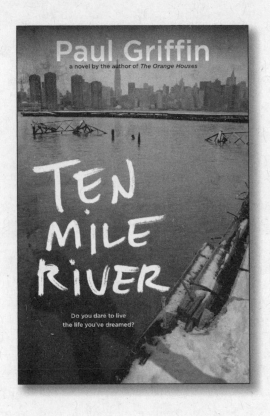

Ray and José have been best friends from juvenile detention to foster care. Now Ray's decided to clean up his act, but José still can't seem to escape trouble. Soon they'll have to choose to go their separate ways, or embrace a whole new life . . . together.

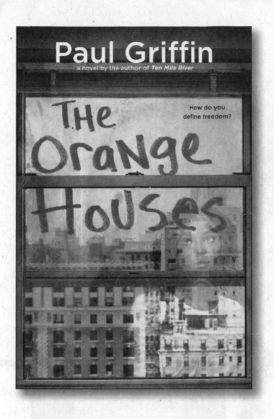

Paul Griffin
a novel by the author of *Ten Mile River*

How do you
define freedom?

THE
OraNge
HoUSes

Fifteen-year-old Mik is deaf. But that makes it easy to shut out
all the noise in her complicated life. When she meets Jimmi, a
struggling street poet, and Fatima, a lonely refugee, they form an
unlikely friendship that will change each of their lives forever.